PAPER
MOON
LANDING

by

Jeremy M. Wright

STONE
GATEWAY
PUBLISHING

Copyright © 2024 by Jeremy M. Wright

Cover design by Lance Buckley

First edition by Stone Gateway Publishing November 2024

Paperback edition
ISBN: 979-8-9855225-7-0

Printed in the United States of America.

This one goes out to the kids.

Austin, Alec, Lexie, Myah, Gabriel, and Jillian.

Where there is mystery, it is generally suspected there must also be evil.

Lord Byron

Also by Jeremy M. Wright

Fiction

Chasing Daylight

Man of Exile

From Shadowed Places:
13 Darkly Twisted Tales Volume I

From the Darkest Hours:
13 Darkly Twisted Tales Volume II

Young Adult Fiction

The Good Ship

PAPER

MOON

LANDING

Chapter 1

When the first bell rang and the girl grabbed a fistful of my button-up plaid shirt, nearly yanking me out of my sneakers and into the empty classroom, I had decided that I'd just about had enough of Paper Moon, Florida.

So far, the small town was miles away from winning any kind of love and affection in my heart. If it weren't for the promise to my brother, Josh, I would have locked myself in my bedroom until the next move inevitably came around. With a sincere attitude, I swore to Josh that I'd try to make a few friends, fight less, spend fewer hours in the principal's office, and even show my teachers at the new school a small amount of respect.

"You're the new kid, J.C. Graham, right?" the girl in the purple dress said.

It was common to hear someone mispronounce my first name. Often, people pronounced it as initials, as if combining my first and middle names, until I correct them.

"It's Jayce. You know, as in it rhymes with ace."

"You shouldn't be here."

"You pulled me into this classroom. Remember?"

"No, I mean, you shouldn't be in this town."

"Believe me when I say that I wholeheartedly agree with you," I said and massaged the back of my neck as one of my obvious signs of discomfort.

"If I were you, I'd go home, repack everything, and tell your brother that you're better off moving back to Colorado."

"How did you know where I moved from? How do you know about Josh?"

"This town doesn't have many secrets. Although I'm taking it upon myself to uncover the secrets that do exist here."

"What's your name?" I asked the girl.

"I'm writing an article. I'm going to publish all my findings in the school paper at the end of the school year. Make sure you get a copy when it comes out."

"But you just told me that I should move back to Colorado. What's your name?" I asked again. The girl was a little strange, but there was something interesting about the bluntness and mystery of her nearly one-sided conversation.

"There are dark forces thriving in our cozy town. You probably shouldn't get wrapped up in it. That's why it's best for you to leave as soon as possible," the girl whispered.

"Do you have a name?" I pushed.

Students moved past me and took their seats.

"I'm going to blow the lid off a lot of things going on around here. There are people that don't want me to write the paper. There are probably even people who would do harmful things to me to keep the article from being published."

"How about if I call you jabberwocky?" I decided, as the name seemed to fit.

I noticed over half a dozen eyes now watching us. My discomfort level jumped up a few notches. I didn't know any of these students, but for some reason I felt embarrassed about being caught speaking with this girl. She was probably the deranged classmate no one spoke with, and now they wondered why the new kid, of all people, had befriended her.

"The dictionary defines jabberwocky as meaningless speech or writing. I do neither. There's always a point I get across. Right now, my point is that you're late for class," the girl said, and the last bell rang.

"Well, so are you."

"I disagree," she said, turned, and took her seat.

I wasn't sure if the girl's entire purpose all along was to make me late for class or to put out there that this town was even more insane than I'd already figured.

"You're not in my class, young man. Off you go," Mrs. Edelstein said, and she motioned for me to take flight.

Before the door closed in my face, the girl turned in her chair, smiled, and with all politeness said, "By the way, I'm Katrina Mossgrove. Everyone calls me Kat. Welcome to Paper Moon."

I thought the girl was the perfect definition of being off her rocker. If she didn't wear her hair in a braided ponytail, substituted her glasses for contacts, and had a conversation like a normal person, she might be pretty and possibly interesting to know.

I noticed the deserted hallway and began running to room 104.

All eyes turned on me when I opened the door and slinked inside. Just before my butt found the seat, Mrs. Driscoll turned in my direction. I couldn't tell if she was smiling or scowling. The reason for this is that Mrs. Driscoll wore a black veil that hung from a black hat. She also wore a black dress and shoes. She looked as if she were going to or coming from a funeral. Three days into my new school and I had yet to see my algebra teacher's face because she wore the outfit every day. I wondered if any of her students had ever seen her face.

"So good of you to join us, Mr. Graham. I couldn't say how things worked at your old school, but here you'll be in your chair with your book, notepad, and pencil at the ready when the second bell rings. The world doesn't wait for you. This is your third tardy. That's not an outstanding record, considering this is your third day at our school. Are we understood?"

There was a wave of snickers and tongue farting noises that immediately stopped when Mrs. Driscoll snapped her fingers like a firecracker.

"Yes," I said.

"Yes, what?"

"Yes, I understand," I said doubtfully, not knowing what else she expected.

"Yes, what?" she said with irritation.

Then I got it and said, "Yes, Mrs. Driscoll."

"Good. Now get your things out. You've already put me behind schedule. Now everyone, turn to page seventy-two."

I quickly found the page and then buried my head in my hands and prayed for the next bell to ring.

On the days when the Florida sun was mild and without the hint of an oncoming storm, the students were allowed to spend lunchtime in the courtyard. I thought this was a pleasant treat that I hadn't experienced at any of my previous schools.

The lunch lady flopped mashed potatoes onto my plate, followed by a bubbling ooze of brown gravy, a cluster of chicken nuggets, and a large spoonful of applesauce. I searched the busy courtyard tables for a somewhat familiar face. Three days into my new school and I'd only had a few passing conversations with several of the kids. I thought that with another half hour of lunchtime passing, I could strike up a conversation. Hopefully, it was possible to say goodbye to my outcast title if I could work at making a friend.

In my search for one familiar face, I was unaware that Regan Evans and his noble band of followers moved in for the kill. As the story goes at most schools, here every fresh kid becomes an immediate target for Regan and his crew. Punishment meant humiliation, diminished character, and the occasional bloody nose if the timing and lack of witnesses were right. Regan Evans was the reason one would believe that Satan and his unearthly minion often escape Hell to torture kids for the pure enjoyment of it.

As my eyes were elsewhere, the palm of Regan's gorilla hand struck the bottom of my lunch tray. The force of the blow dislodged the tray from my grip and sent my entire lunch sailing across the courtyard. Applesauce went down some kid's striped shirt, and he leaped from his seat in protest. Potatoes and an ooze of gravy landed in a spattering mess in a girl's tangled blonde hair, which caused her to release a screech that brought an immediate hush to the entire lunchtime crowd. A half-dozen chicken nuggets hammered three tables like dropped missiles, and finally the tray hit the cobblestone with a thunder crack.

The crowd erupted in laughter, applause, and stout whistles.

"Nice going. You dropped your lunch, Graham Cracker," Regan said, offering a nickname I'd often heard.

"I'm sure that was by accident on your part. Right?" I asked.

"Yeah, totally an accident," Regan said with a sneer, and his crew joined the rest of the group in laughter.

5

"And I'm sure you wouldn't mind helping me clean it up? Or are you planning on standing around looking like the king of the morons?"

A small wave of astonished sounds, mostly vowels, traveled across the courtyard.

"I bet you think you're hilarious," Regan said as his hands pumped into fists.

I shrugged and said, "Most of the time. Today I'll just have to improvise, because I'm feeling a little off my game."

"I'll have to improvise your face into the ground," Regan so wittingly countered.

"I'm not sure what that means. I'm sure that in that tiny mind of yours, that's got to be the joke of the century. Let's get this over with," I said. I raised my hands and waited for a fight that wouldn't take long until my backside met the stone ground.

I thought that on my third day in a new school I was going to get creamed in front of the entire school body, but fortunately, I saw a look on Regan's face that only took a moment to decipher.

I turned and saw Mr. Clark quickly cutting between tables, and when Regan saw the science teacher moving in, he tried to make a stealthy retreat.

"Hold it right there, Mr. Evans. Plant your feet," Mr. Clark demanded.

I used my thumb to remove a spatter of potatoes from my right cheek.

When Mr. Clark stepped up to us, he placed his hands on his hips and surveyed the disaster. His tongue clicked several times, and then he fixed hard eyes on Regan.

"I can only imagine you had something to do with this," he said.

"No, sir. The new kid must have slipped or something," Regan claimed.

"Slipped, huh? What do you say, did you slip, Mr. Graham?"

Now this was where my experience from many schools came into play. I know the consequences of ratting out bullies to a teacher. The aftermath was always pain and suffering and sometimes a loss of school days until the internal bleeding stopped.

"Ah, no, sir. I didn't slip. I sneezed," I said.

"You sneezed?"

"Yep. It gets pretty violent sometimes. It's a whole-body reaction. This Florida climate differs from what I'm used to. You know, allergies and all."

"Uh-huh," Mr. Clark said, eyeing us. I figured he was waiting for the pressure to crack one or both of us.

"Sorry. I'll find the janitor and get the supplies I need to clean this up," I said.

"That won't be necessary. Get yourself another serving and find a seat. Try to hold back any more sneezes until you set the tray down. Mr. Evans, don't you have somewhere else to be?"

"Yeah. See you later, Graham Cracker," Regan said. He punched me in the shoulder hard enough that I was sure a black bruise would surface before long. He took the opportunity to high-tail it while the offer of a clean getaway was still open.

Mr. Clark turned and made off to find the janitor for the clean-up. The rest of the students realized the show was over. Since I'd avoided a hospital trip, they went back to their lunch and conversations.

The blonde girl pulled mashed potatoes from her hair, flopped what she could on her empty plate, and then licked her fingers clean.

I shrugged as a silent apology. I found my place at the lunch line and made my way through a second time.

Ten minutes before the bell rang, I found a seat next to Stevie Bradford. Stevie was a skinny kid, with enormous glasses and a vicious cowlick that stuck up in the wind like a flapping flag. He had a shyness that only dissolved when he could let himself trust someone enough. Stevie was in my fourth-period woodshop class. He was attempting and epically failing at making a pine nightstand for his mother. The thing was missing an imperative fourth leg, and the table surface angled so much that Mrs. Bradford's iced tea would no doubt slide off the edge and succumb to gravity with a jarring crash.

"I'd say you skated out of that beating with style. I've never seen anyone dumb enough to talk to Regan like that," Stevie said. He pushed his glasses back up his nose and ate a spoonful of chocolate pudding.

"I'm not highly invested in the brains department."

"That's for sure," he said and snorted.

"Regan is his own worst enemy. All the teachers know he's always up to no good. I'm sure they go directly to him when something bad happens at school. The police probably make his house the first stop when trouble shows up in town."

I noticed a kid sitting by himself. He was leaning against a tree on the far side of the courtyard. The kid was small, almost frail. His wiry frame barely held his clothes on. He was eating a sandwich from a brown bag and sipping from a juice box. I wasn't sure what it was about the kid that intrigued me. It wasn't that he was sitting alone, because I'd sat alone many times during lunch in the many schools I'd attended. Sometimes kids were loners, or just felt the need to be without company for a time. Maybe he interested me because he seemed confidently arrogant. It was almost like he had an invisible wall around him, protecting him from the evils of the world. He took a bite from his sandwich and put it down. It was at that moment when the kid's entire body went instantly rigid. His face suddenly paled, as if he were nearly ready to black out, and his eyes drifted skyward.

I followed his gaze but saw nothing except a stretching blue sky.

"So, you probably don't like our school so much," Stevie said as he finished his pudding by wedging his tongue into the cup.

I looked at him, shrugged, and said, "There's nothing better or worse about it than any other school I've attended. Teachers, friends, and even the scenery come and go. Everything is a hit or miss of whether I'll bother trying to remember it after I've gone."

"I'm not sure what that means, but okay, if you say so."

I shifted my sight to the loner kid again, but he was gone. There was a weird emptiness where he had been. His sandwich lay half eaten on the brown bag, and the juice box had tipped onto its side.

I rotated on the bench seat and searched the courtyard. I didn't see the kid anywhere.

"Where did that kid go?" I asked.

"This place is packed with kids. Which one?"

I pointed and said, "The kid who was sitting by himself next to that tree."

"I don't know. I wasn't paying attention to him. Maybe he went to pee."

"He was there one second and gone the next."

"Maybe he really had to pee," Stevie offered.

The school bell rang to finalize lunch. Students stood, gathered their backpacks and lunch trays, and began heading inside. In the bustling crowd moving through the doors, I turned, and, on tippy-toes, I could see the tree. The kid hadn't returned for his partially eaten lunch.

Kat Mossgrove was suddenly in front of me, blocking my view.

She said, "Something interesting out there, new kid?"

"None of your business," I said with irritation while trying to keep my focus on the tree. I was still bitter about her making me late for class.

"And just maybe the kid who was over there a moment ago is none of your business. I think you should concentrate on making it to class on time, since you're not very good at it," she said and pushed past me with a hard body check.

"What's your problem?" I called after her, but she didn't turn around.

Stevie said, "You should stay away from her. She's a total whack job. She's like one of those people that reads supermarket tabloids and believes everything written in them. Her whole family is bizarre. Her twin brother is even worse. He thinks he can time travel or something. His name is Anderson. Who gives their kid a last name for his first name? Wouldn't it be funny if his last name was also Anderson? Anderson Anderson."

"So, this Anderson said he can time travel?" I asked.

"Sure, what kid can't time travel?" Stevie said mockingly. "He's got a lot of weird stories about how he went back in time and helped change our future. He's just another kid creating stories for attention. I'm sure you've seen a bunch of kids like that in some of your other schools."

"Well, I've never actually known a time-traveling kid before, or even heard of one. But in my last school, one of the students won the regional hot-dog-eating contest. He downed twenty-eight hot dogs in all."

"Yeah, well, you've just seen the tip of the iceberg for weirdness around here. Later," Stevie said and took off down the left hallway to his next class.

I wondered if the kid next to the tree was the one Stevie was talking about. It would almost make sense for his sister Kat to get defensive when she saw me looking for the kid who vanished, maybe even literally, from the lunchtime crowd.

I thought that this school, and even the town, was becoming stranger than a bad Saturday night science-fiction movie. I almost hoped it was. I desperately needed a break from the monotony of a normal life. I looked at the wall clock and ran for my next class before the tardy bell rang.

Chapter 2

The gym teacher, Mr. Miles Dexter, who was also the track coach, was wearing a pink shirt that claimed, "Pink brings out my winning personality." He was also wearing florescent green shorts and neon blue flip-flops. Although his hair wasn't very long, he styled it in spikes that reminded me of a thorn bush. His whistle howled whenever he felt someone wasn't doing their very best, which happened every ten seconds or so.

The thing about Mr. Dexter was that he was the brother of Robert Dexter, who was the mayor, the chairman of the School Board, owner of the Honey Hill Inn and Dexter's Hardware. He was also a former All-Star running back for the Florida Gators from 1984 to 1988. But because of a knee blow-out during a practice game his senior year, the NFL dream train slipped away. Every town loves its celebrities, and Robert Dexter was Paper Moon's pride and joy.

Miles Dexter, on the other hand, had a bad temperament that landed him in the custody of several fine law enforcement facilities across the state during the '90s. Being that Robert Dexter dreaded his celebrity status would crash and burn because of his brother's troublesome ways, Robert saw that Miles' Physical Education degree should come in handy at Paper Moon High School. The school board awarded Miles Dexter the position of PE teacher, track coach, and assistant coach of the Water Moccasins.

I figured the coach had lost not only his good manners but also his common sense and his ability to dress himself properly somewhere along the way.

"All right. I want five rows. We're going to run two hundred meters. Whoever wins from each group gets a five-minute rest. I want to see major effort out there, ladies and gentlemen."

Silently kids gathered, formed lines, and waited for the ear-piercing whistle. Somehow, without even trying, I found myself in the first group of runners.

I hated running. I believed that it should be reserved for evading hungry bears or a runaway cross-town bus ready to squish me into the pavement. Josh had said that I needed to take part in at least two extra-curricular activities each school year. My brother claimed it would build character, competitiveness, and friendship. I thought it built an overwhelming exhaustion, sore muscles, and a desire to raid the refrigerator with serious hunger pangs.

Strangely enough, I knew three of the other runners. Stevie, Kat, and Regan were in line with me. At first, the race hadn't meant much to me, but now I suddenly felt the desire to make my legs hammer faster than they ever had before. There was no way I was going to let a girl, a kid half my weight, or a hulking, bumbling, stupid baboon beat me in this race.

"I've got you now, Graham Cracker. You better run like I'm chasing you and gonna beat the snot outta you when I catch you," Regan said on the other side of Kat.

"You will be chasing me, since you'll be behind me the entire time. See if you can find the finish line in my trail of dust," I said. Even though we were running on a concrete track and no dust would form behind me, I thought I got my point across just fine.

"Keep dreaming, loser."

"Clever," I muttered.

Before the whistle screamed, Kat whispered, "Hey, whatever you do, don't laugh. It'll be a death sentence if you do."

"Huh?" I asked.

The whistle sounded with another ear-bleeding shriek, and the runners were off down the track.

Kat's statement puzzled me, and I hadn't expected the signal. She had purposely done it again. Earlier, she made me tardy for class, and now she had cleverly thrown me off focus and left me half a dozen strides behind the others. With bold determination, I got my legs moving.

I was sure I could catch up. I was sure I could even win the race if it hadn't been for what I saw in front of me. There were two things I noticed at the same time. The fifth runner was no longer an unknown kid. Mr. Dexter had swapped the runners when I wasn't looking. The kid who had been eating his lunch next to the tree now held the position, and he was freakishly fast. Second, Regan Evans was running in an awkward skip, or maybe a prance. Truthfully, the kid looked as if he needed to go a number one and a dire number two and was trying to find the closest bathroom before messing himself. He ran with his legs spread wide as if he were straddling a horse. His hands were down at his sides with the palms held out, almost appearing as if he were stepping on something distasteful. Even though Regan's movement was hilarious, the kid was fast in that special run.

I couldn't help it. The laughter started somewhere in my eyes, migrated to my brain, and, like a plague, eagerly traveled down. From there it branched out, infected my lungs, made each breath labored, and turned my determined leg muscles to jelly.

I caught up to Kat, but the laughter threw me off-balance, and we collided hard enough to clack my teeth painfully together.

Kat pin-wheeled her arms to keep from crashing down. In turn, she smashed into me. The whole thing seemed like a pinball game gone horribly wrong. We became a tangled mess, veered to the right, and collapsed onto the grass field. There was a shout and a scream, one of laughter and the other of pain. The other runners paid no attention, as they saw a better opportunity for victory with two runners down.

There was a long, angry scream coming from Mr. Dexter's whistle. He was coming down the track toward us in a fast-paced shuffle that was neither a walk nor a run. He looked like a bull in flip-flops charging a waving flag.

"Get off me, stupid," Kat said as she firmly planted her palm on my face and pushed.

"Hey, watch it," I said and tried to stand.

"You did that on purpose. You made me fall."

"I didn't. I'm sorry. Did you see how Regan was running?" I asked with laughter that didn't want to quit.

Mr. Dexter bellowed when he stopped and towered over us. "I don't even believe what I just saw. Are you kidding me right now? That kind of behavior and lack of sportsmanship doesn't fly at my practices."

"I'm sorry. I lost my balance. I didn't mean to run into her," I said.

I finally got my legs under me and stood. After I brushed the grass from my shorts, I held out my hand to help Kat to her feet. She slapped my hand away viciously and stood on her own.

15

"That certainly isn't what I saw happen. I saw you push her, Mr. Graham."

"Accidentally pushed her," I clarified.

"Purposely," Kat countered.

"Don't get ahead of yourself, Ms. Mossgrove. I saw you push him right back," Mr. Dexter claimed and placed his hands on his hips like adults do when scolding someone.

Kat and I immediately began protesting, but we were quickly silenced when Mr. Dexter held up his hand.

"Do you know what we do to kids who lack sportsmanship around here, Mr. Graham?"

"No, sir," I said and instantly realized all my laughter had taken flight.

"Well, we make sure that classmates with disputes will get along from now on. I have one method that I particularly enjoy enforcing. Both of you come with me," he said.

Kat rolled her eyes and gave me a hard look, obviously knowing what form of punishment was rapidly on its way.

Mr. Dexter stopped in the center of the track field. He motioned for me to stand in a specific spot and Kat to stand two feet to my left. Next, he took my left hand and Kat's right and put them together. He stepped back and appraised the sight of the two of us standing in the open field and holding hands for all to see.

"There. That's much better. Now smile. I want you to stay like that for five minutes. If you don't keep smiling, I'll keep adding minutes until practice is over. Actually, you kind of make a cute couple," Mr. Dexter said and chuckled.

Kat smiled. I reluctantly failed to find the desire to force a smile.

"That five minutes just turned into six minutes. Smile, Mr. Graham," he said.

Kat quickly drove a left fist into my ribs, and my smile magically found the surface.

"Ah, there we go. Play nicely, kids. Next group, get ready," Mr. Dexter shouted and stuck the whistle back in his mouth and headed for the start line.

The humiliation was undeniable. I could see the entire track team bubbling with laughter. Even the kids hanging around the track bleachers after the last bell rang were enjoying themselves. There were howls, hoots, and stout whistles of appreciation for the entertainment Mr. Dexter had so graciously provided.

I wanted to dig a hole all the way to China or some other place where this story would never be spoken in a language I understood.

"Happy now?" Kat asked fiercely through an awkward smile. Her grip was powerful, grinding my knuckles painfully together.

"There's no need to be bitter over this," I said through clenched teeth.

"Thanks for making my day, Graham Cracker," she muttered.

"Who won the race, anyway?" I said, while trying to switch my mind and the conversation in a new and more comfortable direction.

"My brother, of course. I didn't even have to see it. He always wins. He's the fastest runner in the school."

"So, the kid sitting by the tree at lunch is your twin brother?"

"Duh. We look exactly alike."

I looked at her and then at the kid moving to the start line again. I didn't see a resemblance at all. In fact, there weren't any features they shared, but I kept my mouth shut about it.

"Stevie told me that your brother can time travel." It was difficult trying to have a conversation while smiling stupidly.

Kat's face went slack when she looked at me. Her eyes were hard, almost threatening pain if I continued this conversation.

"You think he's crazy, don't you?" she asked.

"I didn't say that. I just think he's got a vivid imagination. Hey, there's nothing wrong with wanting to be somewhere else sometimes. I can tell you right now that I'd love to be anywhere else except here."

It took a moment to realize that Mr. Dexter's whistle was calling, but it wasn't directed toward our track mates, but at us.

When my head snapped around, I could see him pointing at his grinning face. Caught up in our conversation about Kat's time-traveling brother, neither of us realized our smiles had fallen flat. We quickly gave Mr. Dexter what he asked for without protest.

"That's another minute added. Keep it up and you'll be here until dinner. I've got all night," he said.

I shook my head and said, "I'm sorry I got you into this. It certainly isn't right that a teacher is allowed to humiliate us like this. We should go to Principal Swann."

"It wouldn't do any good. All the teachers are in league with each other. Mr. Dexter's brother is a serious controlling force in this town. He's a nice enough guy, but none of the adults challenge him. Don't worry about it. Before too long, everyone will forget about it. This isn't the first time I've been forced to stand here and hold a boy's hand."

"It isn't?"

"No, and just for the record, each one of them became my boyfriend after and we did a lot, I mean a lot, of kissing."

"Are you saying you want to date me or something?" I asked, even though I instantly detected her sarcasm.

"For crying out loud, I'm just messing with you. I'm not sure I even like you very much, so I certainly don't want to kiss you," Kat said.

Her hand pulled free from mine when Mr. Dexter blew his whistle and motioned for us to rejoin the team.

"I'm not even sure we're from the same planet," I said as I followed her.

Despite the conflicts with Kat Mossgrove throughout the day, she caught up to me after I left school and headed home.

"So, why do you move so much?" she asked.

"Believe me, I don't like it. My brother goes where the jobs are. If he gets fired or gets laid off, we sometimes move to another city, or even another state."

"I don't get it. Why do you have to follow your brother from place to place?"

"Josh is my legal guardian. He has been since my parents died."

"Oh," Kat said with a lingering finality.

I knew she wasn't going to press the matter, but I was sure she wanted to know how my parents left the Earth.

"My mom and dad were the adventurous type, from what I've heard. They spent a good deal of their life savings doing a lot of traveling, seeing the world and stuff like that. They were attempting to sail to Europe when they got caught in a severe storm. The boat overturned, and they went into the water. The boat and their bodies were never recovered. We couldn't even have a proper funeral for them."

"Oh, that sucks. I'm so sorry." After an uncomfortable moment of thought, Kat said, "I think I'd rather have no parents than the ones I got stuck with."

"It's no picnic looking after yourself all the time. Usually, I feel like a burden to Josh. I feel like he got stuck with me out of pity. He knew that if he didn't take legal custody of me, then I'd probably be stuck in some hellish foster home. Josh had a bunch of plans lined up, but when my parents died, he had to abandon his dreams to take care of me. It isn't fair to him, and it isn't fair to me."

"I'm sure. My mom doesn't even live with us. I'm not entirely sure where she is now. She shows up once every couple of years, brings us gifts, tells us how much she's missed us, promises to stay this time, then my parents argue, and she disappears again. My father is completely nuts in his own way. Anderson and I spend as little time as possible at home."

"Life sure isn't what it appears to be on television sometimes. At least not the programs I've seen. Those people have such elite schools and fantastic family lives. What a crock," I said.

It felt good to vent to someone. Kat was a pretty good listener. She understood how family could sometimes suck the life right out of you. Being a teenager was no picnic, and most of the time, it felt like the entire world was working against us.

"Hey, do you have to get home right now?" Kat asked.

"No. Josh won't be home from work until seven o'clock or so. I'll have to make dinner for him, but that shouldn't take very long. What's on your mind?"

"You're new in town. I thought I'd show you a few things that might convince you that this town is a light-year past normal."

"I've already figured that out. But I'm up for whatever you've got in mind," I said and followed Kat to the business section of town.

We stepped onto Ready-Set-Go Avenue. I had already noticed the oddness of the street names and decided to ask Kat about them.

"What's with the street names?"

"What about them?"

"The names are so weird. They're not usual names like Pine, Birch, or Oak Street."

"So other towns name their streets after trees?"

"That was just an example."

"I wouldn't know. The names have been the same since I was born. Maybe it's all the other towns that are the weird ones. Maybe it's just all about originality, you know, like me."

Chapter 3

"Check this out," Kat said as she motioned for me to follow her across Ready-Set-Go Avenue in an awkward crouch.

"Are we trying to hide out in the open or something?" I asked as I mimicked her amusing, squatting shuffle.

Kat pressed her back against a brick building as if hiding from enemy fire, then leaned to her left to peer through the window of the town barbershop. She snickered and whispered something I couldn't understand.

"What's so special about this place?" I asked.

"Shh, he's putting on his cape and coming out. Just act natural and, for God's sake, don't laugh, especially like you did earlier at Regan."

Cape? I thought.

I didn't know what Kat was talking about until the man stepped from the barbershop, turned, locked the door, and began walking toward us.

The man was well over six feet tall and a solid two hundred and fifty pounds of defined muscle. He had a square jaw, a prominent forehead, and an enormous nose. He also had a tanned complexion, his black hair and goatee spotted with white. The obvious thing was that the man was wearing a crimson tunic, a black cape that was fur-lined at the collar, a silver crown, and white sneakers.

At his waist was a leather strap, and hanging in a scabbard at his side was a sword.

I was sure the clothing was something commonly worn during the Middle Ages. At my last school, before I moved, we had been in the middle of a class study in which we were discussing the Renaissance era. In a way, the class fascinated me. It reminded me of how my current life situation compared to the overwhelming poverty-stricken people of those times.

"Ah, children! So good to see you this fine evening!" he bellowed as we stepped up to him.

"Good evening, Sir Reginald Spree," Kat said, and lowered her head. She crossed her feet, bent her knees, grasped the hem of her dress, and bowed slightly at the waist.

I looked at her for a long, uncomfortable moment.

"Kneel, stupid," Kat said from the corner of her mouth.

For the second time today, Kat gripped the front of my shirt and pulled forcefully. My lower back gave, and my knees buckled to her command. She was incredibly strong for a teenage girl.

"A glorious evening it is. And who is this gallant young man?" Sir Reginald Spree said in a voice that echoed across the busy street.

When we straightened, Kat said, "I would like to present Jayce Graham. He's an incredibly simple-minded new arrival at our township."

"An ally, I hope."

"He's nothing more than a court jester. He's certainly not a nobleman such as you, Sir Reginald Spree."

"Well, all the same, it is a pleasure to meet you, young master," he said and nodded slightly. The sun winked at me off his crown.

"We're looking forward to watching your dominance at the tournament of champions this year," Kat said. I could see a smile hiding behind her eyes, and the corners of her mouth were curled in silent humor.

"It should be quite a conquest for me this year. Have you heard that Evan Plurge has already put forth a challenge? Imagine the gall of that man, believing he will unhorse me! Me!" He placed his hand on his chest to emphasize his shock.

"What a buffoon he is! I cannot foresee such a man overtaking you. Your quick wit and stamina will outlast all challengers," Kat said and bowed again.

"I greatly appreciate your confidence, young lady."

"It's our pleasure, Sir Reginald Spree. We must be off. Have a lovely evening," Kat said. She took my hand and pulled me past the oddest man I'd ever met.

"It was nice to meet you, Sir Reginald Spree," I called over my shoulder.

"Likewise, young master. I expect you'll be rooting for me at the games!" he said.

I saw several people on the sidewalk bow to him as he passed.

When we were a block away, Kat released my hand and slowed her pace.

"Okay, explain that whole thing," I said.

"Explain what?" Kat teased.

"Hilarious. I mean, explain the lunatic in the old-time outfit who's carrying a sword."

"Oh, that. Well, not much to tell. Sir Reginald Spree is our current Knight of Arms champion."

"And in current times, that means what, exactly?"

"He conquered all the challengers at last year's tournament. Oh, and he's also the town barber."

"Great, he's going to have to cut my hair one of these days. I sure hope he doesn't use the sword. So, what part of the last five minutes had any level of sanity?" I asked.

"Probably none of it. Honestly, the tournament games are fun to watch every year. It's kind of like stepping back in time for a few days. The entire town comes to watch or participate. There are even vendors who supply the type of food you would expect to see during medieval times. A lot of the townspeople show up in costumes because it adds authenticity during the event."

"I've never heard of any town doing something like that. Who started it and when?"

"I'm not sure. It's been going on for decades. Heck, even my dad remembers the games from when he was a kid."

"How come I've never heard it mentioned on the news or seen it in the papers? I would think something this unique would be on the news," I said.

"We keep tight a lip on things around here. The tournament is only welcome to those living in town. The mayor doesn't even allow outsiders to attend, especially reporters or news cameras."

"Outstanding. When is the tournament?"

"There will be postings for the tournament date soon. You'll see them stuck up everywhere, on telephone poles, in store windows, and probably in your mailbox. Come on, I've got someone else I'd like you to meet. He's a real gem," Kat said and led me to the outskirts of town.

The dirt road was like a wet, sliding snake through the dense woods. Kat and I were walking in the grass to the right of the deep ruts and desperately trying to keep our shoes clean. It seemed like we had walked the entire length of the county when she finally nodded toward a clearing.

"It's just ahead. Do you see it?" she asked.

I narrowed my focus. After a moment, I saw where she was pointing. There was a run-down structure. At first, I thought it was a barn. As the trees thinned out to a wider clearing, I saw it was a house. Well, it had once been a house, but now it was beaten down and sagged from years of weather abuse and a lack of upkeep. The cedar siding had severe splits, and many planks had fallen away and were left on the ground to rot. The roof bowed in the middle and looked on the verge of total collapse. Someone had boarded over several windows, and the frames still able to support glass were so filmed over with muck that no sunlight could break through.

"Is this place abandoned?" I asked as I watched Kat move up the front porch.

"I told you there was some else I want you to meet. Come on."

The wood steps bowed under her weight. The porch cracked and popped as she moved to the door and knocked on the oval glass.

"You shouldn't be up there. The wood might give out," I said.

"Quit being such a sissy and come on."

Kat knocked again, and without receiving a response, she opened the door and poked her head inside.

"Mr. Bixby? It's Kat. I've brought a friend I'd like you to meet. We're coming in now."

"This is a terrible idea," I said as I followed her inside.

When I closed the door, the sunlight immediately died out. Except for a dozen burning candles in one of the rear rooms, there were no overhead lights to help chase away the shadows.

Something caught my right sneaker and began clanking and moving after me in the darkness. I quickly turned and nearly fell over a stack of newspapers. At first, I thought that I'd disturbed a sleeping dog and now the thing was in attack mode. The clanking came to a stop, but the thing on the floor kept shifting forward.

I stopped and kneeled, and in the soft glow of the distant candlelight I saw what it was. The thing on the floor was like one of those toy monkeys clanging symbols together. Instead of a monkey, it was a robot that looked as if someone had constructed it from a dozen separate toys. Instead of symbols, it was small metal pots that probably went to some old tin toy set.

Its eyes came to life with white sparks behind the clear lenses, and the toy kept after me like a relentless ankle-biting dog.

"Stop it," I yelled to the toy and kicked it over when it bumped against my shoe.

Lying on its back, the wheels continued to spin. The pots that it had instead of hands began clanking again, and the eyes flickered with bold determination.

"Intruder alert," Kat said over her shoulder.

"You could have warned me."

"What fun would that be? You should have seen the look on your face. Priceless." Kat laughed in a way that reminded me of a honking duck as she moved to the next room.

"How did you even find this place?"

"I've been out here tons of times. A few years ago, I was in the woods near here and found this place. I didn't know anyone was living here. I just thought it was a house no one bothered to tear down. Of course, when I came inside, there was a different story than what I expected."

"And then she found a frightening old man with a second head and hellhounds for pets," a low voice said from the shadows of the armchair beside the fireplace.

As I tried to see the person, something whirled beside my head and was quickly off. I stopped, swatted at the air again, and searched for the flying thing that had grazed my ear. More than anything, I thought it was a bat, and those beady-eyed flying mice were high on my terror list. I looked at Kat to see if she had a clue what sort of thing was stalking the surrounding darkness. Kat was only smiling, paying no attention to me, and moved toward the man as he stood from the armchair.

With the firelight behind him, I could see the outline of a man, as he claimed, with two heads. No, that wasn't possible. At least I didn't think it was possible. I figured the firelight was playing with my eyes and made it appear as if the man had two heads. But when we stepped closer, I realized that two pairs of eyes switched from Kat to me.

A part of me, the cowardly part, began operating my feet. I felt myself unwillingly turning back to the door. I would have made a break for it if Kat's hand hadn't clamped onto my shoulder. She knew the action I was about to take before it was even a solid thought in my head. She was letting me know that there wasn't anything to fear in this place.

With Kat's reassurance, my panic lifted a little. Thankfully, the man didn't have two actual heads, but he was supporting an eerie-looking mannequin head on his right shoulder. His shirt even had a second collar that fit tightly around the dummy's neckline.

The white mannequin head was female. It had curly blonde hair, brown eyes lined with makeup, and lipstick. The thing looked more lifelike than I felt comfortable with. The eyes shifted to me, looked me up and down, and then turned to Kat.

"Who's the cute fellow you brought along?" The jaw worked up and down on hidden hinges. The voice was female and came from somewhere unknown.

"This is my new friend Jayce."

"Good to meet you," the man said and held out a hand that was certainly male.

I stared at that hand with the thick black hair popping out between the knuckles and decided that this one time I would have to be rude and refuse to shake someone's hand. That idea was short-lived as Kat rammed an elbow into my side. For a girl smaller than me, she had a hidden strength I was quickly beginning to acknowledge. I figured I probably had nearly half a dozen bruises courtesy of my new friend.

I reached out and shook. His handshake was gentle as he pumped my hand twice and released it.

"Jayce, this is Mr. and Mrs. Bixby. They're not fond of strangers, but since you're my friend, it's okay."

"Surely do it's all right," Mrs. Bixby said in a thick southern accent, and then looked me over again.

Those eerie, almost realistic roaming eyes were unnerving in the worst possible way. I couldn't believe Kat willingly came to this place and stayed for any length of time.

"Please, let's get comfortable," Mr. Bixby said and motioned to the chairs beside the fireplace.

As I sat, something lightly kissed my right ear. My hand automatically went into frantic motions. I swatted blindly, as if trying to ward off the attack of an entire bee colony.

"What on earth are you doing?" Kat asked, watching me as if I'd lost my mind.

"Something keeps touching me. Did you see it?"

"Careful, young man. If you hurt our pets, my husband will get quite upset," Mrs. Bixby said.

I turned fast enough at the sound of her voice that I caught Mr. Bixby slightly moving his lips. So, the answer was simple. Mr. Bixby, lost in his own world of craziness, wanted a companion so much that he had attached a partial mannequin to his body. He brought her to life by a clever manipulation of strings to operate the eyes and jaw and used his own voice in the style of a ventriloquist.

"What exactly are your pets?" I asked, scanning the darkness.

Mr. Bixby reached into the shadows beside his chair. His fingers played with something I couldn't see until he took hold of it and gently brought it closer.

What I saw was a thin string running straight up. Seeming to balance on the tip of the string was a yellow and blue butterfly. Its wings beat smoothly in the air. Its direction shifted toward the brightness of the fireplace, but the captured string prevented it from reaching its destination.

"Oh, Sally, I surely don't think you want to play over there," Mrs. Bixby said as her doll eyes watched the butterfly.

Kat stood, slowly walked around the room, and reached out every so often. When she came closer to the fire again, she was holding nearly a dozen colored strings in which different species of butterflies fluttered from the ends. It looked odd, as if she were holding a bundle of colorful balloons substituted with real butterflies.

"Incredible," I said, and then gently took the assortment of strings.

The butterflies moved in various directions, all of which were trying to break free from their tethers. A blue butterfly landed softly on my nose, studied my eyes, and

30

took flight again. I opened my hand, and all of them sailed off into the darkness once again.

"How on earth did you fix the strings on each butterfly?" I asked Mr. Bixby.

It was Mrs. Bixby who answered. "Very carefully. We must give them a gentle sedative through an aerosol. We tie a string that matches the color of each butterfly to their body. Don't worry, the string doesn't interfere with their flight and won't harm them."

"I've brought you something," Kat said and dug into her backpack.

"Oh, good. You must have picked up the supplies I asked you to get," Mr. Bixby said.

"I did." Kat removed a plastic bag filled with red rubber bands of various sizes and another bag with an assortment of springs, some of which were small enough to fit inside a wristwatch, while the others probably operated larger clocks or some other mechanical devices.

"How come you don't have any house lights on?" I asked.

"They don't believe in having electricity," Kat said.

"Of course we don't. Modern technology never really interested us. Besides, they expect you to pay for it. Look here," Mr. Bixby said and reached into his pocket.

He opened his hand, and sitting there was a small metal object the size of a tennis ball cut in half. He placed a tiny key into the top, wound it, and put the metal object on the hardwood floor.

The thing ticked like an old-fashioned explosive, and for a moment I thought it would go off like a cherry bomb. Instead, it came to life. It slowly rose from the ground as metal legs began uncurling from inside. There were small springs at the hinge of each joint. A tiny orb on the front of the thing rotated, and a single red eye stared at my sneakers. When the thing finished transforming, it was nearly four inches tall. It moved slowly at first on its spidery legs but then picked up speed and was nearly crawling up my leg before I could retract my feet up the chair.

Kat began laughing so hard she snorted uncontrollably.

"It won't hurt you. It's just a toy, you wuss," Kat said.

The metal spider bumped against the wooden leg of the chair several times. The red orb of its eye rotated up and inspected the chair before it folded itself back up with a series of clicking metal. After a moment, it was half of a sphere again.

I picked the thing up and turned it over. Mr. Bixby had designed it well. The spider's legs were locked together so tightly inside the sphere that I couldn't see the mechanics of how it operated.

"A gift for my new friend," Mr. Bixby said.

"Oh, no, I can't accept this. I appreciate the offer, but—"

"Think nothing of it. I offered a similar gift to Kat the day we met. She accepted it without question. I hope you'll do the same."

"Oh. Sure. I suppose if it's a gift of friendship, then it would be rude to decline."

"It would," Mr. Bixby said.

"Thank you. It's wonderful. I'll call him Fred," I said, as I couldn't think of anything wittier to say.

"A delightful name," Mr. Bixby said and clapped. He held out the winding key, and I took it.

Kat said, "Mr. Bixby is an inventor. You've so far seen only a few of the things he's created. That's why I buy him rubber bands and different-sized springs. He's awesome at making things out of ordinary items that you wouldn't think would make a good toy. I sell the toys he builds at the monthly flea market. His items sell out every time. People around here love Mr. Bixby's inventions."

"I simply can't keep up with demand," Mr. Bixby said and held out a dish filled with hard candy.

I'd always heard that taking candy from strangers was a bad thing to do. Mr. Bixby was without a doubt the strangest of them all, but, again, I didn't want to be rude and decline something offered to me. I plucked a yellow candy from the dish and popped it in my mouth. It was a lemon drop with a hint of cherry.

"Thank you. It's good," I said.

"We should probably be off. Jayce needs to get home," Kat said.

"Well, I suppose we'll see you next week?" Mrs. Bixby asked.

"Of course. I'll bring more supplies for you."

"Wonderful. Do be careful on the way home. It looks like rain," Mrs. Bixby said as her wooden eyes stared out the dirty window.

A roll of black clouds was moving in. I knew we'd get soaked before even making it halfway home.

As we moved toward the front door, I stopped as I spotted a black-and-white photo hanging on the living room wall. It was a train derailment. Someone had taken the photo from nearly a hundred yards away. Eight box-cars had plowed into the ground after tipping off the tracks. Dozens of men wearing protective suits were situated across the area.

"Wow. When did this happen?" I asked.

"My father took that photo during the Second World War. The train was carrying God knows what to MacDill Air Force Base. One thing or another caused the derailment. The military locked down the area, but my father found a path through the woods and took that photo."

"They're wearing chemical suits. At least I think that's what they are. Do you know what was on the train?" I asked.

"Hmm, no idea. My father said it was a powerful chemical that burned his nose and eyes. He said it appeared as if nearly all the containers had ruptured. All I know is that it took less than a day to clean up the wreckage. It was a tight-lipped operation, because the local paper didn't even get wind of it until the military was long gone."

"Come on. The storm is moving in fast," Kat said, tugging my sleeve as the sky grumbled.

"It was good to meet you," I said as Kat pulled me away from the house.

"Careful as you go," Mrs. Bixby called after us from the front door.

The wind was at our backs, and the intensity of the rain wasn't far behind.

"I can't believe you willingly go to that house all by yourself. The man is completely off his rocker," I said.

"Mr. and Mrs. Bixby are harmless."

"In case you didn't notice, Mrs. Bixby is a mannequin head with a moving mouth and eyes."

"Shut the front door. I hadn't noticed that before. Thanks for the insight, professor. He's an inventor. Inventors are hermits by nature and sometimes a little out there. He just created Mrs. Bixby to have someone to talk to. I'm sure you talk to yourself sometimes."

"Sure, who doesn't? But I don't have a fake head on my shoulder that I talk to as if it's a real person. The guy even has butterflies tied to strings. He's even named each one."

"You worry too much, Graham Cracker. I've been coming here for a few years. Mr. Bixby never seemed dangerous or made me feel awkward. No one is twisting your arm to come back here again," Kat said over the thunder rolling across the darkening sky.

A moment later, the rain came down like a waterfall. We broke through the cover of trees to the main road, and immediately the downpour caught us.

"This is where we part. My house is that way. Your house is that way," Kat said as she pointed down the road toward the west side of town.

Kat knowing where I lived didn't surprise me.

"Okay. I'll see you tomorrow at school," I called out and ran for home.

Chapter 4

My brother Josh is the easiest person in the world to cook for. He quickly gobbles up everything I cook or bring home. He has a cast-iron stomach that's never upset with what he consumes of any ethnic foods. A year ago, I challenged the strength of his stomach and his ability to contain and digest whatever went down his throat. While living in Colorado, I had stopped at a Japanese restaurant on the way home from school. I spent what little allowance I had and bought a platter of sushi, raw squid, and live octopus.

When Josh got home and eagerly opened the brown bag and the containers inside, I thought he'd shoot back on the couch and look at me as if I'd lost my mind. Instead, he opened each container with interest. He asked me how he was supposed to eat each item. I told him to eat everything right out of the container like you would with any meal. Except the hostess had explained that he needed to pinch the small live octopus between the chopsticks and wrap the squirming tentacles tightly around the body. Then he could dip it in a sauce and place the entire thing in his mouth and chew.

To my surprise, Josh took a pair of chopsticks, opened the container filled with salt water and two octopus, plucked one, wrapped it, dipped it, and then crammed the entire thing into his mouth with no hesitation. Not once did his face contort in disgust or show any signs of spitting the thing out and heading for the bathroom to puke. He chewed thoughtfully and swallowed. When he was done, he said that once he got past the suckers sticking to his teeth, tongue, and gums, it wasn't half bad. He pointed to the table that had the remaining octopus, which had escaped its watery confinement, and was squirming for freedom. He offered it to me. I declined the moving mass of snot and told him to enjoy the meal. I cooked myself a hot dog instead. Josh finished everything I had brought home and offered thanks with a long, loud belch as he turned on the TV.

Today I had no special surprise for him. Since I was running late from spending hours with Kat and several of the strange people of my new town, I simply cooked burgers on the grill with a side of macaroni and cheese. My timing was perfect as I pulled the burgers off the grill just as Josh came through the front door.

"Smells good, twerp," Josh said as he dropped his tool belt beside the living room chair.

"Hopefully it satisfies. I'm sure you're hungry."

Josh went to the sink and washed his hands and face. He sat at the kitchen table and groaned as he bent to untie his work boots. He removed them with a sigh of relief and leaned back, his spine offering several loud pops. I placed a plate in front of him, followed by the ketchup and mustard.

"Long day?" I asked.

This was the typical way we communicated. I asked about his day, and then he asked about school.

"I've got to say that construction isn't one of my favorite jobs, but the thing is, I see how rewarding it is when we're done. I kind of enjoy building houses. When it's complete and sold, a family is going to move in there.

They'll have experiences of good and maybe some bad memories to last a lifetime."

"You sound like a Hallmark commercial," I said as I scooped up a spoonful of macaroni and cheese.

"It's kind of like that. I never really thought about it before I took this job. It's awesome to know that I'm helping build something that's going to be around for a hundred years or more," he said.

"Yeah, I guess that sounds kind of cool."

"So?" Josh asked as he eyed me over the burger bun.

"What?"

"Any trouble at school?"

I shrugged. "Not really. Nothing serious at least."

I told him about my unusual day that had started with being late for class and ended with spending a short time in the house of Mr. and Mrs. Bixby.

"So, the school bully runs like he just went to the bathroom in his shorts, the town barber is a knight, and your girlfriend is friends with a two-headed man. Oh, and there's a kid at your school who can time travel. It sounds like you had more of an interesting day than I did." Josh chuckled and started working on his macaroni and cheese.

"She's not my girlfriend. She's just a friend."

"Yeah, sure. The way you talk about her is the way a boy talks about a girl he likes. Don't try telling me otherwise."

"She's almost as nutty as the other people I've met today, but I like her as a friend. Not, I repeat, not as a girlfriend."

Josh held up his hands. "Hey, pick your girlfriends however you like. It's none of my business. Here's the thing, I don't want you going to that house in the woods again. It doesn't sound at all like that man is right in the head. Besides, if the house is as bad as you say, the roof might collapse while you're there or something else bad could happen. Just promise me you won't go there again."

"Mr. Bixby is harmless. Kat said she's been going over there for years."

"If your girlfriend is smart, she won't go there anymore, either. Listen, stay away from that place. For me, please?"

"You're worrying for nothing. Kat's smart. She knows what she's doing. I trust her when she says that Mr. Bixby is harmless."

"He isn't mentally there if he's got pet butterflies on strings, or a fake head that's supposed to be his wife."

"He's also an inventor. Check this out," I said and pulled the mechanical spider from my pocket. I wound it and set it on the table.

Like the ticking of a clock, the thing slowly came alive as it uncurled its legs. The silver orb of its eye rotated until the red lens showed. It moved steadily toward the other side of the table. The look on Josh's face was comical as he watched the spider scurry toward him. I'm sure it was the same look I offered when I first saw the thing skittering at me. I thought Josh was going to stand and step away as the mechanical spider's legs clinked against his plate. Instead, he reached out and took hold of the silver body. He turned the bottom up and inspected it. Josh's face scrunched as he studied the underside of the spider.

"I have no idea how this thing actually works, but it's kind of cool. Did you look at the underside of it?" Josh asked.

"No. This is only the second time I've seen it open. The first time, the legs retracted before I even touched it."

The clicking stopped, and the legs refolded. I took the spider back, stuck the key in the slot, and turned it. I held it out at arm's length and watched the legs unfold. What I saw inside wasn't what I expected. There weren't small gears activated by the turning of the key. Instead of gears, dozens of small rubber bands unwound while stretching from side to side as tiny springs extended and retracted. It made me think of the bags of rubber bands and assorted springs Kat had brought for Mr. Bixby.

"Unreal," I said.

The rubber bands finished their twisting and extending motion. The springs retracted and pulled the legs in again. The eye rotated closed, and the thing was still.

"That's brilliant. That guy should sell those things. He'd make a killing," Josh said.

"He does. He says he has more orders than he can keep up with."

"Well, unlike you, I haven't met anyone in town except Mr. Barshell when he showed us several of the rental properties."

Even though Josh and I live in Paper Moon, Josh couldn't find a suitable job close to home. The rent here was more manageable than the neighboring town of Coral Key. It was in Coral Key where Josh had to find work. I was glad Josh had decided we should live in Paper Moon instead and he would commute. We had originally looked at some rentals in Coral Key, but the place seemed too uppity for us. I'd never forget the snobby looks we got driving through town in Josh's battered, rusty truck. They offered looks of disgust not only to our vehicle but also our casual, worn-out clothing. I always disliked people who thought they were better than someone else.

"Oh, I almost forgot to tell you. There's going to be a tournament sometime this summer. From what Kat tells me, it's a three-day event between individuals living in town. There's jousting, sword fighting, and an archery competition. It's like a whole medieval event. It sounds like a blast, and I'd really like to go."

"Does it cost anything to get in?"

I knew that money was always tight. If there was an entrance fee, Josh would have to shoot down the possibility of going.

"I didn't ask Kat. I don't think so. It's just for residents. They won't let anyone else in."

"We'll probably have to wait until we know what day it's on. You know we can't plan on something that far away," Josh said and took his dinner plate to the sink.

Yeah, I knew it all right. For all I could guess right now, Josh might lose his construction job and this time next week, we could be living in Maine.

I didn't say what was on my mind. Doing so would only start another argument where I'd go running off to my room and not speak to Josh for several days. If someone moved as often as I did, they'd feel the same way.

"Okay," I finally said.

Josh went to the couch and began cycling through the TV channels while I did the dishes. When I was done, I went to my room to finish my homework. It wasn't easy focusing on the assignments, as my mind kept wandering through the events of the day. This town was such an odd place in the world to land. Before my parents went missing somewhere on the Atlantic Ocean, I remember my mom telling me that the universe has a funny way of putting everyone where they're meant to be. I wondered if Paper Moon was a place I was meant to stay. I bet my parents never thought the universe had a place for them at the bottom of the ocean. I'm sure it never crossed their minds until the boat went over and the waves continued to crash down on them.

Chapter 5

I couldn't say for sure what had woken me. Whether it was a dream, a good or bad one, or an outside noise, my brain simply signaled that I was finished lying around for the night. Either way, my eyes were open and refused to close. Coming through a part in the curtains, a dim morning light and the lingering darkness of tree branches played shadows across the wall. I tried to see pictures in those movements, forcing my mind into a slow cranking state, hoping I could fall back to sleep. Maybe it was the fact that I was in another town, in another state, still running down the too-familiar road Josh and I had traveled far too long. We never settled long before Josh was looking for another job. I never knew if his inability to keep a steady job had to do with him being unable to learn, unwilling to cooperate with management, or if he subconsciously sabotaged each job field because he knew in his heart that he wasn't fit for the position.

When I felt my mind slipping back a little to the world of fantastic dreams, a scream tore through our quiet neighborhood. My eyes went wide, my body rigid. At first, I wasn't sure if I had fallen asleep and the scream was born in the dream world. The shadows on the wall faded as the light outside grew brighter.

I slipped from the bedsheets and went to the window. Looking outside, I couldn't fully understand what I saw. I knew what an uncontrolled fire could do, of course, but never in my fourteen years have I seen anything consumed as fiercely as I did right now. It engulfed a house across the street in yellow, orange, and red flames.

People stood on the sidewalk, looking unsure of what to do. Swirling red and blue lights shot across the neighborhood as a fire truck rushed down the street.

I hurriedly put on my shorts and shirt. Moving into the hall, I pounded on Josh's door and entered before he even said anything. Josh could sleep through nearly anything. I imagined it was from the exhaustion of a physically demanding job. His eyes shot open after I shook him several times. I never had to wake him up so abruptly before, so his mind gave me immediate attention.

"What's wrong?" he asked, alarmed.

"A house across the street is on fire."

With no more questions, he ripped off the covers, threw on clothes, and headed for the front door. I followed close behind.

We could feel the heat of the fire as we ran to the gathering crowd. The volunteer firemen erupted from what I guessed to be the only fire truck in town.

"Is anyone in there?" Josh asked the gathering neighbors.

They looked at us. Silently watching the two young men new to a town where all others had probably lived for generations.

"That's the McCreadys' house. I don't see them out here," a man with a white beard and thin hair told us.

Josh didn't hesitate. He grabbed my shirt and hauled me across the street, closer to the burning house.

"There might be people in there," Josh yelled to the firemen who scrambled to uncoil the hose and hook it up to the nearest hydrant.

"Sir, step back and let us work. You're only getting in our way," one of them said and ran back to the truck.

A police car was now coming down the street. I knew what Josh was thinking. If someone was inside, the firemen were going to be too late to get them out by the time they had everything hooked up and were ready to fight the fire.

"Come on," he said and grabbed me again.

We went towards the back of the house, going against the calls of the crowd for us to come back and let the firemen handle the job. Josh was never one to sit by, especially when someone needed help.

The intensity of the heat grew every step we took as we rounded the back of the house. We moved past children's toys, a bike, and a sandbox. At that moment, we realized that children might be trapped inside the burning house.

"Stay back, I'm going to try the door," Josh said.

The area of the back door wasn't as consumed with fire as the rest of the house. This allowed Josh to peer through the window and try the knob.

"It's warm but not hot. We've got to check and make sure no one is inside." Josh then delivered a hard kick just to the left of the knob.

The door exploded inward, and a rush of heat ran out at us. The opening of the door gave the fire a rush of oxygen, and the flames instantly doubled. Just like an insane dream, Josh ran inside, disappearing into the black smoke and eager flames. He screamed a moment later, a scream not of pain but of panic. I heard responding cries from others inside. They were upstairs somewhere, trapped by the fire.

I didn't give it a second thought. I ran to the side of the house, unraveled the hose from its hook, and turned the faucet on full. Blindly, I followed Josh's lead. Going through the kitchen, I doused everything in my path. I must have passed the stairs in the smoke as I reached the front living room. There were blankets lying across the back of the couch and a loveseat. I directed the hose at them and soaked them as quickly as I could. I dropped the hose, wrapped one wet blanket around me, grabbed the other, and retrieved the hose. I headed back toward the kitchen and found the hallway with the stairs heading up.

"Josh! Where are you?" I called and coughed into the wet blanket.

"Jayce, get the hell out of here!"

I ran, not out, but up. I'm certainly not a hero, but I'm no coward either. One of the few relatives I had left in the world was in this burning house. There was no way I was leaving him. The fire followed me up the stairs. I sprayed the carpet to knock the flames back, making sure our return path was clear. The slack in the hose ran out when I hit the top step. I had no choice but to abandon it.

In the thick smoke, I found Josh crawling on the floor, exiting a bedroom. I threw the other wet blanket over him. He grabbed a corner and breathed through the waterlogged fabric to help filter the air. A weak call came from down the hall. I crouched to get below the heavy upstairs smoke and saw a closed door at the end of the hall, and it was on fire. Joshed kicked at the bottom of the door until it gave out. Inside, we found a woman and a young girl of about five lying on the floor. The mother cradled her daughter protectively. Their eyes were closed, and neither of them moved.

Josh crawled to them and said a moment later, "They're alive but unconscious. Can you carry the girl on your back?"

I nodded.

45

Josh helped, and seconds later, the girl's limp body was strapped across me. Since she was unconscious and couldn't hold on, I had to lean forward to keep her on. Josh threw the wet blanket over us. He draped his blanket over the woman. He slid one arm beneath her knees, and the other around her back and hefted her up. We moved fast toward the stairs.

The gushing hose soaked the stairs, but the wall to our right was fully on fire.

We kept tight to the railing when Josh said behind me, "Hurry, Jayce. I'm on fire."

In the middle of the house's inferno, nothing could have frozen my blood faster. Looking back, I saw flames had grabbed Josh's right shirt sleeve and now crept toward his face. He didn't want to put the woman down. He didn't want to drop her. He didn't want to take time to slap out the fire. He just wanted to get out.

We hit the bottom landing as the front door exploded in. Two firemen wearing protective gear and respirators stepped inside. One held an axe, the other controlling a hose as he quickly hammered every nearby flame. They saw us at the bottom of the staircase, holding the mother and daughter as we tried to reach safety. They saw Josh on fire. The fireman turned the hose on us. The water's spray was like a million needles shot from a cannon. Even through the pain, there was a welcome relief from the heat of the house. After the firemen quickly doused Josh's shirt, they moved aside, and we ran into the front yard. Our muscles gave out as we reached the grass beside the fire truck. The woman tumbled from Josh's arms and the girl slid off my back.

Two paramedics carrying medical kits ran up to us, asking if we were all right. Through a series of hard coughs, we said we were. Josh told them it was the girls who needed the help. The paramedics placed oxygen masks over the nose and mouth of Mrs. McCready and her daughter.

We all watched in stunned silence, waiting for something to happen. I didn't expect the two to jump up laughing in joy or any kind of nonsense like that, but I expected them to open their eyes and whisper to all those around that they were all right.

I was not disappointed. The young girl was the first to open her eyes. Her ocean-water-blue eyes searched each face closest to her. She released a series of violent coughs, forcing out any remaining smoke. When her eyes found her mother, her tiny hand reached out and gripped three fingers. Maybe it was maternal instinct, but that gentle touch of her daughter made her come around. Her focus instantly found her daughter, and then her arms took her in.

The crowd came alive then. It seemed like an odd thing to hear people clapping while someone's house and all their earthly possessions became black ash, but the two people were alive. Those closest to us began smacking our backs, telling us what a fine job we did, what a brave thing we did, what a crazy thing.

I didn't think of it that way. They were just people who needed help, and we had the opportunity and the desire to give it to them. Part of me maybe even wanted to argue that what we had done was a completely stupid thing. There could have been four victims consumed by the fire instead of two. But after all, we left the house with nothing more than a few minor burns and some scorched lungs. I was glad Josh had run inside and that I had followed.

"A hell of a thing. I don't think I've ever seen anything like that. You boys deserve a medal at the very least," an officer said. He took off his cap, scratched his head, and then clicked his tongue. "A hell of a thing, all right. I didn't think anyone was inside."

My face was hovering over the grass as I coughed hard, trying to find clean air. I had a hard time focusing on anything, so I stared at the mud around the sole of the police officer's shoes. There was a glossy shine on the tops of his shoes and that shoe polish had a strong chemical smell to it. Maybe it was a combination of that smell, the fiery smoke still in my body, and the surge of adrenaline and jangled nerves. The result was I threw up on the officer's shoes.

He leaped back in surprise. He muttered a few curse words but then caught his tongue as he realized there were children around.

There wasn't much left in my stomach, as it had been nearly eight hours since I had last eaten. Most of what came out was a green bile, and the acidic rankness of it burned my already scorched throat on the way out.

"I'm so sorry. I didn't know that would happen," I said as I wiped my mouth with the back of my hand.

"It's all right, kid. You just caught me off-guard is all," he said as he did his best to use the grass to wipe off the vomit.

One paramedic asked Mrs. McCready if there was anyone else in the house. Through the oxygen mask, she told them it was just the two of them, and that her husband was away on business until Friday.

The fire raged on. All attempts to douse the blaze seemed to do no good. The streams of water only enraged the fire. It was defiant to die until it had consumed the entire structure and every bit of personal items left inside.

It wasn't long before the firemen gave up the fight. Instead, they focused their hoses on the adjacent houses to keep them from going up in flames as well. There was nothing worth saving anymore. I was sure the crowd of onlookers also realized it.

I couldn't imagine having everything I owned suddenly and violently taken away, never to be cherished again. Josh and I had little in the way of possessions anyhow, so the sting wouldn't hurt as much. But the McCready family probably lived their entire lives in Paper Moon. All they owned was now in flames. Clothes, toys for the little girl, furniture, kitchenware, photos, and the entire house itself gone forever. Long after the flames died out, workers would haul away the rubble to the local dump to become lost in Florida soil.

I saw the realization of those facts cover their features. There was nothing left for them but the pajamas they wore. The woman cradled her daughter as they watched the flames reach for the night sky. The house offered a mocking, constant belch of black smoke blown away in the night breeze.

I turned my attention to Josh. The fire had burned his right sleeve away, and the skin was an angry red where the flames had grabbed him.

"Are you going to be all right?"

"I think so. Hurts a bit like a horrible sunburn, but I don't think there will be any lasting damage."

"You still need to have them look at it. Maybe they've got some ointment to put on it to help soothe it."

"They need to worry about those two before they get to me." He hugged me then. It was a hug of relief. "I wanted you to stay outside. That was a stupid thing you did by running inside."

"I was just following my idiot brother. We already lost our parents. I wasn't going to lose you as well."

He smiled. "Yeah, well, I'm glad you had my back. I wouldn't have been able to carry both of them out. That was a smart thing you did with the hose and wetting the blankets. Where did you get that idea?"

"I saw it in a movie once. The fire leaves you alone when you're soaking wet, and the smoke has a hard time getting through wet fabric when you breathe through it."

There was an awful groaning of tortured wood. The second story suddenly sagged about a foot like a giant getting ready to sit for a rest.

"She's going to drop! Everyone move back!" the policeman with vomit on his shoes yelled.

We didn't have to be told twice. Those of us still too close instantly scrambled up and ran for the street. The rest of the crowd had already made it back to safe territory. When we got to the other side of the street, the structure gave out. It made a horrible cry, like a beast being swallowed into an abyss. Wood, shingles, siding, fractured windows, and anything else on the second floor quickly came down to the first floor like a crazy magic trick. A million angry fireflies burst out of the collapsed structure and flew in every direction, including right at us. One of them got caught in the corner of Josh's left eye, and he swatted at it to get that burning ember knocked loose.

"I believe that house is still trying to kill me," he said as he rubbed his eye.

The collapse had taken much of the fire's eagerness, and the flames had dramatically died down.

Nearly an hour had passed since the full rage of the inferno had begun. Now a little more than half a dozen small fires remained. The crowd soon lost interest and headed back home to get ready for work or school. Most of them offered somber apologies to the McCready family and told them that if they needed anything to just stop by and ask.

Before we headed home, Josh, a boy who quickly become a man when our parents died, went a step further than all the others.

He walked up to them and said, "Mrs. McCready, I'd like to offer both of you a place to stay after they check you out at the clinic. I don't want to hear that it isn't necessary. You're not putting anyone out. I would like very much to give you a roof over your head until your husband gets home and helps you get everything sorted out."

She said, "That's very kind. We don't have any family in town, so I'll take you up on the offer. How can I turn down the men who saved our lives?"

That's how Mrs. McCready and her daughter, Lily, stayed with us for the next two days. Josh suggested that Mrs. McCready and Lily take his bed. I could have slept in my room, but I wanted to be with Josh on the fold-out sofa. It was nice being close to him when most of the time we only saw each other in passing. The second night after the fire, we talked into the late hours. We talked about the new town, my school, his new job, and, of course, about the fire that gave us houseguests.

I drifted off shortly before one in the morning. In my dreams, I became an investigator on a mission to find the reason behind the fire that consumed the McCreadys' possessions. There was a dream about fiery chaos. I dreamed of awful things happening to good people. I wouldn't know it then, but fate also had such a strange plan for me.

Chapter 6

Everyone's business in Paper Moon is rarely private. Small towns spread local news like a lightning crack. If even the hermit, Mr. Bixby, was aware of Josh and me running into a burning house, it wouldn't surprise me.

Because of the attention surrounding me, I managed to avoid another confrontation with Regan Evans. During the week, both students and faculty were always close with questions about the fire event. I was tired of explaining my actions and resisting everyone's claims of me being a hero or a moron. I promised I was no such thing. Maybe the moron part, but definitely not a hero. I enjoyed having a few close friends, when possible, but I couldn't stand overwhelming attention. If I could step back into my ordinary life prior to the night of the fire, I gladly would.

I didn't see much of Kat or Anderson during the rest of the school week, and not at all after classes. It wasn't until Saturday that I found out what they had been up to.

One of Josh's coworkers was doing remodeling on his home and asked him for a helping hand with a carpentry project for a generous wage. So, Josh jumped on it. Being left alone as usual, I spent Saturday morning and early afternoon enjoying the book *The Martian* by Andy Weir. Books were the one thing that traveled with me every time we moved. I often picked up thrift shop copies or excellent finds at garage sales in every new town. They were cheap, plentiful, and a wonderful distraction equaling hours of enjoyment. They were also the primary source for my word building and the reason I always aced English studies. After plowing through two hundred pages of incredible humor and mind-blowing engineering in the name of lone survival on a barren planet, I needed to step away from Mark Watney's desperate attempt to go home. The itch to get up and go outside took its hold, and so I answered.

I had no destination in mind. I simply started walking down our street. My sight briefly caught the blackened debris of what remained of the McCready house. I had spent the week talking endlessly about it, so I wanted to push it far from my mind this weekend.

Many people were outside doing yardwork, children playing in yards, and others going for a walk like me. A few blocks later, I left the neighborhoods behind and ventured into the woods. After a few dozen yards following a narrow path, I ran into two kids I knew. I was honestly glad to see them.

"What are you doing?" I asked.

Kat was crouched beside the stream with her back to me. To her left was Anderson, trying to skip stones downstream.

Kat quickly stood and whirled around. She was holding a plastic vial of water. She screwed the cap on and said, "What are you doing, hot-shot hero? Did you follow us?"

"No. I didn't even know you were out here. I was just exploring the woods. There's nothing to do at home, so I came out here. Are you taking a water sample or something?" I asked.

"Something like that," she said as she pushed the vial into her front pocket.

"Sounds secretive if you're not willing to tell me. Come on, I can keep a secret. You know I can. I don't have any friends, so I've got no one to tell anyhow."

Kat looked at Anderson for approval. He shrugged and turned his attention back to the skipping stones.

"All right. I had an idea. Do you remember when I took you to Mr. Bixby's house?"

"Of course. I'm sure I'll never be able to blank that one from my memory."

"Well, I was thinking about that picture you pointed out. I hadn't really thought about it before. After Mr. Bixby told us his father witnessed the cleanup of the military train wreck, I started thinking about what could have been in those train cars. Remember that the pictured showed the military men were wearing protective suits? What if whatever was on that train was some horrible chemical that had absorbed into the ground? What if they didn't really clean up the chemical, but left it where it spilled? They cleaned up the train wreckage quickly and got out of there before anyone knew what was going on. It could have been some bad stuff that leaked out into the soil."

"Ah," I said. "I think your paranoia is in overdrive. I know you love creating so-called conspiracies, but so what if there was a chemical spill eighty years ago? What does that have to do with the water in that stream?"

"Everything. We don't know if that chemical spill was something potentially toxic or something that could have long-term effects on all the people in or around town."

I looked at Anderson to see if he agreed with his sister's far-fetched idea. Anderson wasn't paying attention to us. His intense focus was on the steady run of the stream. His mind seemed a million miles from here.

I walked down the path closer to Kat. I held out my hand for the water vial. She removed it from her pocket and handed it over. I held it up to the sun breaking through the trees. The water was crystal clear.

"I think I know what you're getting at. So, you're thinking that a military chemical spill has been leeching into our town's water supply from the ground soil, right?"

"Exactly. I've been taking samples from several streams, the two closest lakes, and the tap water. There's a reason the people in town act so oddly," Kat said.

I looked at Anderson again, and then turned to Kat. I wondered if Kat believed that they were exempt from the town's strangeness. Between a time-traveling kid and a girl who believed that every person in the world had a secret agenda, they were a far reach from being omitted from the large group of abnormal people.

"You're going to need some serious proof if you plan on battling against the government. Even if you have the water analyzed and they find something, there's no way you can point your finger at a military train wreck that happened so long ago. No one will believe it."

Part of me was trying to reel in Kat from the idea that everything was a cover-up. She seemed like a girl who needed these excuses as an explanation to why the world was the way it was. Reality was simple. The world wasn't a perfect place. People weren't perfect either. Far from it. When you combined the two, you had a serious problem with never knowing what things were meant to be like. My father used to say whenever a problem came around, "It is what it is, and trying to find an answer for it will drive you mad."

I handed Kat the water vial. When I looked upstream, I noticed Anderson was gone. Searching across the forest,

I didn't see him anywhere. There was also the lack of foot-steps moving through the forest.

"Where did your brother go?"

Kat glanced at that empty spot. There were shoe prints leading to the edge of the water where Anderson had been, but no prints walking away. There was a ripple of water where a thrown stone had just landed.

Kat shrugged and said, "He must be on one of his jour-neys through time. I've got an idea. We could look through old articles in the newspaper at the library. Maybe there's something in there about the train wreck that Mr. Bixby didn't know about. Maybe we can even find out when the people in town started acting so strangely."

This was a good idea, I thought. I wasn't on board to learn about some chemical spill covered up by the mili-tary, but I wanted to prove that Kat's belief was a light-year from accurate. I thought that maybe this way she would stop grasping for conspiracies.

I looked again at where Anderson had been. Sarcas-tically, I said, "The time-traveling kid is off to save the rest of the world again, while leaving us to save this town."

Kat delivered a knuckle-stinging punch to my arm and said, "Hey, leave him alone. He's got enough to deal with. He never asked for the things he gets. I assure you that Anderson doesn't want them. So why don't you keep your nose out of his business, okay?"

I tried to rub away the numbness and said, "That hurt. Okay. Whatever he does is no concern of mine. I'm sorry for existing."

Kat's anger quickly faded. She looked at the ground, maybe feeling bad about hitting me again.

"So, what do you say? Should we head to the library and see what we can dig up?" she asked.

"I don't see why not. I've got nothing better to do."

The public library was a busy place on Saturday afternoon. Some of my classmates were there, as well as a dozen adults roaming through the stacks for the next great read.

We found an empty table near the back wall and set our stuff down. I wasn't sure where to start, so I looked at Kat and waited for her to figure things out.

"We need to speak with someone and find out where they keep the microfiche of old newspaper articles," she said and moved toward the librarian's desk. "Excuse me, Ms. Tunstill. We're working on a class project about the effects that Paper Moon may have suffered during the Second World War. Could you point us in the right direction to where we could find local newspaper articles or microfiche that describes how the people of town got along during that devastating time?"

"Projet de la classe, yous dire?" Ms. Tunstill said.

"Right," Kat shot back.

"Suivez-moi," Ms. Tunstill said.

She came around the desk and headed for the east end of the library. We followed her downstairs to the basement and passed overloaded bookshelves. Half the lights were out in this area, and several others buzzed and flickered with the promise of going out for good.

"Tout ce que vous recherchez peut être trouvé dans les," she said and pointed to a stack of drawers.

"Great. Thank you very much, Ms. Tunstill," Kat said.

"Si vous avez besoin de quoi que ce soit d'autre il suffit de le demander," she said and headed back to the stairs.

When the librarian was out of earshot, I said, "I'm not even sure what to make of that. Doesn't she speak English?"

"Don't you speak French?"

"I've only taken Spanish courses."

"She speaks English, but I suppose she likes the sound of French better," Kat said and started searching through drawers.

"But she deals with people all day. How many people in town speak French? Did you understand her?"

"There might be a few people in town who speak French. I don't. I didn't understand a word she said. I never do. I just ask a question and follow her to wherever she takes me. She pointed to these stacks of drawers. So, I figured we'll find what we're looking for in here. Look," Kat said as she opened the fifth drawer.

There were brittle yellowed envelopes neatly categorized by date. Kat fingered through them until she reached a certain year. She pulled twelve envelopes from the drawer and then moved over to the viewer.

"This is the entire year of 1942. If I remember right, the U.S. joined the war in December 1941 right after the Japanese attacked Pearl Harbor. So, we'll start at the beginning of 1942 until we figure out when the train wreck happened and maybe find out what was on it," Kat said and inserted the first microfiche slide.

We were looking for two important things. We wanted to know if The Paper Moon Recorder had any information about the train wreck or other articles talking about noticeably strange behavior observed in town. Even though this really wasn't a school project, as Kat had claimed, it sure felt like one. I wasn't thrilled about spending a Saturday in the library searching through old newspaper articles.

One slide followed another as one hour moved to the next. We went through all the slides of 1942 and 1943 with no luck. I didn't figure we'd find anything until Kat stopped her search and focused the viewer on a certain article.

I looked over her shoulder and read aloud the headline and the rest of the brief article.

Military train derails three miles north of Paper Moon.

I received a report early Tuesday morning that a massive train wreck occurred just outside of town. The cause of the derailment and casualty numbers are unknown. I could not get near the accident as military men stopped me on the access road that passes near the wreckage. The men posted on the road would not answer questions about injuries or what the train was carrying. It's assumed, but not verified, that the train's destination was MacDill Air Force Base 170 miles north of town before it derailed. A series of large cranes moved past the blockade during the next hour and were moving out again ten hours later. After the military left, I could use the road to get closer. Aside from the repaired damaged ground in which I suppose train cars plowed up the dirt, nothing much else was noticeable. However, there was an overwhelming odor that I couldn't identify. The pungent smell could have a connection to something previously transported on board or simply the southern wind carrying the musty smell of the Everglades from the south of town.

"Okay, so now we know the train wreck happened in April 1944. So, since we didn't come across any articles before that date about people in town acting strange, let's read through the articles after the train wreck," Kat said and switched microfiche.

Kat inserted the slide of May. We skimmed the articles and then switched them out for June. Then June switched to July. There was something interesting we discovered during this month. An article in July 1944 announced the city's approval to begin construction on the arena in which the annual games would take place. The article didn't specify who first came up with the strange suggestion, but the entire town believed it was a fantastic idea.

Kat said, "The article says they built the arena to help people take their minds off the war. I would think creating an arena for battling each other would be more of a reminder than anything else."

Kat's theory was gaining a bit of ground with me. This had to be our answer. They cleaned up the derailment of the train car but not the contents of what spilled out. The military then denied the ordeal ever happened, leaving no blame to be assigned.

"What if all these water samples you're gathering reveal something major?"

"What do you mean?"

"I mean, what if the chemicals found in the water are some really serious stuff? Maybe something that causes cancer, like eventually melts your brain into a gray pudding kind of toxic mess?" I asked, as I was now thinking about how much tap water I'd consumed in the short time I've been in this town.

"Honestly, I can't think of a single person in town who has cancer. Let's send these samples to the lab I found online. Once we get the results, we can decide what move needs to happen next."

Chapter 7

The following Saturday, as we rode our bikes along Downside Up Street, Kat asked, "Have you seen a gator before?"

"Of course. Who hasn't seen one?"

"I mean, have you ever seen a gator in the wild?"

"I saw a bunch of them in a cage at the zoo. My parents took us just before they died. It was one of the few things they ever did with Josh and me before they decided to see the world and let us take care of ourselves."

"But have you ever seen a gator in the wild? Have you ever been so close that you could tap one on the snout with a stick?" Kat persisted.

"No. Why would you hit a gator with a stick? That seems like a dumb thing to do."

"I'm not saying I would, only that I could. Are you up for a bike ride out of town?"

I shrugged. "I don't care. I've got nothing better going on."

When we finally hit the top of the hill, Kat said, "Okay, even though we're going downhill, I want you to pedal as fast as you can. When we hit the bottom of the hill, stop pedaling. The momentum will take us nearly a mile because it's dead flat at the bottom."

Before I had time to even catch my breath, Kat was on her bike, shooting down the hill while cycling fast enough that her feet were a blur.

I hopped on my bike, kicked off the concrete, and quickly pedaled. She had gained a sizable lead, but her bike was old, rusted, and in dire need of oil to smooth out the chain and gears. My bike was old, yes, but since I was sure that this would be the last bike I would own in the years before I hit adulthood, I took great care of it. Extra money in my household was unheard of, and if my bike gave out completely, then the rubber soles of my shoes would take the place of rubber tires. Josh had made it clear that the things I had needed taken care of if I chose to continue enjoying them. He said that the only reason he'd take out his wallet for me was to buy secondhand clothes from the town thrift shop. This didn't bother me all that much. I was getting used to doing without certain things. Heck, after a while, I didn't even notice when some unimportant item was gone to the trash or just gone.

The speed was incredible. The hill was steep, but adding our almost frantic pedaling was rocketing us at insane speeds. I thought that if a car drove into our path from one of the side streets, there wouldn't be a possibility of stopping in time.

Our bikes found the bottom slope of the road. Now the road lay dead flat and arrow-straight for as far as I could see. Kat was right. The built-up momentum seemed able to carry us all the way to the Florida Keys if I resisted using the brakes.

Kat then did something that stunned me. She shifted from her hunched aerodynamic position, sat upright, tilted her head back so that she saw nothing but clear blue sky, and then she let go of the handlebars. Her arms spread wide like an eagle's wings. She looked as if she were trying to swan dive into that endless sky.

"Try it, Jayce. Just try it. It's like flying! It's incredible!" Kat yelled out.

Kat was fearless. She was a girl who believed she had nothing to lose, and because of this belief, she had everything to gain.

The problem was that, unlike Kat, I worried about everything. I thought I got it from my mother, but I wasn't sure. I worried that if I let go of the handlebars my front tire would by chance run over a small rock, or dip into a pothole, and this action would throw off the front tire's steady line and the result would be a hard crash followed by an ambulance ride to the hospital. Then after my hospital stay, Josh would endlessly bark about how stupid I was and whether I had a clue how much the hospital trip cost.

Like most kids, the battle between common sense and my body's eagerness for the experience was short-lived. I wanted the enjoyment Kat was absorbing. I would have to pay the consequences of a crash if it came to that.

Mimicking Kat's movement, I tilted my head back and then cautiously pulled my hands away from the handlebars. My muscles began relaxing and trusted Kat's guidance when the blast of a car horn directly behind me caused me to jerk forward. The bike wobbled from my movement, and the front wheel began turning. I grabbed the handlebars just as my bike veered right. I quickly steadied out before the bike dared a hard flip. My front tire rubbed against Kat's rear tire, and I saw her quickly change position as she gripped her handlebars and got her bike back in a straight line.

I pulled up next to Kat. When we were sure we weren't going down in a horrific skin against concrete slide, we looked back. Strangely enough, I wasn't surprised to see who was behind us.

In the passenger seat was Regan Evans. He was rocking back and forth, his mouth wide with howling amusement. We could hear his hut-hut-hut laughter through the closed car windows, sounding like he was getting ready to hike a football.

Sitting in the driver's seat was an older boy who looked as if he'd just escaped prison. His hair was long, oily black scraped back on his scalp. His eyes were nearly as black, steady, and menacing, with no hint of playfulness. I was sure that at any moment they would run us over like animals on the road and keep going without a glance back.

The vehicle moved to the left lane as we skirted the dirt shoulder. They pulled alongside us, and Regan rolled down the window.

"Where's your girlfriend taking you? Are you heading out to the woods for a little alone time?" Regan asked, and then he smacked his lips in a kissing motion.

"Jayce has already seen more action with a girl than you will by the time you're thirty," Kat barked at him.

I immediately knew that what Kat said was going to come back and bite her more than she expected. She was pretty much giving Regan permission to tell the entire school body that we were a secret couple. I could see future rumors circling through the school, running wildly out of control.

"Is that so, Graham Cracker?" Regan asked.

Without warning, the car made a hard swerve at us. We quickly shifted to the right, and our tires dug deeply into the wet ground of the shoulder. I thought that the sudden deceleration would cause Kat and me to vault over our handlebars and land roughly in heavy Florida mud.

"I don't think my brother likes you very much. He just got back from an all-boys school up north. They kicked him out because he didn't play well with others. He almost beat a teacher to death with a textbook because the teacher wanted him to reread a chapter. Rory doesn't like reading."

"I didn't know you morons could read," Kat yelled.

I was only half listening as I tried to get my bike back on the road or to the right, where the sucking mud gave way to thick grass and stable ground.

I'd never been in a situation like this. Not only was I dealing with a mean, crazy schoolmate, but now I had to contend with the crazy schoolmate's psycho brother, who had no interest in rules or authority. This was a kid who wanted, maybe even needed, to crush everything that stood in his path.

Somehow, Kat and I worked our bikes from the devilish grip of the mud by popping our front tires back onto the street. Thick globs of mud spun off the rear wheel, splattering my tee shirt and the back of my head. I gritted my teeth, holding back the anger, and wished for this stupid confrontation to finish.

I had only hoped that Kat would do the same. I believe I've mentioned that Kat was a girl with little tolerance for this kind of thing. She spoke her mind the moment something came around and, win or lose, she let the situation go whichever direction it wanted.

Kat did two things at once. She kicked at the car with her left foot, and she thrust up her middle finger. The kick ran a mud smear up the metallic blue paint of the passenger door, caught the side mirror, and knocked it out of place. The flying bird of her middle finger did far more damage than I expected.

I thought that Rory's expression was that of a potential future serial killer. His face shifted from flat-line angry at the entire world to a narrowed focus at two people who were within easy slaughtering distance.

In fact, I was pretty sure Kat was trying to get us killed. It was the only explanation I could come up with.

We both saw it coming and acted well before the car crushed us to the ground. Kat and I heaved our bikes into the air. It was a trick that took a lot of upper strength and practice for a kid, but it became effective when you needed it most. Our bikes left the street, sailed across the muddy shoulder, and landed smoothly on the grass.

"I think we should break to the right," I said, while looking for a gap between the branches.

I was sure that the woods beside us were our only means of escape. I didn't wait for her response, certain she would follow. My bike cut a hard path through the tangle of undergrowth. The weeds grabbed at my feet, the pedals, and even the gears as I tried to get away from Regan and his evil brother.

Kat had listened to my advice and was cutting a path beside me. She muttered words someone her age shouldn't. I think she was even directing some of those words at me as our bikes dodged between the trees, traveling deeper into the woods.

"Nice one. You tried to get Regan's brother to kill us," I said as I stopped pedaling, trying to catch my breath.

"Are you afraid of everything? He wouldn't have done anything that stupid," Kat said and then looked back to make sure there weren't two figures running through the woods toward us.

"I wasn't afraid until you antagonized them. That wasn't very smart to kick his car. He could have run us down and kept driving and no one would have known why there were two splattered kids on the road."

"You're such a baby sometimes. It might be shorter this way if we cut through the woods."

"Take back what you said," I demanded.

I was ready to turn my bike around and head home. The attitude Kat was giving me reminded me of the day we met. I hadn't liked it then and I didn't like it now.

Kat frowned. It only took a few moments until she realized she sounded exactly like the bullies who had chased us into these woods.

"I'm sorry, but punks like those get me worked up. They think they can push anyone around. Sometimes someone needs to push back."

"I understand more than you know. Let's get going. This place gives me the creeps," I said, and then started pedaling again.

After twenty minutes of making our way through cobweb-infested woods, we came out of the forest onto a gravel road. There was a large metal building, and beyond it came an insane amount of animal sounds. I guessed that Kat had dragged me to a type of zoo. Above the front door was the largest gator skull I've ever seen. Actually, it was the only gator skull I'd ever seen. The rows of large white teeth held a human arm, plastic, hopefully.

As I started down the road, Kat grabbed the waistband of my shorts and pulled me back to the edge of the woods.

"Not so fast. I'm not sure if anyone is around. We'll have to sneak around until we know for sure that no one else is here. Let's leave the bikes here for now," Kat said and crept along the tree line.

"You mean that we're not even supposed to be here?"

"Not really. Don't worry, they've probably gone home for the day."

"I thought you were taking me to a tourist place. I didn't think we'd be trespassing."

"You need to get some backbone. Where's your sense of adventure?" Kat asked as we moved closer to the building.

"I have a sense of adventure, as long as it doesn't land me in trouble."

As soon as I finished speaking, the side door swung open, and a rugged man in faded blue jeans, a stained plaid shirt, and a straw hat came out. His eyes immediately spotted us. His lips widened, revealing the eager teeth of a predator spotting prey.

"Gotcha," he said as he shot towards us.

"Run, Jayce," Kat ordered.

I didn't need to be told twice. I left my bike, and my feet were in motion before Kat could finish my name.

"Got one taking off north through the woods, Grady," the plaid shirt man called out.

I heard a squeak of hinges. I turned and saw the front door fly open and an equally dirty, dressed man sprinted through it. Even though I had a head start, the second man was fast. I was aware that he knew the woods far better than me, but if I found a good hiding spot, I could wait for him to pass and then I'd head in a different direction.

I turned to say something to Kat but realized I was alone. Looking back to the dirt road, I saw Kat standing beside the other man, who had exited through the side door. Kat was laughing.

The moment of distraction caused my left foot to ram between the ground and a log. The uncontrolled balance caused me to pitch forward, and I hit the forest floor hard enough to punch out my breath.

The man following me was quickly hovering. His features no longer looked like a determined hunter but now a gentle giant. His massive hands grasped my arms gently and pulled me up.

"Easy now. Did you hurt yourself?" he asked in a gruff but calm voice.

I was leaning over, waiting for my breath to return. When it finally did, I said to the man, "I'm okay. I just lost my breath for a second."

"I'm glad it was only that. It could have been much worse. Your friend has a wicked sense of humor. Did you hurt your ankle?"

I rotated my left ankle. It was slightly stiff but definitely not broken.

"I think it will be all right. What do you mean she has a wicked sense of humor?" I asked, even though I thought I already knew, because Kat stood beside the other man and laughed at my bumbling escape.

"Oh. Kat called us earlier and said she wanted to play a joke on a friend. We figured we'd go along with it. I would have felt bad if you had gotten hurt."

"I'm fine," I insisted.

So, Kat set this whole thing up. She had gone out of her way for a practical joke that left me feeling foolish. There was something about her behavior sometimes that made me wonder why I ever decided to be friends with her. If she treated all her friends this way, then I really hated to see how her enemies suffered. I was sure a muddy sneaker mark up the side of Rory's car wasn't the worst that could come around should the two dare to push their evil ways.

We reached the road where Kat and the other man waited for us. Kat's ear-to-ear grin quickly transformed into a frown as she noticed I favored my left ankle.

"What happened to you?" she asked.

"What do you think? I was looking back to see where you were, and I tripped over a log. I got the wind knocked out of me as well, if you're interested," I said bitterly.

"You fell?"

"All thanks to you."

"I'm sorry. I was just trying to give you a scare."

"It's bad enough you nearly got us run over by the Evans brothers, but now you set up this whole thing that almost broke my ankle," I fumed to Kat.

"Hold up. Who are the Evans brothers and why did they try to run you down?" the big man next to me asked.

Kat said, "Rory and Regan. They're two morons who love to terrorize other kids for the sheer fun of it. They're mean and hateful bullies who get away with most of the despicable things they do. I wish someday someone would teach them a hard lesson in humility."

The other man shrugged and said, "Most of the time, boys like that get exactly what's coming to them. You just wait. It'll happen eventually."

"Well, I guess I should introduce you. Jayce, that is Grady," Kat said, pointing to the mammoth man beside me. "And this is Carl."

I told them it was nice to meet them and shook hands.

"Jayce started at my school a few weeks ago. I thought I'd bring him out here and give him a taste of the south."

"Well, since we're all friends again, then I think Jayce wouldn't mind having a look around and see just what it is we do here," Grady said and patted me on the shoulder.

"You bet," I agreed.

We passed the metal building the two men had exited and moved down the dirt road. Now I could see that this place was an actual tourist spot. Maybe not a hot spot, but the place certainly intrigued me.

There was a decent-sized gravel parking lot. On the other side of the lot, there was a building with wood siding and a cedar-shingled roof that was four times the size of my house. The sign above the glass double doors had a hand-painted thrashing gator and half a dozen slithering snakes and lizards. The sign said:

Grady's Wildlife Rescue and Retreat.

"How come it isn't Grady and Carl's Wildlife Rescue and Retreat?" I asked as we headed to the main building.

Carl said, "Grady started it years before I came along. He's actually the one who captures all the alligators, snakes, and lizards. You could say he's a critter wrangler. I never once saw him get nervous about trying to grab something that could kill him."

"Sure, I get nervous. I just have a great way of not showing it. If you show the monsters fear, they'll swallow you whole," Grady said.

We stepped out of the Florida heat and into the pleasantly air-conditioned building. I knew from my first step in the door that this place was off-the-charts exceptional.

Earlier, I had been thinking about the medieval games and how Josh wouldn't put any extra money in my hand for any kind of fun. I had been trying to figure out a way to earn extra money in the coming summer months.

I blurted it out even before it was a solid thought in my head.

"Would you guys be looking to hire someone part time, maybe for a few hours a day after school? I bet the cages and stuff need some cleaning and whatnot."

Grady scratched his chin. He watched Carl with a questioning look and then fixed back on me.

"You wouldn't by chance know someone who's look-ing for work?" Grady asked and smiled.

That was how I landed my first job, and a pocket full of hard-earned cash that finally offered the opportunity for me to have some fun in life.

Chapter 8

Grady rubbed his chin as he thought about it. He looked me over, measuring me up for whatever daily tasks he could create. He then studied Kat's expressions as if this would give him a sign of my work ethic.

"Does four days a week and two hours each day suit you all right? Maybe I could give you about twelve dollars an hour. I'm going to have to pay you in cash, as the state won't allow me to hire someone as young as you. So that money is yours to keep. The IRS won't know anything about it if you keep a tight lip. You'll keep busy cleaning cages, feeding animals, mopping floors, and anything else we decide needs done. Does that seem like a fair deal?"

He held out his hand, and I couldn't shake it fast enough.

"It's a deal. Whatever you need me for. How about if I come twice during the weekday after school and twice on the weekend until school is out? Then I can come any day and time."

He nodded and gave a satisfied grunt. "Well, we can start your education now. Carl and I were about to head out and find us a catch if the two of you want to tag along."

"Catch?" I asked.

Kat held up her hand to silence Grady's answer and said, "Oh, wait, you shouldn't answer that. I want him to enjoy the surprise."

Ten minutes later, the four of us squished into Grady's blue pickup and headed south. I wasn't stupid. I knew what was found south of town. There were a couple thousand square miles of raw nature known as the Everglades. What our mission could have been was beyond me.

Nearly forty-five minutes later, we turned off the paved highway and onto a rutted dirt path surrounded by thick woods consumed with heavy moss. We reached the edge of where wildlife and plant life thrived in the wetlands. Grady parked in front of a shack built on stilts to accommodate the changing water levels. It was a small building, not much bigger than my living room. I would have thought the owner had abandoned it decades ago, but a man came out at the sound of the truck doors closing.

"It smells like a locker full of dirty gym socks out here. What did you get me into?" I asked Kat in a whisper.

"You caught yourself in the snare of this job. I just came along for the ride. Plus, I really want to see the look on your face when you find out exactly what you got yourself into. It'll be priceless."

Kat took off running for the shack as a massive man in filthy overalls came down the steps. She nearly knocked him off balance as her body slammed into him and her arms wrapped around him the best she could. He was smiling, his gray bearded face showing genuine happiness.

"Hank! Hank, it's been forever since I've seen you!" Kat called.

"Hey there, young kitten. I've been missing you something awful," he said and stroked Kat's long blonde hair.

I wondered if the man was Kat's relative or just a good friend like Grady and Carl.

"Looks like you brought an extra pair of hands for your day of fun in the sun," the man said.

"Hank, this is my friend Jayce Graham. You can call him Graham Cracker because he likes it. He doesn't know what's in store for him today. So don't spoil it," Kat said.

"Our greenhorn is going for a boat ride today, Hank. We're going to show him the ropes on how to yank a gator out of the water with our bare hands," Grady called out while retrieving a red bag from the truck's bed. He then instantly looked at Kat with a silent apology, as the secret was out.

With the surprise instantly spoiled, I felt the blood completely drain from my head. I seriously felt near passing out. They were all looking at me, maybe waiting for me to hit the ground in a faint or throw up from the unexpected information.

I refused to give them what they wanted. Even though my upper lip was trembling, I smiled the best I could. I told Hank it was nice to meet him and that the day sounded like a good time. Although my inside voice was totally screaming, sounding like a little girl ambushed by a fat spider. The voice told me to head back to the road, if necessary, hitchhike a ride back to town, and scratch Kat's name off my list of friends. Or I suppose I could have refused and waited in the truck until they came back, but I knew how pathetic that would make me look. If I couldn't even get into a boat with gators, then how could I feed them for weekly pay? Backing out of this experience might make Grady rethink his decision to give me a chance at the wildlife retreat job.

Apparently satisfied with my answer, we went around the shack, where the property ran into mossy water that traveled as far south as I could see. A rickety dock reached out about twenty feet, and at the end of the dock was a battered aluminum boat with an outboard motor. The boat was barely large enough to fit our group without adding an angry, snapping alligator into the mix.

Luckily, Hank wasn't joining us on our Everglades tour, as the bulk of the man would have outright sunk the boat. Carl pulled the cord to kick the motor on, and with a coughing sputter of black smoke, it came to life. We found our seats, and then the motor was humming a loud, even tune as we pushed away from the dock, moving deeper into the wild. The boat picked up speed, zigzagging around trees and through islands of reeds, as Carl was a perfect navigator in this amazing landscape. I wasn't sure how far we were going until Grady pointed to the left, and then Carl cut the engine back to a dull grumble.

We angled toward a tree that must have been a couple of hundred years old, because it was as wide as a mid-sized car and seemingly tall enough to reach low-flying planes. We slid beside the tree, and Grady grabbed a white rope anchored by a thick spike to the tree. When he pulled that rope, it came up with no resistance. From the water came a heavy-duty hook, and wedged on that hook was something long dead. I couldn't identify what it was, because the bait had turned gray and mushy from being water-logged.

Grady flung it back into the water and said we might have better luck with the next one. But the following three held the same results. It seemed to me like the creatures here were getting smart about what they snapped onto. I didn't know how many traps Grady, Carl, and dozens of other men had set up across these endless miles. I figured it must have been enough to keep money in their pockets. Otherwise, why would anyone do it to risk their skin?

However, our fifth stop became a different story. Even I could tell right away that something was on the taut line, and it vibrated with anxious anger as the boat pulled closer.

"We've got ourselves a winner. Now you two stay clear until we see what we see. There could be almost anything on this line. If it's something we plan on keeping, I want the both of you to do exactly, and I mean exactly, as we say. You hear?"

Kat and I agreed. Then Carl and Grady began gently pulling the line. Whatever was stuck on it came up to the surface with little resistance.

Carl looked over the edge of the boat. He gave a small grunt and said, "Just as I figured. We hooked a—"

He didn't finish whatever he was going to say, but I quickly found out the end of that sentence. A geyser of water erupted as something exploded from the surface. We were all instantly covered in foul-smelling water. From the depth came a tangled mess of muscle and hissing fury. I couldn't immediately take in the full view of the thing because it happened so fast.

The thing thrashed on the line as its weight pulled it back into the water. Carl went off-balance by the unexpected fight, and he nearly toppled into the water after the thing. As I saw it wriggling, I realized it was a snake as thick as a battleship's anchor chain. I had never seen a snake of such thickness and length. If I hadn't known any better, I would have thought Carl, Grady, and Kat were pulling a mean prank on me and that the thing was nothing more than a rubber decoy. The terror on Kat's face said otherwise. I thought maybe she could have learned to run across water and back to the safety of the dock if she had half a mind to do so. She began rocking on her heels from the motion of the boat. I grabbed her arm, terrified she was going for a swim, and pulled her low to the bow. Wrapped around each other, we watched the two men battle the enormous snake with unmatched strength and anger.

It only took another moment before Carl pulled a knife from its sheath at his belt and drew it across the line. Just like that, the fight was over. The snake thankfully sank back into the watery depths. The boat slowly rocked itself out as Grady and Carl took a seat and used handkerchiefs to mop sweat and water from their faces.

"I about decided I wasn't all that interested in trying to save that hook from its mouth, if you know what I mean," Carl said.

"I do," I told him. For some strange reason, I started a wild laugh that caused me to slip off the seat and fall to the bottom of the boat.

The three of them watched me as if I'd lost my mind.

"I'm a beginner at this, and here the three of you looked more terrified than me," I told them.

"Mr. Hotshot with the cool head. If I had thought of it, I would have snapped your picture. By the look on your face, I'd say you unloaded in your pants when that snake came up," Kat said irritably.

"I didn't, but it was a close thing," I admitted. "What kind of snake was that?"

Grady said, "That, young man, was a Burmese python. They're big, strong, and develop a piece of the devil in them when they get hooked. They can get big enough to swallow a full-sized alligator. They'll get their teeth in you, wrap you up like a Christmas present, and when you're done fighting and breathing, they'll swallow you down inch by inch. A kid your size, sneakers, and all, makes a good meal to last them well over a month."

Grady grabbed another large hook from a tackle box and then tied it to the line. He then pulled a piece of dead flesh from a white bucket and worked it onto the hook.

The bait went overboard and into the water to snag some other vicious things that ventured past.

Carl revved the engine, and we tore through the reeds to the next stop. I realized that men living a life such as this were insane. They might have been smart, but willingly wrestling massive snakes and gators for extra money meant that men like that didn't have brain cells firing on all cylinders. Only lunatics would choose such a career. Of course, I had asked for a job at such a place. So, I guess that spoke volumes about my state of mind.

Our last stop offered what Grady and Carl desired. Much like the line that held the snake, this one was also pulled tight and cut through the water with an agitation far more threatening than the snake. Whatever was stuck on that hook didn't like it one bit. It wanted freedom. I figured if it could, it would yank that hook all the way through the roof of its mouth in order to get away.

It took several minutes for Carl to get a firm grip on the line. When he finally did, I could see the instant struggle on his face. Whatever was on that line didn't want to come up. It fought like the devil to stay on the murky bottom. Grady quickly joined the battle, and side by side, they strained every muscle to haul it up.

A moment later, it must have decided to give up, because both men sighed with relief at the sudden slack in the line. I offered a small moan of terror when the thing hit the surface. There were thick scales, mischievous yellow eyes, and a row of white, rounded teeth. I'd seen nothing so fearsome before in my life. It looked like an ancient monster pulled straight up from hell.

The powerful tail slashed the water in a warning once, twice, and then after the third time, its entire body came alive for a final fight. The men had been expecting this, as the alligator didn't get much room to move around. It managed a solid hit to the side of the boat, punching a small crater and offering the roll of thunder. It was a move forceful enough to send our boat in the opposite direction of the gator.

"Get the tape," Grady barked as he took a face full of water.

Carl let go of the line, rapidly dug through the tackle box, and came out with a roll of black tape.

Grady gave a swift, hard pull on the line, and the gator's head saddled up next to the boat. Instantly, his large hands seized the upper and lower jaws, pinching them closed. The gator thrashed, pushed off the water, and nearly broke loose from capture.

When the gator rose and dropped, the shift of weight offset the balance of the boat. I felt Kat's hand grasping for me, but it only snagged a small piece of my shirt before losing grip. Other hands were trying to find me, but the suddenness of the moment was too unexpected. No one could save me from going overboard.

I went over, and just like that, I fell right on top of the creature. Kat would later tell me it looked as if I were trying to ride the thing, as if it were an amusement park attraction. I landed head-to-head, and feet to angry whipping tail. For an awkward moment, I realized I was nearly kissing the Everglades monster.

The gator was just as stunned as I was, because it momentarily ceased its fighting. Its devilish eyes rolled up and locked on mine, causing an icy river to course through my body. Then it found new life and spun its body in a wild death roll. Just like that, I was flung loose from the horrifying ride. I hit with a hard splash as the bright May sun quickly turned to murky, black wetness. The water closed around me like a dark sky. I opened my eyes but quickly clamped them shut again as the dirty water stung.

I didn't know where the gator was, but I could hear it knocking against the boat as it fought to get away. I popped to the surface like a cork and took in a welcome, deep breath.

"Jayce, swim to the bow," Carl called after me. They were trying to direct me away from the snapping jaws and toward the only-slightly-less-threatening whipping tail.

The gator caught a glimpse of me as I swam for the boat. I would have thought it was more focused on getting away, but apparently, the opportunity for an easy meal appealed to its reptilian instincts. Its entire body abruptly turned and nearly brought Grady and Carl into the water with me.

The last thing I saw before going underwater were large teeth, a pinkish white blend of an open mouth, and a throat that seemed to go on forever. It was either brilliance or pure stupidity, but I dove under the gator's belly. I knew about the agility of alligators in the water, so I figured if I stayed below its hunting eyes and teeth, it couldn't find me. Plus, I was sure Grady and Carl still had a hold of the line. My best bet was to swim to the boat's other side to get back on board.

A hard rush of water churned above me, and something tugged at my shirt, briefly having a hold before releasing. I pushed for the surface, but something quickly halted my desperate reach for air. Something had clamped onto my right sneaker and viciously pulled me back several feet, shaking the held breath from me. I kicked, fighting for life, for air, for the single purpose of not becoming a messy glob inside the gator's stomach. The pressure on my foot was enormous, and then something popped. It vibrated through my body and ran through the water, but I felt no pain.

My foot broke free. All muscles went into action and pushed against the water. Seconds later, I burst from the surface and took in the damp air that couldn't have smelled sweeter.

"He's here," Kat yelled.

"Grab him up," Carl told Kat. Then to me he said, "Get your butt in here, boy."

Kat was looking at something behind me. I expected to see teeth closing over me a second before being swallowed down whole.

"For God's sake, don't look behind you," Kat said, calmly enough that I was sure she was messing with me.

"What?" I asked with heightened panic.

"There's another gator going for the water," she said.

Looking over my shoulder, I saw she was dead serious. An alligator just as large as the one fighting for freedom slid from the muddy bank into the water and disappeared beneath the surface.

"Get me up! Get me up!" I screamed, clawing at the edge of the boat, trying to pull myself from the water attraction of relentless death.

Kat had handfuls of my shirt and, working together, we were able to remove me from the water and fell back into the boat with a hard crash. After catching my breath, I looked down, expecting to see my right foot completely gone and a remaining bloody mess where it had been. I figured the adrenaline rush and the power of the gator's jaws had delayed the screaming of severed nerves. What I saw instead was a foot where a foot had always been. However, my sneaker had suffered a morbid death. I now understood that the popping sound was the foam padding and the rubber sole tearing free. That part of my shoe had gone to become the monster's afternoon snack.

Carl and Grady had finally gotten tape around the gator's jaws. Now that the fear of losing hands or fingers was gone, they easily pulled the thing from the water and into the boat with us.

"I just got away from this thing and now you want me to sit next to it?" I asked them with wide eyes.

Grady dropped a towel over its eyes, and just like that, the fight entirely left the reptile.

As if reading my confusion, Grady said, "Covering their eyes calms them down considerably. Once I get the rest of him bound, he won't put up much of a fuss until we cut him loose again."

"Well, look at that," Carl said as he pointed to my back. "Looks like you got yourself an honorable badge of courage. You've just become a genuine gator wrangler."

I couldn't see what he was talking about. Kat stood, looked, and said, "Whoa, that gator's claws tore your shirt from shoulders to butt. There's only a little blood, so I think you're going to make it. No trip to the morgue for you. Sorry."

"You guys owe me a shoe and a shirt. Next time I'm staying in the truck with the windows up," I told them. I was mad, but more than that, I was thankful to be both alive and unmaimed.

It didn't take much time at all before they secured the gator, and the trip back would hopefully be without further incident. Of course, all of us were practically sitting on the thing.

Kat started laughing. It was a bellowing call, sounding like a crane echoing across the Everglades. We all looked at her in confusion.

When she was able to catch her breath, she yelled over the roar of the motor, "You should have seen the look on your face when you were trying to get back in the boat. It was absolutely priceless!"

I held up my sneaker and showed her the missing rubber sole. I said, "You wouldn't be laughing if it was my foot missing instead of just part of my shoe. Plus, the other gator was coming after me, too. I don't think you would have been any braver than me."

"Good thing your clothes are wet, otherwise the pee stain would be totally noticeable," Kat said.

When we made it back to the dock, Grady, Carl, and Hank carried the thing from the boat to the back of the truck with obvious effort. On the ride home, I kept looking back through the window. I half expected to see the thing broken free of its restraints, ready to shatter the rear window, crawl into the cab, and finish off the job it had started. The thing just lay there in surrender. It may not agree with where it was going to live, but it would no longer have to hunt for food every day or worry about someone skinning it to make a pair of fancy boots, a jacket, or a belt.

My first day at work was terrifying, to say the least. I was pretty sure this was only a taste of what my exhilarating Florida wildlife job would offer. Twelve dollars an hour didn't seem like quite enough if today's insanity was the baseline for expectations, but I was going to run with it.

I arrived home about ten minutes before Josh. I buried my shredded shirt in the trash. I didn't yet want to tell Josh about the new job, because I knew that if I did, today would be my first and last day. I didn't think he would have a problem with me having a job, only that the one I had chosen was far too dangerous for only twelve dollars an hour.

I decided to shower later. For now, I changed into clean clothes and headed back to the kitchen.

Josh walked in the door, looking physically beat-down as he did every day. He removed his work boots and then slumped in the dining room chair. I was in the process of putting dinner together from a mix of leftovers available from the fridge.

"How was your day? Anything exciting happen?" he asked in a deflated voice.

I wasn't sure if he could smell the pungent odor of the water on my skin or in my hair. I don't know how he could have missed it. I looked at the front door where I had dropped my shoes, the right one ravaged to death.

"No, not much," I said.

The nine o'clock news began with a breaking story. The man behind the desk looked up from his notes to the camera and instantly jumped into the report.

"Paper Moon's local law enforcement, with the assistance of Coral Key's investigative units, were able to piece together clues left behind at several local fires. The arrest of Nelson Reynolds, a Paper Moon resident and ninth-grade science teacher in Coral Key, came early this morning. Mr. Reynolds was taken into custody during his fourth-period class. Much to the dismay of students, fellow teachers, and parents, Mr. Reynolds' arrest came about with unprecedented evidence found during a search of his home. Our cameras captured this major story unfolding as detectives walked the teacher inside the police station to begin processing. Mr. Reynolds is currently facing charges of five counts of arson and two counts of attempted murder of Mrs. McCready and her daughter, Lily."

Mr. Reynolds wore the face of a man completely lost in the events he currently suffered. It was hard to believe a man who looked so kind could be the person responsible for burning down five structures in Paper Moon.

"Well, they've got the man and the evidence that drives the nails in his coffin. Sounds like it's a slam-dunk case for the prosecution. He should get everything he deserves from this point on," Josh said.

"I can't believe a man like that almost killed a woman and her daughter."

"He nearly killed us, too."

"Yeah. I suppose so."

I couldn't shake it, though. The dumbfounded look on Mr. Reynolds' face haunted me. He looked as if he'd been instantly plucked from his pleasant reality and dropped into a nightmare that made no sense. A new life had clamped unyielding jaws around him, and every possible dream once attainable was now beyond reach on the other side of steel bars.

Josh stretched and then flicked off the TV, as bedtime had come around.

Though the news story was gone from sight, it wasn't over for Mr. Reynolds. It wasn't over for me either. In fact, I was going to find myself dropped right in the middle of the entire mess. I didn't know it yet, but I was even going to bet my life in pursuit of the truth.

Chapter 9

"You know, you're the one who fought him the most. Carl and I just plucked him from the water. So, I think it's reasonable that you name him," Grady told me on the Wednesday following my Everglades near-death adventure.

Standing in the enclosure, I fished in the bucket, grabbed a handful of slimy, raw chicken legs, and tossed them to the edge of the pond. Four alligator heads, mostly submerged in mucky green water, momentarily watched us. They then pushed forward to the edge to check out the offered meal. Those heads rose from the swampy water, becoming large, scaly bodies as they moved onto land. The Flintstones, Fred, Wilma, and Pebbles, each cocked their heads and snagged a chicken leg. With their heads jolting back, working tongues forced the chicken parts into their gullets, and they were gone for good.

It took every ounce of courage for me to not drop the bucket and run for my life as they moved toward me. During my brief employment time, I'd learned much from Grady, mostly by watching. By keeping those chicken pieces between them and me, they'd have no desire for my leg instead. Gators were creatures of opportunity. They'd rather accept an easy meal instead of exerting energy and risking bodily harm to capture wild prey.

"I've never named a gator before. Actually, I've never named any animal before."

"Well, it's your call."

I threw more chicken, and that was when our newest guest went into action. He was either extremely hungry or finally found the moment to display his dominance. His momentum was both humorous and terrifying as his agility on those stumpy legs startled the Flintstones enough that all three moved off to the side. Their deep-throated gurgling was a warning, or maybe worry, that their new pond mate failed to understand that they all got an equal share of food.

That was when the name came to me. A year ago, a school bully with a matching temperament to Regan Evans hit puberty and developed a severe case of facial acne. Not only that, but the changing of his adolescent voice from a squeak one second to a low tone the next was endless amusement. During these voice alterations, he would get aggravated and offer a deep, throaty breath, trying to clear the high pitches. It was much like trying to dislodge something from his windpipe that simply wasn't there. Between the gator's growling and the scales that reminded me of acne, I had the name.

"Frank. His name is Frank," I told Grady.

"Hmm. Frank. Yeah, I can see that. Why not?"

He didn't ask where the name had come from. Maybe he figured I had my reasons for selecting that specific name. If he had asked, I don't think I would have given him the story. It was a mean thought that brought the name out, and I didn't want Grady thinking I was some horrible kid making fun of another for things beyond his control. I would have just told him the name popped in my head and left it at that.

"Frank, meet the Flintstones. You're all roommates now, so play nicely," I said. I upended the bucket, spilling the remains of chicken across the concrete pad, and then I backed out of the enclosure.

We watched the four gators lumber toward the pieces, snapping them up instantly. All of them got a reasonable share. I was glad to see Frank getting along with the others and not hogging the rest of the food for himself. I wondered if he would like it here. There was no need to search for food. There was no longer a need to worry about being hunted by men in boats, either. But it made me wonder. Could caged animals be happy about this sort of arrangement? They no longer had to worry about anything at all. But then again, their freedom to roam the wilds of this wonderful planet was permanently removed. I couldn't bear the thought of being stuck in a cage all day and night, even for free meals. It seemed like a horribly boring life.

"The little birdie has flown the coop," Grady said as he tucked his phone back in his pocket and closed the gator cage.

I looked around, expecting to see one of the park's exotic attractions flying free in the Florida sky.

"Excuse me?"

"Local news app just beeped my phone. The arsonist, Nelson Reynolds, escaped custody an hour ago. They've dropped a net on all roads going out of Coral Key. Though he's on foot, I don't think he'll be using roads to hightail it out of there."

"I can't believe he escaped after only four days in jail. I wonder if he'll come back here. Maybe the fires will start again."

Grady grunted and said, "Doubtful. Everyone around these parts knows what he looks like. He's going to have to travel far to reach some town where he can blend in.

He's possibly facing the rest of his life in prison. So, common sense would tell him to hop a freighter and find some country with a non-extradition treaty with the U.S. Cuba would be his closest bet for a getaway."

I agreed that we'd seen the last of Mr. Reynolds and could now enjoy peaceful nights where no more fires consumed Paper Moon structures.

We were both wrong.

Chapter 10

I saw the first flyer in our mailbox on May 31st. I saw another flyer stapled to a post on Traveler's Avenue. After that, I began seeing them everywhere. Someone taped fliers to all the store windows on U Buy N Buy Street. They were also on the windows at the town clinic, the local bars, and even both churches I passed. I think the only place that wasn't littered with flyers was the school, because it got very few visitors as the final class ticked away last Friday.

Many of the flyers were different. The one in our mailbox simply said: *It's coming on Thursday, June 20th.* And below that statement was a well-drawn picture of two knights on horseback, dressed in armor and sporting lances.

On the window of the barbershop was a flyer showing archers lined up, watching arrows taking flight toward distant targets. I looked through the shop window and saw Sir Reginald Spree cutting a man's hair with clippers. Of course, Sir Reginald Spree was wearing his medieval outfit. I'd never seen him wear anything else. At his side was the sword he'd probably use during the event. I wondered if he would again conquer all competitors at this year's games and become the returning champion at the Knight of Arms tournament. He saw me watching him. I smiled, pointed to the flyer, and then gave him a thumbs-up. He returned the smile, waved, and then turned his attention back to his customer. I wasn't Kat, so his interest in me was a simple courtesy.

I saw the last flyer pinned to a wood pole at the end of the block. It displayed two men dressed in full armor with their swords clashing. I couldn't speak for anyone else in town, but my blood was surging with anticipation. The thought of having to wait weeks was sheer torture. Of course, this was a common plan to build up enthusiasm and get people talking. When the games finally started, the entire town would be buzzing with eagerness.

I looked at my watch and realized I was going to be late for work if I didn't get going.

Someone had named Broken Road accurately. It was long neglected by the town's road crews. It desperately needed tearing up and re-pouring with concrete. There were sections of concrete badly sunk and other sections jutting up. If someone drove it at a fast clip, tire and shock damage were a sure thing. I figured the town council wanted it that way, as it would be crazy to have a nice even road on a block that was labeled "broken." As I've said, the town had a bizarre outlook on things.

I stopped pedaling and rested on the sidewalk. What grabbed my curiosity was the business of Clean Sweep, or what used to be a business. It was vacuums and other cleaning products that had gone up in a raging fire and thick smoke two weeks ago. Now the building stood like a severely rotten black tooth among a row of thriving businesses.

I looked around. Most people passing barely gave the place a second glance. However, there was one person who had fixed his attention on the condemned building. Ahead of me, sitting on a sidewalk bench, was one of the sheriff's deputies. He was not in uniform now but dressed in street clothes. I recognized him because he was the same officer whose shoes I had thrown up bile all over the night of the fire on my block. Not only was he staring at the building with fascination, but he also snapped several pictures with his phone. Even in Paper Moon, this was a little odd. Of course, it was possible that he had an interest in photography, and such a wreck of a building was art to some people.

The deputy turned his head, and our eyes locked. I tried to look away and pedal off down the road, but my body wouldn't let me do anything except stare at the man I didn't even know by name. I could imagine our minds asked each other questions that would get no answers. He was no doubt wondering why he had caught my interest. I was wondering about something entirely different. He broke eye contact first. I took advantage of this and leaned on the pedal and was off again down the street.

A thought occurred to me, and before I realized it, my bike braked next to the bench. He was busy pushing his phone inside a small carry bag and zipping it shut. I guessed he was in his early thirties. He looked athletic, probably spending free time at the local gym. He looked up at me and smiled. His mouth smiled, anyway, but his eyes narrowed with suspicion.

"I remember you. You're the kid who puked on my shoes a couple of weeks back," he said.

I'd figured this was a memory we would share about our first encounter.

"Yes, sir," I said. "I saw you over here and I thought I would stop and say hello."

"By the time I got home, that puke had dried on my shoes. I had to scrub the hell out of them to get them clean. Then I had to polish them."

"I'm sorry about that. I guess it was from the smoke and all the excitement."

"It sure was an exciting day. It's a hell of a thing to see a house go up in a fire like that."

I looked to my left, staring at the blackened decay of the building.

He followed my sight and studied the burned mess again. The edge of his mouth turned up in a smile.

"This was the last building Nelson Reynolds burned down before we nabbed him. It was excellent police work that picked up the clues and put him behind bars. It's a shame a bunch of incompetent employees run the Coral Key police department. They should have never given him the opportunity to escape."

"Oh. Well, I've got to get to work," I said as I tried to find a fast way out of this man's company.

He looked at me. "You're awfully young to have a job. Where is it you work?"

"At Grady's Wildlife Retreat," I said and then silently called myself a moron. Kat was right, I had the brains of a dung beetle. Grady paid me in cash because the state wouldn't allow me to work at his business at my age. That meant that he was illegally employing a minor, and I had just spilled everything to a police officer.

"So, do you take care of the animals and such?" he asked.

"Yes, sir. I clean cages mostly. It was nice talking to you, but I really must get going."

"Well, off you go. You be careful in traffic."

"Yes, sir."

I made my way down the block before I turned into an alleyway. There was a man dropping a trash bag inside a dumpster. He only glanced at me before heading back inside. I turned and peered around the corner of the candle shop. The deputy wasn't looking my way. He was up and walking toward the other end of Broken Road with his pack slung over his shoulder.

I figured it was a bad idea, but I was going to be late for work. My curiosity was a curse, and I wanted to know where the deputy was going. I wasn't a professional at following someone, even though I'd seen it done dozens of times on television. By keeping far enough back, I had time to react if he simply looked over his shoulder. I kept my eyes on places I could quickly duck behind. It didn't matter, though, because he never looked back, not once. He only glanced left and right as he took in the view of town. He walked with quiet arrogance, as if he balanced the entire world on a fingertip. When I spoke with him, I got the impression that he was a man always in control of situations. Even in those circumstances that were beyond his control, he would do a superb job of faking it. The fact is, I didn't like him. I'd moved around a lot across this country and connected with tons of people. So, I'd become pretty good at reading people I'd just met. There was something about the deputy that didn't sit right. Maybe it was the way he stared at the wreckage of the building with a gleam in his eye. Maybe it was the way his mouth formed a soft smile when he shouldn't have. I guess I couldn't be sure what gave me that awkward feeling, but it was the reason I needed to follow him.

The business section of town gave way to wealthy neighborhoods. The lack of people pressed me to stay back nearly a block in case he checked over his shoulder. If he saw me, there was no excuse in the world that he would accept. I was sure he knew Grady's place was in the opposite direction. At the end of Hiccup Avenue, he stopped in front of a pale yellow, two-story house with white trim and shutters. He unslung his pack, unzipped it, and removed his phone. I stopped behind a row of bushes where only the top of my head peered over the leaves. He looked in both directions of the block and, seeing no one, he snapped several pictures of the house. He then slid the phone back into the pack and was on the move again.

Five blocks away, he walked up the front path of a for-est-green house with a yellow Dodge Charger in the drive-way. He fished inside his front pocket and pulled out a ring of keys. He slid a key into the front lock, opened the door, and disappeared inside.

A part of me wanted to stay at a distance, but the other part craved to give in to the curiosity. The curiosity won over. I pedaled down the sidewalk, ready to aim for the cover of bushes if I saw him come back out. No one else was on the block, but that didn't mean someone couldn't see me through a window. I tried to act like I belonged in his neighborhood and that I wasn't following a sheriff's deputy for unknown, stupid reasons.

As my wheels found his property, I saw a light come on in the basement window. The window had a curtain, but it wasn't fully closed. I scanned the neighbor's back-yard before I felt comfortable enough to peek inside. No one was paying attention to me. Leaning my bike against the corner of the house, I kneeled and peered inside the lit basement. It was full of junk. There were stacks of old pa-pers and magazines to my left. To the right was a mixed-up pile of worn-down electronics like radios, televisions, and several microwaves. There was furniture in there too, buried under heaps of stuff.

I figured that basements in Florida were a rarity due to possible flooding issues, but Deputy Kline had either pur-chased an unusual gem within the area, or he had dug out a partial basement himself.

I saw the deputy at the base of the steps. His hands were on his hips as he looked over his garbage piles. He moved to his right down a narrow pathway that snaked through his odd collection. He stopped at one wall of the house and began moving boxes away from the wood paneling.

Something crashed behind me. Although it wasn't loud, to me that noise was like a plane slamming into the earth. I looked over my shoulder, expecting to see someone standing there, but saw my bike lying on the ground. It had tipped over from its resting place against the house. I looked inside the house again. The deputy was crouched, a stack of boxes in his hands and his head turned. His eyes were on mine, at least the one eye he could see through the crack in the curtains. My blood turned to winter river water. As earlier, I froze in place, unable to look away. His mouth moved, but I couldn't hear anything. Maybe questioning himself why this kid had trailed him home. Why was this kid watching him through the window? What was this kid's obsession? I couldn't answer, because I didn't even know the reason.

My muscles unlocked as the deputy stood. I grabbed my bike and shot down the road, only glancing back when I passed the neighbor's house and saw the deputy watching me from the basement window. His eyes were hard and mean. I didn't like that look.

A quick thought ran through my head. I could go back and tell him I was sorry, and that I didn't know why I had spied on him. I was a curious kid and people fascinated me. It sounded like a stupid idea and only put me within the deputy's reach. I pedaled harder when a car came up behind me. I was sure it was the deputy coming to interrogate me, but they were only townspeople passing by. I looked at my watch and saw I was already fifteen minutes late for work.

Reaching the long driveway to Grady's place, I saw dozens of cars in the gravel lot. Stopping my bike at the entrance, I saw the out-of-state license plates and realized tourist season was in full swing. People from everywhere were visiting this part of the world, interested in everything the Sunshine State offered. Even after working here for several weeks, I was still fascinated by many of the attractions.

I leaned my bike against the side of the building. Opening the front door, a blast of blissful air conditioning rushed me, making my manic pedaling worth it.

There were a few customers inspecting the glass cages containing a variety of spider species. Through the rear windows of the building, I could see Carl and Grady in the back lot, feeding the Flintstones and Frank. Enthusiastic guests watched them throw raw chicken, which was instantly snatched up by the large gators.

In the back room, I began gathering supplies to clean cages before moving out into the display rooms to feed all the critters and creepy-crawlies. I started with the snake enclosures. Empty cages needed to be scrubbed and fresh wood shavings dropped in so that I could move snakes from dirty to clean cages. I went to one of the glass cages sitting on the back bench.

My mind was all over the place. Focusing on my tasks wasn't easy as I kept thinking about my encounter with the deputy. Why had he visited a fire-destroyed building in his free time and taken pictures? He told me it was an exciting day when Josh and I had rushed into a burning house. Was there something to that? Was there something else that happened during his shift that made his day more exciting? Why had he stopped on his way home and taken pictures of an ordinary yellow house? What was he doing in his cluttered basement? Were the boxes he'd moved a possible answer to something? What would he do now that he saw I had been spying on him? I realized he knew where I lived. Would he come to my house and tell Josh I'd been snooping on him, or would he show up when I was home alone?

I removed the cover of an empty glass cage. Reaching inside, I started pulling all the shavings to one side so I could dump them in the waste barrel. A moment later, something tugged on my right forearm. I jerked my arm out, not understanding what had happened. Two holes just above my wrist were looking at me like a pair of eyes. I stared back stupidly as red tears leaked from those eyes on my arm. Inside the cage was a diamondback rattlesnake. Its body coiled tightly around itself. Its yellow, hellish eyes fixed on me, a forked tongue going in and out, tasting the air. Then the rattles of its tail went to work. An announcement of danger far too late. My brain finally connected the holes in my skin with the snake in the cage.

I hadn't seen it hiding beneath the wood shavings. The cages on the back bench were supposed to be empty. I staggered back and bumped into the door. I began thinking about what Grady had told me when I first began working here. He had given me loads of helpful knowledge about all the creatures I would be dealing with. I was trying to think back to what he'd told me about the various snakes at the facility. He made it clear which ones were poisonous and which ones weren't. He had told me what needed to be done right away should one of the poisonous breeds ever get fangs into me. I couldn't think fast enough. Then it came to me. I had to calm down. The more I panicked, the faster my blood pumped. The faster my blood circulated, the quicker the poison surged through my body and attacked vital organs and my nervous system.

I drew in long and slow breaths. The pain was intense. It felt as if someone brutally jabbed a thousand needles into the already damaged skin. There was a myth about people being able to suck out poison from fang wounds. Grady had told me this was completely incorrect. He told me that the poison entered your system well before you even realized the snake's fangs had punctured. One of the few things that could save a life was antivenom.

I backed out the employee door and onto the main floor. Several customers looked at me strangely. I was still hot from the outdoor swelter, but now my body was pouring out a panic sweat. I was cupping my hand over the wound as I slowly walked to the back of the building, where I had seen Grady and Carl outside.

"Are you all right, kid?" a father of two little girls asked me.

"Snake bit," I managed to mutter. Then I pulled my hand away and showed him the two holes above my wrist.

"Snake bit?" he asked and then looked around at the floor, maybe expecting to see something slithering toward his kids.

I looked out the back window. Grady was no longer talking to customers. Instead, he was looking right back at us. I saw concern on his face, as if he just knew something bad had happened. He put down the bucket of chicken pieces, left the enclosure, and headed my way.

My head spun, and my breathing became more difficult.

"Diamondback," I told the man before a blackness filled my eyes and I felt myself going face-first to the floor.

I didn't know how long I'd been unconscious. I was lying on Grady's bed in his small apartment at the back of the main building. Grady and Carl were hovering over me. I saw concern and then relief in their expressions.

"You were petting the snakes when you shouldn't have," Carl joked.

I looked at my wrist. Grady had wrapped a white bandage around my fang-stung wrist.

Grady held a cup close to me, then put the straw in my mouth and told me to drink. I did. The water was cool and appreciated.

"Not too fast or too much," he said.

I took a deep breath and said, "Am I going to be all right?"

Carl said, "Well, no, you see, you died. Instead of Heaven, you're in Hell and you're going to have to stare at our ugly faces until the end of time. Sorry, but it's a real bummer for you."

Grady said, "It's a really lucky thing you told one of the customers what breed of snake got you. It's also lucky that we just got done milking that snake of all its venom so we could begin processing another batch of antivenom. I can honestly tell you I've had my share of slip-ups. Fangs have caught me half a dozen times. Carl has had more bites than all snake wranglers combined in North America."

"And I'm proud of it," Carl said.

I thought of what Josh might say when he found two spots punched into my skin.

"Will I have to go to the hospital?"

Grady and Carl looked at each other. Grady said, "We can certainly take you there if that's what you want, but there's really no need. There isn't anything doctors can do for you that we haven't already done. Like I said, that snake was depleted of venom. From here on, we just need to keep the wound clean and dry, and it'll heal up just fine."

If Josh found out, this would be the last day I ever got to work here. Somehow, I would have to keep him from seeing the bandage or fang-struck wrist. I figured long sleeves were going to be in fashion every evening at home. Josh would think I'd lost my mind wearing long sleeves during a summer swelter, but I couldn't think of any other way to cover it up.

"No," I decided, "I don't think I need to go to the hospital. I just want to lie here a bit longer and then get up and move around some."

They stood. Grady said, "It was likely a panic attack that made you black out. Well, go ahead and rest awhile. We'll be out there when you're feeling a bit better."

Grady flicked off the light and closed the door behind them. I lay there in the air-conditioned silence. As I began drifting off, I thought of those yellow snake eyes watching me. The eyes remained the same as the snake's head morphed into the face of the deputy. Those sinister eyes studied me, searching for any secrets or suspicions I might be keeping.

Chapter 11

Grady brought me home in his rickety truck that was a small step above Josh's rust bucket. Not many people spent much of the midday outside if they could avoid it. Even the brief time it took to exit Grady's vehicle with its constant shuddering air conditioner and enter into the cool embrace of the house was unbearable. Living so close to the ocean and so far south, the air itself was waterlogged, and at times it was hard to breathe if you were out in it for too long.

I was home for only a few minutes before I heard Josh pull into the driveway. There was no way I could run, but I hurried the best I could to my room to grab a long-sleeved shirt. I returned to the kitchen to clean up the dishes from this morning when he walked through the front door. He pulled a handkerchief from his back pocket and mopped the sweat from his face. Just like me, he enjoyed the air-conditioning blast when he walked inside.

"I don't know how you work out in this kind of weather all day. I couldn't do it. I'd probably pass out and someone would find me later drowning in my own sweat. The weather here is definitely a drastic change from Colorado. Especially this time of year," I told him as he collapsed into the dining room chair.

"People can get used to just about anything." Josh was quick to catch on as his eyebrow arched while watching me. "Speaking about heat, exactly why do you have a long-sleeved shirt on during the summer?"

I shrugged. I couldn't think of a quick answer.

"What's going on?"

"Okay. So, please don't freak out. I took a job a while back. Just outside of town is a wildlife habitat. I just wanted to make some extra money. So, Grady and Carl hired me to clean cages and help feed the reptiles, amphibians, and such."

"Why didn't you tell me you got a part-time job? You probably figured I wouldn't approve because there must be dangerous creatures, something like snakes and gators, huh?"

"Yeah, and other stuff."

"All right. What does that have to do with wearing long sleeves?"

"Um, well, today something went a bit wrong. I had a lapse in focus that caused something to bite me."

Alarm overcame his features, but of course, all my bodily parts were still whole, so he kept his older brother panic-mode in check.

"I was just trying to cover it up. I didn't want you to worry. Grady took care of it. There wasn't any need for antivenom."

"Antivenom? A poisonous snake bit you? For crying out loud, Jayce. I need to see it."

I pulled up my sleeve and slowly peeled back the gauze pad. Two perfect circles, spread an inch and a half apart, marked my wrist.

"Sweet Jesus. Are you sure that Grady guy knows what he's doing? We should probably at least take you to the clinic here in town. I mean, shouldn't we double-check that there's no lasting effect from the bite?"

"Grady and Carl just got done milking venom from the snake. There wasn't any injected into me. The clinics and hospitals in southern Florida get their antivenom supply from Grady's habitat. There isn't anything more a clinic could do."

"Okay. All right. You should at least go lie down on the couch. I'll get you some water."

I didn't feel like resting, but I did. Josh set a water glass on the wobbly coffee table. He lifted my legs, sat, and laid my feet on his lap. He began rubbing my back. It was a little weird at first, but then I relaxed and enjoyed it.

The thing about Josh was that he was a good brother, but he didn't show it very often, if that makes any sense. He never really raised his voice, or ever struck me in anger, even though there were times I did stupid things and deserved it. Most of the time, it seemed as if his attention was only half there when I was talking about something that either happened during or after school. He worked a lot, and I didn't blame him for being tired all the time. Usually, he wanted to do very little after work, mostly just zone out on the couch in front of the television. Becoming an adult after graduation must suck when you're immediately enslaved by the workforce, and then they finally release you when you're a withered old person who's too damn broken and tired to do anything fun.

"Since it's summer, I thought that one of these days I could go to work with you."

"Why would you want to do that?"

"I think it would be fun to try out for a day. Maybe I could just be the gofer who gets stuff for people, like tools and material."

"When Mom and Dad were alive, all I wanted to do during summer was sleep until noon and lie around watching TV and playing video games. I didn't even want to think about working. Of course, most of that time I took care of you when they were at work. I was always having to get up because you were getting into some kind of mischief."

"I'm sorry if I stole part of your childhood."

He looked at me sincerely and said, "Don't apologize for that. Truthfully, I wouldn't have changed any of it. I always liked having a brother, although a sister would have been a bit less stressful, probably."

"For sure," I agreed. "I've put you through the wringer. It's been a wild ride since the day we came here. There isn't anything normal about this place. You wouldn't believe the things I've seen and done in the last month."

Josh quit rubbing my back. When I looked over, his eyes were closed, and his breathing was slow and steady. Just like that, he was out for the count.

"I like having a brother, too," I said to him.

He offered a small grunt. I wasn't sure if it was in acknowledgement or a response to a passing dream.

Josh did ask his boss if it was all right for me to work with his crew one day, acting as a helper for any needed task. His boss claimed that if an unpaid worker was on the job site and injured by a rusty nail, or even a twisted ankle, the developer would be liable for that injury and could even face a lawsuit for negligence.

If I couldn't go to work with him, then that left me with the only option of getting into more trouble.

I wandered over to Kat's house, but her father had grounded her and Anderson for not taking care of chores earlier. We got to a bit of talking until her father, already sounding slightly drunk, started hollering about closing the door and not letting the air-conditioning out.

I hopped back on my bike and headed down the street. I had no destination in mind, because I had nowhere to be. I knew I didn't want to go back home. So, I decided to swing by Grady's. I figured I'd show him that there was no further concern following the snake bite.

I decided on taking a different path to the reptile habitat. It ended up being the same path that Kat and I had taken the day Regan and his brother had nearly spattered us across the street.

When I cut through the tangle of weeds on the shoulder of the road, the forest immediately swallowed me. The woods had dramatically thickened since early spring. I figured the blazing sun and constant damp air made such plant life thrive.

After ten minutes of pushing through the rugged terrain, I made the decision to travel back to the road, because these woods weren't suitable for a boy and his bike. But when I turned around to follow the path that I thought I had beaten down, I saw the path was gone. The weeds and brush had sprung right back after my passing and showed no signs of being disturbed. I looked from one tree to another, and one patch of thick weeds to another. I had no idea which direction I had come from or which direction to go. Panic set in then, because I knew these woods could lead me to places I didn't want to go. The Gulf Coast was somewhere beyond this stretch of woods. I could also reach the Everglades by going another way. It was hard to see the sun through the canopy of trees, so following the direction of its arch was impossible. The only thing I could do was to not second-guess myself. I had been heading steadily in one direction with confidence before I paused, so I would keep going in that direction.

After twenty minutes, I became aware that my mental compass was no longer functioning. I should have reached

Grady's nearly ten minutes ago. I made a ninety-degree right turn north and walked for thirty minutes. I didn't find a road or any other signs of life. So, I again made another ninety-degrees right turn and walked for half an hour. My logic was that I had walked about a half an hour through the woods in one direction at first before turning, so if I changed direction and walked another half an hour at some point and found nothing, changing direction again was eventually going to get me back to the road. My logic was a failure, because I was sure I'd made one large oblong circle.

Something was burning. Breaking through a clearing, I found a camp with a smoldering fire, a blanket beside it, and a small pile of prepackaged food and cans of soda.

"What are you doing wandering out in the woods all by yourself?" a hard voice said from behind a cluster of trees.

I spun. A thin man dressed in orange stepped out from the trees. I immediately recognized his outfit. It was the standard-issue clothing for many prison institutions. His light brown hair was short, but his face had a thick beard.

"Nelson Reynolds," I said, instantly recognizing him from television. Southern Florida news stations had highly televised the coverage of his arrest for burning three homes and two businesses in Paper Moon. I had also seen the coverage of his escape last week, only three days after his arrest.

"What's that name mean to you?"

"Ah, nothing really, sir."

"So, you know who I am, but I have no idea who you are. What's your name, kid?"

My brain went into lockdown. I couldn't for the life of me think of a fake name to give him. I couldn't even think of classmates' names from school to offer.

I felt my body automatically start to turn, wanting to take to my heels.

"There isn't any place to go. Running from me wouldn't do you much good. If you found me this deep in the woods, then it means you're lost."

He walked over to the tarp and sat down beside the fire.

"I'm not going to hurt you, if that's what you're worried about. Come sit next to the fire. It might be ninety degrees out here, but the fire is still soothing."

He was right. I had nowhere to go. Besides, I had a feeling he really didn't mean any harm. I don't know how I knew this. I just knew. I sat on the opposite side of the fire and watched him closely over the dying flames. I had made full preparations to run if I saw him make a move to grab me.

"So, what is your name, if you don't mind me asking?"

"I'm Jayce," I told him. I had no intention of giving him my last name.

"Nice to meet you, Jayce. How is it you came to get lost so deep in the woods?"

Strangely enough, he held out his hand, and I shook it, as if we weren't an escaped prisoner and a scared kid.

"I was trying to take a shortcut to Grady's reptile gardens when I took a wrong turn."

"Ah, I know exactly where that is. I've spent nearly a week in these woods. After we have a discussion, I'll point you in the right direction to get there. But first, I need to have your word that you'll tell no one that you found me out here. I want you to promise. A promise is something every man should keep, and if he doesn't, then he should rot in misery for it."

"I promise." I would have told him anything to get out of here quickly.

He eyed me suspiciously over the low flames. "Tell me again and then you can go."

"I promise," I said again. Even I noticed the second promise had more sincerity in it.

He pointed to his right and said, "Go that way just short of a mile and a half and you'll reach your destination. It's been good meeting you, Jayce."

I stood and started pushing my bike. My body really wanted to run, but then I stopped.

"Can I ask why you did it? I mean, why you burned those houses and businesses down?"

"Have you ever heard the saying 'innocent until proven guilty'? I have yet to start my trial. They haven't given me the opportunity to prove my innocence. I'm wanted by the law now, but that doesn't mean I did anything wrong."

"So, you're saying you didn't burn anything down?"

"That's exactly what I'm saying. Someone set me up for all that. They say they have my fingerprints on a book of matches left at a crime scene. Besides what's in front of us, I haven't started a fire in years. Come to think of it, the last time I struck a match was a July 4th cookout at my house two years ago. I told the police I wasn't one of those people fascinated by fire. It's destructive and uncontrollable once it really gets its hunger going. They said they had my blood as well. They said I must have cut myself at several of the houses when I was setting everything up to burn. I showed them my entire body. I showed them I had no recent injuries."

"So why did you run? Why did you escape if you're innocent?" I asked.

"I don't know. It was a stupid idea to start with. I saw the opportunity, and I took it. I kept thinking about a jury claiming me guilty and throwing me in state prison for the rest of my life. I couldn't last in prison, not any kind of prison. There are hard people in those places, and I'm not a hard man. They'd eat me alive and spit out whatever remained."

"But if you're innocent, then they can't send you to prison. It's just wrong."

"There are innocent men in jail. Probably lots of them. Either they didn't get a good enough lawyer, or the system made an example of them, or a dozen other reasons. The lawyer I could afford said the matchbooks are circumstantial, but the DNA left behind is going to be a hard thing to beat. Even though I didn't have any recent cuts, it's still my blood at one crime scene. I can't explain how it got there. Other than the Clean Sweep business, I've never been to any of the buildings that burned."

"So, what can you do, live out here forever?"

"No, not forever, but long enough until I figure out what to do next. I'm still not sure if I'm going to turn myself in and take my chances with the legal system, or if I'm going to try to make a run for Mexico."

"I guess I understand. I sure would hate to rot away in prison for something I didn't do."

"Do you know what scares me the most?"

"What?"

"I was able to get a phone before coming out here. Before the battery died, I saw an article that the real arsonist has already started back up since I escaped. What if next time he kills someone? When I was in jail, he stopped, and people were safe. And then I escaped, and a family lost their home to fire. So now it seems even more convincing to the authorities and the media that I'm the arsonist. That means the police aren't looking for the real culprit, because they're looking for me. But then again, if I'm back in jail, then there's nothing I can do to try to stop him. I think that's why I snuck a ride in the back of a truck from Coral Key to come home. Being a fugitive at least gives me a fighting chance to prove my innocence."

"I understand," I told him, and I did understand. I would want to catch the man who framed me, and I would want to know why.

"I love this town, Jayce. I love it more than I can say. I wasn't born here, but I've spent my adult life here. There's no other place in the world I'd rather live. Why would I want to burn down something I love? I can say that until I'm blue in the face to the judge and jury, but they're not going to believe me because they have DNA evidence that says otherwise."

"I believe you," I told him. I really did.

He smiled as he read my face and saw honesty in it. "Well, score one for me. I'm glad to hear it, but I've got a lot of people to convince before I'm through."

I don't know why I said it, but with a person in need of help, I felt obligated to do something, even when that person was a fugitive from justice.

"I can help you somehow. I can look wherever you need me to look. You can't run around town, because they'll arrest you. So, you can use me. Maybe I can follow someone you might suspect. Maybe I can get the proof you need."

He smiled again, but I saw the refusal in his eyes.

"Well, I would hate to do that, Jayce. If there was a person who I suspected of framing me and I had you follow him, and he caught on to you, he could hurt you, maybe even worse."

"I'll be extremely careful. I'll just be a kid messing around town. No one pays much attention to a kid running around in the summer."

"Sorry, young man, but I'm going to have to say no on the matter. However, there are a few things you might be able to help me with. You can see this orange prison outfit sticks out like a sore thumb, and it's crazy hot to wear in the summer. I sure would like regular clothes, something lightweight. Shorts and tee shirts would be great, but also a pair of blue jeans while I'm living in these woods, so I don't get eaten alive by the damn bugs. Do you think you could find me anything like that in my size?"

"I think so," I said. Although he was a great deal taller than Josh, I thought of someone else who matched his size. This meant I would have to bring another person into the secret.

"Terrific. Could I ask you for another favor? I need some restocking of my food and water supply. I came across a house about four miles to the north and found a storm shelter with some boxes of canned goods, matches, this tarp, and the blanket. I didn't have it in me to go upstairs and take anything else. I hated even taking what I did, but the canned food was near expiration, anyway. Moths have devoured this blanket, so I didn't figure they'd miss it when it was gone."

"Sure. I think I can come up with something."

Chapter 12

The following day, Kat told me to shut my mouth. She said I must have gotten delirious from the heat and lack of water, and it made me see things in those woods that weren't really there. She was in total disbelief that I had run into Mr. Reynolds in the forest west of town. Even after I convinced her to grab some supplies, she still thought I was full of it. She gathered some of her father's clothes and some canned goods, and we left her house to visit a secluded place in the woods to meet the man wrongly accused by the authorities.

Kat was a chattering box of excitement. I couldn't get her to shut up for two minutes during the entire bike ride. She asked me to repeat the conversation I'd had with Mr. Reynolds. I told her she could ask him all the questions she wanted. One thing I worried about was my broken promise to Mr. Reynolds. I wasn't sure how he'd take it. I had promised not to tell anyone, but Kat wasn't just anyone. She was my friend, and someone Mr. Reynolds could trust. I was sure he would understand.

We had left our bikes off the gravel road that led to Grady's place. It was the point at which I had escaped the woods yesterday. There was no sense pulling our bikes through the tangle of weeds to and from the campsite. After a while, I thought for sure I had gotten us lost in the woods, because the campsite was nowhere to be seen. I almost changed direction but immediately knew that would be a bad idea. It hadn't worked well for me the last time. If I hadn't run into Mr. Reynolds, I could have found myself standing on the sunny gulf coast about now.

After ten more minutes of keeping on the same heading, I smelled the fire of Mr. Reynolds' camp.

"It's just up ahead. I hope he's not angry I brought you," I told Kat.

The thundering bark of a dog just about made me jump out of my skin. It had been right in front of us when we came through the thick weeds into the small clearing.

"Hold up there, Jasper," the police officer said and tugged the leash of the German Shepard that had lunged at us. The dog immediately obeyed and sat, but that didn't make me feel any safer.

Two state patrolmen in blue uniforms, wearing dark shaded sunglasses, watched us stop at the tree line. I imagined we looked scared, which we were. I don't think they knew the exact reason for our fears. They probably thought it was the dog that had spooked us. In fact, it was our knowledge of a fugitive's whereabouts and our failure to inform the authorities.

"What are you two doing way out here?" the patrolman holding back the dog asked.

"Ah," I said as I looked around. I didn't see Mr. Reynolds anywhere. The fire was smoking a little, and the handful of things he had taken from a nearby house was beside the tarp.

Before I could come up with an answer, Kat said, "This is our camp, officer. Is something wrong?"

"Your camp?" He eyed me and said, "Is that right? You two are camping way out here?"

I nodded because I thought my voice would fail. I wondered if they had captured Mr. Reynolds while I was gone. Other officers could have taken him away while these two stayed behind to search through his camp. Admitting that this was our camp could link us to Mr. Reynolds and reveal that we were aiding and abetting a known fugitive, which would land us in some serious hot water.

"This campsite is nearly a couple of miles from any road. Why is it you come all the way out here to play?"

Kat shrugged. "This is our fortress, and these woods are our kingdom. We can't go that way because that's Lords of Brimstone territory. And that way is the Guards of Prosperity sanctum. And the Everglades is south. So, we camp here."

The officers' confused looks also matched my own. I had no idea what the hell she was talking about.

She looked at them, smiled, shrugged, and said, "It's just kid stuff. It's summer and there's nothing else to do."

"Then you're not aware that an escaped fugitive was recently spotted on a farmhouse's security cameras near here and that man might be in these woods hiding from the law?"

"No, sir," Kat and I said in unison.

"This isn't a safe place for kids to play. Have you seen anyone around here besides your friends?"

"No, sir," Kat said.

"So, if you just got out here, then who started the fire?" he asked and pointed to the smoldering flames.

"We've been here most of the day. We just pillaged and plundered the Lords of Brimstone's northern outpost. Now we're back to relax and enjoy the fruits of our triumph," Kat said and held out the box of canned goods and clothes we had brought for Mr. Reynolds.

"It's illegal to have an unsupervised fire. If some of these embers got out, it could start a forest fire."

116

"I'm sorry. We didn't think of that. We only had the idea to conquer before we left camp," Kat told them.

"Well," the other officer finally said, "I suppose you're not doing any harm out here. Just remember to keep an eye on the fire and make sure it's completely out before you leave. If you see a man walking through these woods, I want you to run away as fast as you can and tell the police. Do you understand?"

We both said that we did.

The officers and their dog headed northeast. When the forest swallowed them, Kat set down the box of goods beside the tarp.

"Well, I never thought they'd leave," a voice said that seemed to come from everywhere.

Kat and I spun around, searching for the man who had said it, but he was nowhere to be found.

"I suppose the coast is clear," the hollowed knot of a tree told us.

I squinted and focused on the hole in a massive tree twenty feet from camp. The hole was about fifteen feet off the ground, and there was an eyeball in it. The blue orb studied the area where the officers had disappeared and then fixed on us. It blinked, looked to the left and right, and then blinked again. It was the oddest thing I'd ever seen. I was at a loss for words.

"Jayce, that tree ate your new friend," Kat whispered.

In my mind, I agreed with her.

We walked over to the tree, and the eyeball vanished and was replaced with blackness. I heard a series of grunts following the rustling effort of a man working free from a tight spot. We circled the tree, and as we did, the back half of the trunk opened like a small door. Mr. Reynolds' butt came out first and then his head. He stood and whirled around to face us.

117

He thrust out his hand, and, with an English accent, he said, "It's a pleasure to meet you, my lady. I am but a young squire lost in these fair woods. I happened upon your kingdom without permission. A thousand pardons for my intrusion. I beg of you not to shackle me and toss me into the dungeons for the rest of my miserable days. Instead, I ask you to use my knowledge to assist in the defeat of your rivals."

He's as nutty as the rest of these people in town, I thought.

Kat accepted his hand. She also spoke with an accent. "You are welcome in my kingdom, young squire, as long as you have no ulterior motive to double-cross me or my husband, the king," she said and motioned to me.

He bowed. "I would never think of it, my lady. I am at your service for whatever task you might call on me. Your Majesty, it is good to see you again," he said and offered me a slight bow.

I waved and then curiously inspected the tree. Mr. Reynolds had made a perfect door covering the hollow cavity. I closed the door and saw how well it blended with the rest of the tree. I then opened the door and crawled inside the hollow. It was barely spacious enough for me. I had a hard time believing Mr. Reynolds could fit inside without getting stuck. He had cut small notches in the wood and fixed thick branches across to use as rungs. The ladder went nearly ten feet, where daylight beamed through the peephole.

"This is cool," I said and climbed up.

Mr. Reynold had dropped his accent as he said, "I figured I had a little free time on my hands. I needed a place to hide in case the law came around. It's a good thing I made that, because as you know, it came in handy. I found that hollow tree when I set up camp. I made a ladder and then pulled some bark from another large tree. It took me nearly a day to whittle the bark perfectly enough so that someone couldn't tell a rotted center ran through the tree."

"That's smart," Kat said.

"I have moments of brilliance," Mr. Reynolds said. "I've always liked working with my hands. Besides, I have nothing else to do out here."

I reached the top and stuck my right eye against the hole. "There's a pretty good view from here. No one would even know you were looking at them."

"Let me see," Kat called up.

I came down, and she took my place.

"It's a good thing the dog couldn't smell you," I said.

"I don't think that dog knew what he was looking for. They didn't have any of my clothes for him to sniff and track the scent. If he did know what he was looking for, I don't think that tree would have done me much good for protection."

"Oh, this is my friend, Katrina. She goes by Kat," I said. "I know I promised not to say anything to anyone, but she's a good friend and won't tell another person about you."

Mr. Reynolds smiled and said, "I don't blame you for wanting a friend to come along with you. I understand your need to be safe."

"Jayce told me about someone framing you. Is there anyone you can think of who would want to see you in jail?" Kat asked.

"No, not really. I don't believe I've made any enemies. I've been teaching in Coral Key since 2007. I've had my fair share of arguments with students and even other teachers about one thing or another. We all have. None of those encounters ever became anything. I've never been married. I've dated a handful of women around town, but those ended mutually. I thought I was always a well-liked guy. Ever since the police arrested me, I've racked my brain trying to come up with the name of someone who would do such a thing, but I can't. I don't know what to tell you."

"What are you going to do?" Kat said.

"Like I told Jayce, I'm not sure of that either. A part of me wants to turn myself in and have faith that they'll find me innocent. But I escaped and ran when I shouldn't have, which won't help my case. Guilty men run, and that's the way the jury will see it, despite what my lawyer might come up with."

A brown and black shadow tore through the thick undergrowth. In a second flat, it sprang the distance between camp and the hollowed tree where we were standing. It was on Mr. Reynolds before any of us could comprehend exactly what was going on. The thing was a snarling, biting mess of fur.

Mr. Reynolds yelled. The German Shepard growled. It latched onto his left forearm, and its twisting weight threw Mr. Reynolds off-balance. They went down to the ground in a tangled mess.

Kat and I ran forward. Without a second thought, we began swatting at the dog's backside, trying to get it off of Mr. Reynolds. Neither of us took a second to think about the dog suddenly turning on us, and we were no match against an animal with that much muscle and fury.

"Kids, get back!" one of the officers yelled at us as they broke from the forest and ran toward camp. "Heel, Jasper. Heel now!"

The well-trained dog quickly let go of Mr. Reynolds' arm and backed up a pace. Although it still growled and showed a mouthful of sharp and bloody teeth.

The officers leveled their guns at Mr. Reynolds, who was cradling his chewed-up arm and saying something none of us could understand.

"Roll over onto your face and put your hands behind your head now!"

He did exactly as he was told without a second warning. I knew it had to hurt moving his arm back like that, but he only offered a slight groan. The policemen were on top of him. One kept him pinned down as the other rotated his hands behind his back and cuffed him.

"How about that? We got him, Gerald. You and I nailed him," the younger officer said, and then the two men high-fived each other.

"He's innocent," Kat immediately protested. "He didn't do those horrible things. Somebody's setting him up. We were trying to figure out who before you came charging in here."

"I was going to turn myself in. You hear me? I was going to turn myself in," Mr. Reynolds said as they pulled him to his feet.

"I just bet you were. How about that, Gerald? We got ourselves another innocent escaped convict."

"You kids are in a spot of trouble. You see, you lied to the state police. You were helping a fugitive evade the law. We're going to need the two of you to come with us," the officer named Gerald said.

"I've never seen those kids before today. I ran into them just a couple of minutes ago. I told them to get lost and to not dare say a word about seeing me or I'd come after them," Mr. Reynolds said.

"Is that true? Have you seen this man before?"

Mr. Reynolds obviously didn't want us to get in trouble along with him, so he was giving us a way out.

"We've seen him on TV before today, but that's all," I told them.

Kat started to say something that I thought was going to contradict what I had said, so I jabbed her in the side to shut her up.

She glared at me, then smiled at the officers and said, "Exactly what my friend Jayce said. We don't know this man."

Both officers studied us for a long moment. One of them finally said, "All right. Both of you can stay here and out of trouble from now on. Do you hear me?"

"Yes, sir," we said.

They began pushing Mr. Reynolds through the trees toward an unseen police car and back to confinement.

"Make sure he gets his arm looked at. Do you hear me?" Kat called after them so loudly that I was sure that every creature in a four-mile radius in these dense woods had also heard.

"What now?" I asked.

"There is no what now. Mr. Reynolds' fate is out of our hands. It's up to his lawyer."

I didn't like the sound of that. I didn't think Mr. Reynolds had much of a chance in a court of law, especially since he had taken the opportunity and escaped. Like he had said, running made him look guilty, and that was the way a judge and jury would see it.

I said, "It wouldn't hurt to investigate it. Maybe even without his help, we could figure out who might have set him up. There's got to be only a few people in town crazy and mean enough to pull off something like this. It's worth a try. Besides, I don't have anything better going on during the summer. Do you?"

"I've seen him around town plenty of times, but I've never spoken to him before. He's always seemed like a real nice man who minds his own business. I would have liked to have him as a teacher if he taught here instead of Coral Key." Kat looked at the box of goods in her hands and said, "Damn, now I've got to carry this crap all the way back home."

Chapter 13

As we rolled deep into the month of June, the town finally answered the call of my building enthusiasm.

The sound of trumpets reached us from two miles away. The smell of cooking meat over an open flame was noticeable from a mile and a half away. The sound of clanking swords found us a mile away. When Kat and I emerged from the forest path and arrived at the large field where the medieval arena had been built seven decades ago, we could hear and feel the chatter, cheer, and vibration of the growing crowd.

My excitement had started building when I first met the town barber Sir Reginald Spree and learned of the games. When I saw the posters pasted everywhere around town the last few weeks, the excitement went from a simmer to a boil. Now my enthusiasm was bubbling over the rim of the pot, spilling grease onto the fire, and becoming an all-out inferno.

There was just something about men acting like complete barbarians for a few days to liven the otherwise common, if I dared to call it that, life in a small Florida town. I thought that this type of event would appeal more to men and boys instead of women and girls. But when I looked at Kat, probably with my eyes sparkling as if someone had just thrown a handful of glitter in my face, I saw a delight coming from her that I'd never seen before.

I'd seen Kat smile. I'd even heard her laugh from time to time. She was usually guarded, as if someone or something was about to come along and knock her dreams and ambitions back a few dozen steps. Now the usually stern look on her face had slipped away, and a look of excitement had taken its place. The giddy way she skipped toward the arena was something I never thought I'd get to witness. Today she was a girl who had let go of her worries and found a pure happiness that rarely came along.

"Incredible," I said as I took in the sights.

"I told you it was something you wouldn't believe until you actually saw it," Kat called over her shoulder.

Like always, Kat was right. I hadn't expected this. I thought for sure the games would be a display of lame cardboard swords and shields, jesters who acted a moronic part simply to make a few bucks, and the jousting fakery that would throw a man from his horse yards before a lance actually hit him. But I knew there was something special about today. Even before I entered the arena, I knew it would be spectacular.

It seemed that the people at the event were out for blood, judging by the sounds of metal clanking against metal.

The monstrous gray blocks that constructed the outer walls ran as high as thirty feet and were covered in moss. The arena was oval and made me think I would find a football field inside. I couldn't wrap my head around the fact that a bunch of men inside were riding horseback while dressed in chain mail or suits of armor. All of them here for the single goal of becoming the next Knight of Arms.

We ran until we reached the large wooden gates that were open wide in invitation to all the townspeople. I was trying to rush inside when Kat's voice stopped me.

"Hold on. You're going to skip the best part," Kat said, and then moved toward the vendors that lined the outside of the arena wall.

The savory scents of roasted peanuts, sizzling meat, popcorn, and a dozen other smells I couldn't single out loomed over the packed crowd. People were waving fistfuls of money over their heads and calling out orders to specific vendors.

It reminded me of a time when my dad had taken Josh and me to a Red Sox game. Vendors called out, and hungry or thirsty fans would call back, and then food or drink would travel down the row of spectators and money would work its way back. The same apparently goes for medieval games.

"I can't even see what they're selling," I told Kat, as I was sure she knew the menu by heart.

"You've got to try gator on a pig on a peg," Kat told me, and then popped up on her toes searching for a certain vendor.

"A what?"

"It's one of the best things here," Kat said without an explanation of exactly what it was.

She grabbed a fistful of my shirt and hauled me through the small gaps in the crowd. Somehow, we had cut our way through and stood before a long line of vendors. The smell was stronger and sweeter at this spot. My mouth watered. My eyes were wide and taking everything in without trying to miss a single thing.

A booth with freshly fried pig skins, also known as pork rinds, was to my left. Thin strips of some kind of meat hissed on a flat iron plate to my right. Farther to my left was a booth where an older woman worked. At first, I thought she was tossing handfuls of chocolate chunks into a simmering pot of caramel, but then I saw the chocolate chunks were moving. Inside the clear plastic container was a mass of crawling, leaping black crickets.

Handfuls of live crickets took a plunge into the pot. Most of them had tried to leap out, but the caramel had already grabbed parts of their bodies and refused to let go. It reminded me of a fly landing on a strip of sticky paper hanging from a ceiling and the paper holding it until the fight and life finally gave out.

The old woman stirred the pot, dipped a strainer inside, and pulled out a bundle of bodies now encased in caramel. Some of them still twitched, trying to breathe through the thick mass covering their bodies.

Kat dropped five dollars on the woman's table. In return, the old woman plucked a wax bag off a shelf of already prepared and cooled caramel crickets and handed it over.

"Thanks, love. Enjoy," the woman told Kat.

"I always do, Mrs. Leroy," Kat called back, and we moved down the line.

"I hope you have a pet frog that loves caramel crickets," I said.

Kat opened the bag, twisted a gooey chunk loose, and popped it into her mouth. I could hear the crunching of cricket bodies between her teeth.

Unlike Kat, I scrunched my face in disgust that she had actually put a vile mass of once-live bugs into her mouth.

Kat studied me for a moment and, around a mouthful, said, "It's pretty good once you get past the exploding guts."

We passed a vendor that had an entire pig on a spit rotating over a fire. Kat stopped when we reached the next vendor.

"It's ten dollars for a gator on a pig on a peg, but totally worth every cent," Kat said.

The vendor was selling some sort of kabobs. The smell of grilled onions, green peppers, and pineapple smashed between strips of meat folded over another piece of meat made my stomach growl with anticipation.

"Ten dollars?"

"Sure. Do you think alligator meat and pork comes cheap?" Kat asked and wedged in another mouthful of caramel bug goo.

I thought of all the hours I'd spent during the summer cleaning animal pens. I thought of the frightening experiences of handling poisonous snakes and feeding alligators that would be just as comfortable eating my leg as they were eating the chunks of chicken I had thrown to them. That made me think about my hard-earned ten dollars.

"You better be right about it being worth it," I said and dropped ten dollars on the vendor's table.

In return, I received wedges of meat, fruit, and vegetables on a skewer. I studied it for a moment before taking a bite. The onions and green peppers added a little zing, and the pineapple boosted a sweetness to the spiced alligator and pork. The first bite told me that Kat was right, the ten dollars was well worth it. I might have paid double the price if I had tasted it before, especially since the treat only came around once a year.

Kat nodded in agreement as she watched my expression.

"I told you," Kat said, and then she grabbed my shirt again. "Come on, let's find good seats and watch the practice runs."

With probably the entire town in attendance, working our way inside and scouting for decent seats was not easy. But luckily, when we got inside the arena, we saw a small boy waving his arms, attempting to get our attention. He was smiling. It might be the first time I'd even seen him crack a grin. Before today, I hadn't even been sure he had teeth.

"There's Anderson," Kat pointed out, and we maneuvered up the stone steps to the fifth row and halfway down.

"Oh, you're so lucky," Anderson said when he saw what I had bought outside.

"Didn't you bring any money?" I asked.

"No. Dad doesn't pay me to do chores."

I thought about it and then fished into the front pocket of my shorts. I pulled out a fistful of wrinkled bills, selected a ten, and held it out to Anderson. He looked at the bill with astonishment.

He said, "No, I couldn't."

"Yes, you can. Take it. It's a gift," I told him.

A trembling hand reached for it. When he took it, he said, "Thank you. I'll be sure to pay you back when I can."

"You don't pay back gifts," I told him.

He nodded, smiled, got up, excused himself down the row, and disappeared out the entrance of the arena.

"You're all right, you know?" Kat said as she studied me.

"I have my moments. Does that mean you'll be nice enough to stop calling me Graham Cracker?"

She elbowed me in the ribs and said, "Not on your life. The name has a nice ring to it."

Two men dressed in full armored suits clanked swords inside the center arena. This was only mild entertainment for the crowd, as I could see the men putting little effort into actually scoring a hit. Practice or not, I watched with enthusiasm. It was like going to watch a professional baseball or football game for the first time. Of course, this event had its major differences, as I'd never seen anything such as this on television.

I moved around a lot in my seat as more people dressed for battle began shuffling into the arena.

"Do you have ants in your pants or something?" Kat asked.

I settled a bit, but not much.

Anderson came back. His face beamed with savory delight. Around a mouthful, he thanked me again. It made me feel pretty good that such a simple thing had brought someone happiness.

A man with a thick black beard and clothed in Renaissance garments broke off from the rest of the group. He moved to the center of the arena and held out his arms to the crowd.

"Ladies and gentlemen, boys and girls, we welcome you to the 2024 Paper Moon Knight of Arms Tournament."

The audience erupted with applause. There were ear-piercing whistles and hoots of excitement. The stone seats moved with powerful vibrations.

Someone bumped into my right shoulder. I turned to find a man standing there that I figured never went out to public events or even to the shopping market, for that matter. He was looking down at me and smiling. His wife didn't smile, because I didn't think she could. Her expression was always the same, with the exception of moving eyes and a mouth that worked on small hinges.

"Mr. and Mrs. Bixby!" I said and drew the attention of several nearby people.

"Hello, Jayce," Mrs. Bixby said, her eyes rolling over me with interest.

Mr. Bixby simply smiled, nodded, and then turned his attention to the man in the arena.

"I didn't know the two of you attended the annual tournament," I said and briefly thought about how it would be impossible for Mrs. Bixby to go around town without her husband.

The announcer removed a piece of paper from his shirt pocket and said, "I assure you that this will be an evening to remember. Our challengers will battle one another in stages until only one remains. This evening's challengers are Brian 'Bone Breaker' Barra. Randolph 'Devastator' Jackson. Peter 'The Punisher' Malone. 'Ominous' Evan Plurge. Percy 'Ironsides' Stevens. Jefferson 'The Unstoppable' Courtman. Of course, we all know the ground stopped him last year when he was repeatedly unhorsed by the four-time champion Sir Reginald 'The Barbarian' Spree!"

Laughter and cheers filled the arena.

"Sounds like we should be watching Friday night wrestling instead of a jousting contest," I said and was quickly hushed by Kat.

"For the first time in tournament history, we have a contender who wishes to be known only as Anonymous," the announcer shouted excitedly.

The unknown contender dressed in full armor stepped into the arena and bowed. The crowd came alive again to cheer on the masked man.

"The mystery grows," Kat said from the corner of her caramel-and-cricket-filled mouth.

I smiled. Just like everyone else, I love a good mystery.

"Eight contenders will battle each other in three events until one remains standing to be crowned this year's Knight of Arms."

More cheers ran across the stadium in waves.

"The anticipation is killing me. I wish they would get started already," I said as I squirmed in my seat. "Hey, any idea who the mystery contender might be?"

"No idea whatsoever. Would you sit still?" Kat said, but she couldn't help forming a smile at my jitteriness.

"For those of you who don't know how this competition is fought and won, the panel of judges will award points as follows. One point is awarded when a lance strikes the grand guard. When the grand guard is struck and the lance is broken, the judges will award five points. Ten points will be awarded to a competitor who strikes the opponent's grand guard, breaks his lance, and unhorses the opponent. Any competitor knocked from his horse and unable to continue within two minutes will forfeit the match."

"What's a grand guard?" I whispered to Kat.

"It's a steel plate on the left shoulder that's bolted to the armor. It's the only place a lance can strike in order to gain points," Kat said.

"Oh, cool," I said and focused on the announcer again.

The announcer continued, "The competitors will make eight passes along the list. The one awarded the most points after the eighth pass wins the match. Eight competitors will battle in the first round. Only four will move on to the semifinals. When the semifinals are complete, two challengers will enter the finals. First up will be Brian 'Bone Breaker' Barra versus Anonymous. Ladies, gentlemen, boys and girls, shall we begin the games?"

The crowd came alive with applause as the first challengers entered the arena. Aside from one man wearing gold armor with crimson stripes across the shoulders and the other challenger wearing black armor with gold stripes on his shoulders, they looked very much alike. Their horses, however, were very different. One was pure white and built like a locomotive. The other was small in comparison, with a mix of brown and black. It was lean, but no doubt just as powerful as the other.

"What's a list?" I asked, feeling completely dumb bombarding Kat with too many questions.

"The list is that wall dividing the riders. The one in the center of the arena that comes halfway up the height of the horses. I don't mind you asking me questions if you don't know," Kat said, as if reading my mind.

The riders trotted to opposite ends of the arena. Their coaches placed a small set of steps beside the horses, climbed up, and then helped the riders fasten their face guards. The coaches removed the steps, handed up a lance, and then moved the horses and riders to the starting position.

The horses were restless. They kept jumping ahead before the signal, and the coaches forced them back into place. When the flag dropped, the riders thrust their heels into the horses' sides, and they took off with incredible power. The thundering strike of hooves on sand made my heart quicken with anticipation as the riders closed in.

The riders lowered their lances in unison, holding the position for a hopeful score. Anonymous' lance found the center of Bone Breaker's grand guard.

When Anonymous' strike thrust Bone Breaker up from his horse and into the air, that was when the magic of the event became very real.

Chapter 14

There was an unsettling hush of the crowd as Bone Breaker lay perfectly still in the sand. The grand guard of his armor tore free of its bolts, and the lance's deflecting strike had cratered the metal of his helmet where the left cheek would be. Honestly, I thought he was dead. I think the entire crowd thought that as well. The brutal hit had made us all pull back in our seats and offer a sympathetic groan.

Bone Breaker's coach and the on-site medic were kneeling on each side of his collapsed body. A minute later, I saw the armor move. With the help of the two men, the competitor sat up, and then they lifted him to his feet. After a unified sigh of relief, the crowd came alive once again. Stout whistles and hearty applause welcomed the knight as they guided him back to the staging area in front of us. His arm limply raised with acknowledgement, and he settled on the wood bench.

After a minute of discussion between the men, the announcer stepped from the group and addressed the fans.

Holding up his hands for silence, he said, "It should please everyone to know that Bone Breaker is all right. Although, he has unfortunately forfeited the match because of unrepairable damage to his armor and a possible concussion. With that being said, this match win goes to Anonymous!"

The crowd went to their feet, and again the stadium erupted with noise. Anonymous simply offered the smallest nod of gratitude. I figured he thought that this was no way to win a match. Competitors like these wanted a fair-and-square win and not to win by forfeit or default. It didn't satisfy anyone as a noteworthy victory.

After Anonymous galloped off the field, something more shocking happened than Bone Breaker's violent unhorsing. Two naked men appeared on the field. They emerged from the left stadium entrance, bolting across the field. Thankfully, being that many children attended the games, the two had both hands cupped over their groins. After the initial startle fled my eyes, I realized they weren't men, but boys, and they were two boys I knew. It was the Evans brothers. These two constant law enforcement headaches were up to an act I never thought of as a reasonable prank. What person in their right mind figured that running around nude in front of nearly the entire town seemed like a good idea? What could they possibly benefit from doing such a stupid stunt?

I looked at Kat and then at Anderson. They had the largest grins I'd ever seen. In fact, most of the audience had similar smiles. Of course, there were many mothers and fathers shielding their children's eyes from this vulgar act.

As the boys ran around aimlessly, I noticed something was chasing each of them. No, that was wrong, not chasing, but tied to their ankles by lengths of rope.

"Are they drunk? Maybe on drugs?" Kat asked.

I focused on what was behind them. Regan paused a second, just long enough for me to see what was being dragged. Kat must have understood the instant I did. What the brothers towed behind them were three-foot-long yellow and brown-spotted alligators. Now everything made perfect sense. This wasn't a voluntary devious deed, but an action of revenge that I unfortunately didn't get to take part in. Neither did Kat.

Kat rammed an elbow into my ribs and said, "They don't know those gators are fake!" and then she rocked back with laughter.

I recognized those gators, too. They were hand-painted rubber models sold at Grady's gift shop. Never in my life had I seen a toy look so lifelike. If anyone could give authenticity to a rubber alligator, it would be Grady and Carl and not people in a Chinese factory. So, I understood the terror the brothers displayed. In fact, I was sure most of the crowd believed they were real as well. Only us few privileged knew the truth.

Several of the men working the event finally sprang into action. With a casual jog, they headed toward the wall where the brothers had tried to block the crowd's view of their very white butts. When they saw men heading toward them, they bolted from cover. Regan lost his balance, and in order to avoid a face-plant into the ground, he pin-wheeled his arms. Unfortunately, the movement gave the audience a brief look at what he was desperately trying to conceal. It was a part of Regan no one ever wanted to see.

"That's going to haunt my sleep," Kat told those around us.

The boys switched this way and that, trying to find an exit. Regan kept trying to follow his brother. Even with Rory being older and supposedly wiser, it still didn't give him a grasp on any logical thoughts of escape as thousands of eyes watched them.

No doubt exhausted, the boys gave up running, and security instantly tackled them. While security held them face-down on the turf, it gave the audience a long, uncomfortable view of two butts staring back at us.

"Okay, now that's gross," Kat said as she zoomed in on her phone. "And totally going on YouTube!"

"I don't doubt that at all," I told her as I looked across the stadium.

Hundreds of phones were capturing the entire ordeal. Not so much the adults, but every kid once terrorized by Regan was justly recording the most embarrassing moment of his life.

Anderson was also scanning the crowd. He knew the damage this would inflict on Regan's school status as one to be feared. After this, Regan would be lucky enough if he still had one of his lackeys hanging around. This day would be the ultimate reputation crusher.

"Sweet justice," Anderson said, and we bumped knuckles.

Someone brought out several blankets to the security team holding the brothers down. After the men tried to cover them up the best they could, they lifted the brothers to their feet. Both instantly tried to sprint off again once they saw their ankle leashes still had a gator attached. Two of the guards ripped the gators loose from the tethers and shook them in front of the boys. The realization that washed over their faces was relief, anger, and humility all rolled into one expression. This day just reached the top five of the most satisfying moments of my life.

"He'll never live this down. Twenty years from now, when he thinks everyone has forgotten, someone will bring it up again," I told Kat and Anderson.

"Yeah. Even if he moves to another country, I'll find out where and email the video to everyone he works with and lives around," Anderson added.

"Exactly what I was thinking," I said.

With the noise of the crowd, I couldn't hear anything the men or brothers said. As security escorted them out of the arena, Rory pointed to the area they entered and shouted perhaps some kind of demand. But his angry tantrum went unnoticed.

I looked, of course. The angle of my sitting position didn't offer much view of that entrance. Although I did spot one distinct thing over a six-foot-tall section of fencing.

I returned a painful jab into Kat's ribs. She looked like she was going to clock me in the face, but then she followed my eyes.

A sinister chuckle rumbled out of her as she said, "I knew it."

What we saw was a cowboy hat made entirely of alligator skin. The man had told me that he took the gator's skin after the creature had tried to eat him. Actually, it was the first alligator he ever wrangled from the water. It had gone into a vicious death roll on the boat that could have easily killed the man on board.

He couldn't help that his hat peeked out over the fence, because Grady stood at six and a half feet tall. The mountain of a man was not one who could duck and hide easily. With that said, he wasn't someone who needed to hide. No one except those with a death wish would mess with a man like that.

Through the thin gaps in the fence planks, I could see another man. He stood a good half a foot beneath his friend. Obviously, Carl had joined in on today's unexpected festivities of delicious revenge.

I said, "Well, Carl did tell us that boys like that always get exactly what they deserve."

When the boys and security disappeared from the stadium, the announcer returned to the center arena. The crowd tucked away their phones, as tournament policy forbade recording during the event. The announcer held up his hands, demanding silence.

When the crowd complied, he said, "Well, that was a very unexpected intermission! However, the show must go on! Up next, I give you two competitors who know how to win." His left hand swung out, and he said, "I give you last year's runner-up, Jefferson 'The Unstoppable' Courtman!"

Like a lightning bolt, the black horse and his rider took to the arena. In a brazen show of arrogance, with a wide trail, his horse hammered heavily on the earth around the list. For a brief second, I could have sworn the horse exhaled curling tendrils of steam and offered a quick flicker of bright red coming from its eyes.

"Is Satan really riding that thing?" I asked Kat.

"That's Nexus. He's the biggest, meanest horse around. But remember, it's the rider who truly wins the match. The horse has its importance of keeping on a steady run so the rider can aim his lance, but any great jouster can dominate with nearly any horse."

After The Unstoppable ceased his showmanship, he settled in the center of the arena.

The announcer motioned with his other hand to the right side of the arena. He said, "And a decision granted by fate, a rematch became a possibility! I give you the four-time champion Sir Reginald 'The Barbarian' Spree!"

There was a definite favorite in these games, as the fans leaped to their feet and began a cheer that could have muted a bomb going off outside the stadium. I clamped my hands over my ears but got only a little relief. His armor was a colorless metal finish, causing the sun to wink off it. He appeared to be in no hurry, maybe savoring the roar of attention. His horse was absolutely beautiful, even majestic. She came out in a soft prance that was much like a dance. I'm sure I wouldn't even hear her hooves tap the ground, even if the stadium were completely quiet.

Where one competitor had arrogance and ego, the other had grace and honor. To me, it had a distinct pitting of good versus evil. Even the coloring of the horses and armor gave it that impression.

The riders briefly spoke with their coaches, accepted a ten-foot lance, and moved to opposite ends of the list. My heart was in a hard gallop, even though it seemed as if everything at this venue was momentarily at a complete standstill.

The flag went down, and even before the riders could thrust a heel in their horses' sides, the incredible animals knew it was time to battle. They took off with a hard push and quickly seized momentum. As the riders pressed closer, the lances fell in unison, centering aim for a grand guard strike. But the lances parried, causing a deviation of both lances to come off target. The crowd groaned as anticipation of a monumental moment fizzled out. It happened two more times. The competitors were so zeroed in that their lances targeted each other like magnets.

It wasn't until the fourth charge down the list that low expectations hastily reversed. Instead of a parry, Sir Reginald Spree's lance bullseyed Courtman's grand guard. The action was such an impressive hit that the lance blew apart as if filled with cherry bombs. Courtman rode an invisible springboard from his horse, a quick drift through the air before gravity took hold and slammed him onto the sand. It came to us as an even more violent run than the last competitors, which caused Bone Breaker to forfeit the match.

Much to everyone's surprise, Courtman was instantly on his feet without the help of his coach or medic. It was anger that forced him back up. He paced, his armor clanking as frustration vibrated through his body. Finally, he let the quiet tantrum go, walked to the steps, and mounted his horse.

The next run resulted in the same outcome. This time Courtman was slower getting back up. He was apparently letting anger get the better of him, which destroyed his focus. Sir Spree was taking advantage of this distraction. The fifth run had given Sir Spree a broken lance, and the unhorsing of his opponent earned him another ten points, but Courtman caught Sir Spree's grand guard for a single point.

Going into the sixth run, it was twenty to one and Courtman had all but lost unless he could equal Sir Spree's efforts of the last two runs or unhorse Sir Spree and cause his inability to return to the match.

There was an immediate difference on the sixth run. I'd been watching Courtman's posture, and it was apparent he'd found the mental strength to compose himself and find focus. He knew full well this match was a loss unless he shook loose the previous runs and pretended it was a start-over with zero to zero on the scoreboard. This way he could mentally trick himself into believing that this was not a desperate effort to play catch-up.

I believe the entire crowd saw it as well when the run began. Courtman's lance was steady and on point as he rode the up-and-down motion of his horse the last few feet before his weapon bit into the metal target.

It wasn't a shock to me. But it must have been for the rest of the audience. There was an impressive hush that came over the crowd. Sir Spree did a hard rotation to the right, as if hit by a log swinging on a rope. His airtime was nonexistent. The crash to sand was highly audible in the stadium silence. Many people looked to their neighbors as if to confirm what they had witnessed.

I only smiled as I watched Sir Spree lie there.

Now it's a competition, I thought.

Though Courtman was arrogant, I still loved to see an underdog rise to the challenge. Sir Spree literally got knocked from his high horse to face the reality that any competitor could eventually lose.

He finally sat up with a little help but managed to stand on his own. He wobbled a bit as he made his way to his horse, which waited at the start line for another round.

"Even with all the padding inside the suit, that had to hurt like crazy," Anderson said.

"For a kid with no cushion on your body, that hit would have split all your bones in half if you'd been in that suit," I told him.

Mr. Bixby said behind us, "He's in pain. I can tell. But he'll pin it down until the match is over. He loves having fans, and he wants to live up to the reputation of his previous years."

The seventh run was off, and I was sure Sir Spree wasn't physically or mentally prepared. He was loose in the saddle as his body desperately tried to clamp onto his horse. The lance bobbed all over the place as he lowered it for a strike. As if he'd suffered from double vision, his lance aimed at a phantom horseman.

However, Courtman was a steady rider and had a metal plate in his sights. After his lance exploded and Sir Spree hit the sand again, the audience found their new favorite jouster.

Courtman tossed the remains of the broken lance and thrust his arms in the air. The crowd cheered more than ever before. I probably cheered the hardest, not because it was a close match, but happy for the possibility of Sir Spree losing. I remembered our first introduction. His outfit and his laughable notion that another jouster could unhorse him instantly gave me a distaste for his arrogant character.

The eighth and final pass was possible defeat or glory for either competitor. The score now stood at twenty-one to twenty in favor of Courtman.

It was only seconds after the horses took off with a locomotive charge when I saw fragments of wood flying. A lance exploded, but the crowd leaped to their feet, preventing me from seeing over their heads well enough to know the match result.

"What happened?" I asked those around me in an almost panic that I would never know.

Anderson and Kat both shrugged. None of us were tall enough to see.

By the time the crowd settled back down and took their seats, the competitors were off their horses, helmets removed, and patiently watched the referees as they debated.

"If Sir Spree simply touched the grand guard, they'd be even at twenty-one. So, it could even be a tie," Anderson said.

"But I saw someone's lance blow apart. So, it's possible one of them received five points," I told him.

After a brief debate ended, the competitors joined the announcer and faced us, waiting for the verdict.

"With careful consideration, the judges have counted all points. We've awarded five points to Jefferson 'The Unstoppable' Courtman for a grand guard strike, resulting in a broken lance, bringing his total to twenty-six points. Unfortunately, Sir Reginald 'The Barbarian' Spree's lance did not strike the grand guard but deflected off his opponent's arm. So, the judges awarded no points. In conclusion, the match winner is Jefferson 'The Unstoppable' Courtman by six points!"

A quiet shock circled through the audience, but it then gave way to an eruption of cheers. The judges briefly listened to Sir Spree's protests and dismissed them. Courtman did a little victory dance, which was humorous to watch as he shimmied around in all that heavy armor.

"There you have it! Another competitor has dethroned the king," Mr. Bixby told us.

Here's the breakdown of the remaining matches.

"Ominous" Evan Plurge destroyed Peter "The Punisher" Malone twenty-two to one.

Randolph "Devastator" Jackson trumped Percy "Ironside" Stevens by a narrow margin of one point.

The semi-finals pitted Anonymous against Evan Plurge. After a brutal unhorsing, Mr. Plurge's ambulance ride to the hospital brought another forfeit and the advancement to the finals for Anonymous.

Courtman defeated "Devastator" Jackson in nearly the same way he'd won over Sir Spree. By rallying from way behind, he overtook the Devastator by five points.

The announcer came out and said, "Ladies, gentlemen, and our younger viewers, we will take a brief intermission before the final joust begins. Please find some shade and grab something to drink. Don't forget, there's still plenty to buy from the vendors outside. The trumpets will sound before the final match against Jefferson 'The Unstoppable' Courtman and Anonymous!"

I hadn't realized it at first, but someone had been closely watching me during the tournament.

Chapter 15

With the final match coming up, vendors offered discounts on remaining treats so they could have fresh snacks prepared for tomorrow's archery event.

"Are you planning on attending the other events?" Kat asked.

"Um, I haven't totally decided yet. I kind of wanted to work. I could always use some extra cash."

"Jousting is by far the best event they have. The archery and sword dueling are okay, but nothing special. They've been falling behind in popularity over the years."

"Yeah, then I think I'll skip them. It would probably be a letdown after watching the jousting matches."

I got a big cup of cranberry lemonade that was incredibly tart, but a soothing relief to quench my dire thirst. Kat got a popcorn ball for her and Anderson to share. After the wonderful sweet and salty flavor of gator on a pig on a peg I had earlier, the aroma of a pig turning on a spit smelled wonderful. We swung by the booth where an older man in overalls tended to customers. I ordered a large plate of honey-glazed ham. We found an empty picnic table in the blissful shade, and I placed the plate in the middle.

I motioned to the ham and said, "Help yourselves."

They didn't protest but dug in. With the exception of caramel crickets, I would have loved all the treats available at the games.

I folded and wolfed down thick cuts of ham. The others did the same. We swallowed and drank, washing it down until the plate was bare. As I chewed the last bite, I looked up to see Deputy Kline sitting alone under an elm. He was slowly chewing a hot dog and taking long swallows of iced tea. As if controlled by a robotic system, his eyes slowly rotated across the crowd and instantly ceased motion when they landed on me. Then his head swiveled in the same action until he fully faced me.

Even with the scorching temperature, an icy river ran down my spine and made me shiver. I didn't like those eyes. I saw menace behind them. The deputy was a man who knew a lot about the town and its people. I was sure he knew secrets that members of Paper Moon thought were well-hidden from public view.

"What's up?" Anderson asked as he watched me staring into the distance.

Before they turned around to look, the deputy was on his feet, tossed his wrapper in a waste bin, slugged down more tea, and then headed for the arena.

"Hmm? Oh, nothing. My brain was off running somewhere."

The trumpets sounded, and like students hearing the end of the lunch bell, everyone stood and made their way back into the arena.

When we started up the steps, I saw Deputy Kline sitting in my spot.

I grabbed Kat's arm and said, "Someone took our seats. Let's go somewhere else."

"Well, he can just move, since we were there first."

It was an intentional thing he'd done. He knew where we'd been sitting before intermission, and now he was testing my actions.

He watched us with that same eerie, dead stare as I debated what to do. Kat had no idea what I suspected about Deputy Kline. She didn't hesitate to reclaim our seats before the final joust.

"I'm sorry, Mr. Kline, but we were sitting there," she told him.

"It's Deputy Kline. But I am sorry. I wasn't meaning to be a seat-stealer. I got here late and have been watching from near the front entrance. How about if I scoot down?"

Kat shrugged and said, "Sure."

She then rammed me forward down the aisle, forcing me to sit beside Deputy Kline.

I started to step over the seat to grab a spot next to Mr. Bixby, but a group of people had returned from the vendor area with their arms loaded with goods. They managed to fill the bench before I could weasel in. Deputy Kline cocked his head at me and smiled.

I tried to nudge Kat as far down as possible. Too much and we'd drive Anderson onto the stairs. There was a small space, because Deputy Kline had no intention of sliding to the left to fill the two feet of empty space on his other side.

Kat watched me, probably trying to figure out what was going on in my head. I had wanted to tell her, but Kat has a big mouth. She often didn't think before speaking. I was always sure the filter from her brain to her mouth was out of order since birth.

"It's got to be extra exciting for you, Jayce. I still remember my first tournament. I was a bit younger than you are now before my parents let me come. Oh, it had something to do with all the violence and they were afraid I'd grow up to be a violent person, I suppose. Well, I showed them by becoming a deputy. Sheriff Prescott is retiring next year, and I'm the likely candidate to step into his shoes."

He was speaking to me as if we were old friends. I didn't care about anything he said. I wished he didn't speak to me at all. So, I told him that it was good to know and shifted my sitting position toward Kat and Anderson. I hoped things would start soon.

Deputy Kline tapped my leg and said, "Are you still living up to your hero status? It must work well for you with the girls. Yeah, hero brothers charge into an inferno and save a family. The headline had it right. You could have died that night. It would definitely be something I'd have thought twice about had it been me. I couldn't imagine the pain of burning to death. It must be the worst way to go. Or maybe being devoured by piranhas. That could be bad, too."

I tried not to stare, but I wondered why he had said that. Was he planning on dropping me into a tank filled with hungry piranha? Were his thoughts growing more sinister and now he needed to step up, possibly murdering the one kid in town who suspected him of evil actions? I had poked my nose into a bad situation, and my thoughts ran wild about how to escape from it. Then it came to me.

"Yeah, it was scary. I'd do it again if I had to. I'm just glad they caught the arsonist, Mr. Reynolds. I think the town can breathe easy now, knowing no more structures will burn down and no one else will get hurt."

He smiled at that, but his eyes stared into me, as if he thought, *I don't believe you, Jayce Graham.*

"Like I told you the last time we spoke, it was skilled policework that caught him. We were able to link evidence directing us to Mr. Reynolds. The man must have really hated this town to try to burn it all to the ground."

I thought, *No, not him. Not the man I met in the woods. Not the man Kat and I brought supplies to. He's a kind, honest man. But you, Deputy Kline, are a professional liar. You're deceitful and a coward. You framed Mr. Reynolds for whatever reason. Now an innocent man sits in a cell where you should be.*

Thankfully, two riders charged the field, followed by the announcer.

"I trust you all had a quick cool-down and a few wonderful treats, but now the time has come. We are down to the final competitors. Jefferson 'The Unstoppable' Courtman versus Anonymous! I honestly have to tell you that I've been most impressed with both competitors. The Unstoppable has certainly lived up to his name at this year's tournament. Coming from behind in both matches has shown us that he definitely deserves to be in this final match. Now, I can't say much about Anonymous. In fact, I can't say anything at all! Only that he's a brilliant jouster and has proven that you don't even need a name to battle your way to the finals. Gentlemen, take your places!"

The announcer moved off as the riders took positions. It was so quiet that we all heard the huff of the horses' breathing and the soft rattle of metal armor as they settled at each end of the list. The flag went down, and the horses were off.

It was obvious both riders wanted to annihilate each other to take home the championship. Both riders positioned themselves strongly on their horses, and their lances fell with mechanical accuracy. One rider wanted it a bit more. Anonymous's lance blew apart into toothpicks as it dead-centered Courtman's grand guard. The impact threw him from the horse and resulted in a hard impact on the sand. Despite being partially held together by wood fibers, the judges awarded five points for Courtman's broken lance. That was how it went for every run. The judges awarded Courtman with one or five points but never ten points for unhorsing Anonymous. However, for Courtman, each run resulted in him taking a helmet full of sand.

Going into the eighth and final run, the score stood at seventy to eighteen. Anonymous had clinched victory by a huge margin, but only if Courtman couldn't unhorse and knock him unconscious.

Just like the previous runs, Anonymous destroyed his lance for the final time, throwing Courtman from his horse. Galloping across the arena, he raised his arm, showing the remains of his lance, then threw it to the side and leaped from his horse.

Deputy Kline clapped me on the back. In an uncomfortable display, his muscular hand flexed hard on the back of my neck. His hand forcefully ground soft muscles and nerves, making me wince in silent pain.

What I didn't expect was someone else's hand to seize Deputy Kline's. When the deputy's hand pulled back, I turned to see what was going on. Mr. Bixby had removed Deputy Kline's hand with surprising strength.

Leaning forward, Mr. Bixby said, "It doesn't appear as if he likes your attention. So, maybe you should keep your hands off him."

Deputy Kline's eyes switched around, studying the faces of those closest. He fully knew he couldn't lose his composure in front of the townspeople. He offered a false smile and pulled his hand from Mr. Bixby.

"It was quite a show. That's all. I got a little overzealous. Jayce and I go a little way back. He knows my celebration had no ill intent. No harm, no foul."

Deputy Kline's face slipped from a wide grin to flat angry as his attention moved from Mr. Bixby to me and then back to the arena.

The announcer ran out and immediately verified what I'd been thinking. He said, "This has undoubtedly been the most amazing display of jousting I have seen in my fifteen years of heading up these games!"

Courtman removed his helmet. He had the look of a man who struggled between disappointment and rage, as he had yet again given up a championship match to step into second place. When Anonymous removed his helmet, it became the most shocking moment in the Knight of Arms tournament history.

Shaking her long, blonde hair loose from a ponytail, Ms. Tunstill, the town librarian, howled with joy as she pumped her helmet in the air.

If there was ever a moment in the history of the world where a large group of people unintentionally uttered the same word in unison, it was here and now.

"What?" the audience asked. Then everyone studied their neighbors to make sure they were all seeing the same thing.

The games committee must have also kept the announcer in the dark about who the challenger was. His mouth slowly opened and closed, with no words coming out. He looked like a fish out of water. He simply motioned his hand to the librarian, triggering the audience to explode with applause.

I momentarily forgot about Deputy Kline and his intimidation and joined the crowd. I went to my feet with the rest of them and clapped until my hands were numb.

Ms. Tunstill turned each way, offering a hearty bow. If the audience had received red roses at the entrance to throw out to their favorite competitor, I believed Ms. Tunstill would be hip-deep in them now.

As true sportsmen, the other competitors stepped out and joined the audience with celebration.

It was insane to think that possibly one of the greatest jousters this arena had seen in all these decades was a woman. I don't mean that in a sexist way, but more the difference in physical build between a woman who only outweighed me by thirty pounds against some men whose muscles had muscles made it completely baffling as to how no one had unhorsed her.

"It's all in the training," I decided to admit to Kat.

"What do you mean?"

"Not one hit could drive her from her horse. Those blows that landed should have crushed her."

Kat shrugged and said, "It doesn't surprise me at all. Women have always been tougher than men. We just don't feel the need to display it very often."

"No argument here."

The crowd hushed, and Ms. Tunstill said, "Je vous remercie tous pour votre gentillesse et votre soutien!"

Maybe one or two people in the crowd knew what she said. It didn't matter, because we got the idea. We applauded again as all competitors, coaches, and medical staff left the area.

The announcer said, "And that, ladies and gentlemen, is how a jousting competition should end! Mrs. Tunstill has crushed all challengers, ending the final match with a victory of eighty to eighteen! I might have to check the record books, but I'm certain no competitor has ever finished a final match with eight unhorsings. Thank you all for being here! Please join us tomorrow for the archery challenge. Have a wonderful evening!"

When I stood, I realized Deputy Kline had silently left. I didn't see him in the crowd of people rising to their feet. Just like Anderson, he'd quickly vanished from existence. Unfortunately, it wasn't going to be the last time I saw him. I knew that for certain.

As we were leaving the stadium, Kat asked, "So, explain to me what that was about with Deputy Kline?"

I didn't want to dive into it, especially with Anderson and others nearby. So, I shrugged and said, "I think he believes we're friends ever since the McCreadys' house fire. Maybe he bonded with me after I puked on his shoes. I honestly don't know."

I just wanted to enjoy the energy of this incredible day. Allowing Deputy Kline to ruin this nearly perfect experience would be an insult to today's memories.

Kat spent a minute conversing with Mrs. Bixby, and then we left. I really hated it when Kat encouraged the continuation of someone's mental instability. But we are who we are, and Mr. Bixby was around the bend and through the woods bonkers.

It was the frequent tick of something against the glass of my bedroom window that woke me that night. I desperately tried to push my mind back to sleep. I gave up after a few minutes. I threw the pillow across the room, yanked back the sheet, and stomped over to the window. Parting the mini blinds, I stared into a blackness that stared right back at me. No one was at the window. I was about to crawl back into bed when I noticed a car on the street. It was a police car parked just at the edge of the streetlamp's glow. Leaning against the rear fender was Deputy Kline. He was looking right at me. An icy river flowed through my spine and to my extremities. He offered a wicked smile as if he knew I was momentarily terror-struck.

My bedroom lights were off, of course, but he knew I watched him through the parted blinds. He knew where I lived because of the incident with the house fire across the street three days after I arrived in town. I wondered how he had known which bedroom was mine. Had he illegally entered our house while Josh and I were at work? Had he snooped through our belongings?

I thought about waking Josh, but I figured Deputy Kline would be in the wind when we came to the window. This was going way too far. Now the man who I figured to be the Paper Moon arsonist was hanging around my house in the middle of the night. He was attempting terror tactics, so I'd keep my mouth shut. His reason for being here was a simple method to get me to back off. It was working. I fully understood that if I didn't let my snooping go, I would wake up one night to my house engulfed in flames, giving Josh and me a fiery death.

I didn't know what to do. I wasn't sure if he was expecting me to open the window and call out that I understood his point. He made the next move. Deputy Kline started walking toward my house, all the while never breaking eye contact. I thought he was going for the front door but then saw him redirect to the side of the house. He was heading around back. I ran out my bedroom door and down the stairs.

I realized I should have woken Josh before coming downstairs. I scanned the kitchen for a weapon while fully expecting the back door to be kicked in. Grabbing a pot from the drying rack, I held it by the handle, ready to deliver a vicious swing. A cooking pot versus a loaded handgun was far from a fair fight. My belief in overcoming a trained deputy was a laughable fantasy.

Even in the dark, I saw the phone on the small wooden table beside the couch. Who I needed to call was a joke.

The police were already here, stalking and even threatening me on my own property. If I called the dispatcher, would she believe me when I told her that the sheriff's deputy was probably the one behind all the recent fires? Could I convince her that he was lingering outside my window with bad intentions? I didn't think so. The dispatcher would think some crackpot kid had a nightmare and nothing more. So, I waited for Deputy Kline to make the next move until I had no choice but to introduce him to the unforgiving bottom surface of our cheap cooking pot.

The faint sounds of clanking metal came from the backyard. It didn't sound like he was actually trying to get inside, but that he was up to something else. I had to know. I went to the kitchen window as quietly as possible. I didn't pull the curtain aside because I didn't want him to know where I was. Instead, I peeked through the small gap between them. I couldn't see much, because the large oaks fought off the moonlight and kept our yard in near darkness.

A shadow passed the window, instinctively making me crouch. A cracking twig went off at the corner of the house. Footsteps heading away told me he was moving to the front again. I hurried through the kitchen and living room to the front window. Deputy Kline was leaving our yard and making his way to his patrol car. He opened the driver's door and turned to look, even though there was no way he could know where I was, and then he began laughing. The laugh sounded wrong, a fiendish laugh of knowing something I didn't. It was a sound out of place in the late-night hour. He offered a quick wave before getting in the patrol car, fired the engine to life, and drove away.

When the taillights vanished at the end of the block, I finally took a breath. I wasn't sure if I'd been holding it the entire time. My heart was giving up its race and slowing to a calm gallop.

What had he been up to out back? I knew there was no way I was going to get back to sleep tonight, especially without checking the backyard. I unbolted the door and turned on the porch light. At first, I didn't notice anything messed with. When I walked to the rusty tin shed, it was evident what he'd done. He mutilated my bike and cast a dozen pieces across the yard. The carnage was unspeakable. Had this been his message that he would do the same to me if I didn't back off and forget he existed?

I was walking into dangerous territory. How could I really let it go? The man was likely the one burning down houses and businesses in my hometown. If I did walk away from it without saying a word and he eventually burned people alive, how could I live with it? Something like that would haunt me for the rest of my life. I wasn't sure I could go to Sheriff Prescott with this news. What if the sheriff was in on it? What if it was a tag-team effort to destroy this wonderfully bizarre town? Even if Sheriff Prescott wasn't connected to the mayhem of fire, he might unintentionally inform Deputy Kline some kid came in with a wild tale about knowing that Paper Moon's arsonist was really law enforcement.

There was nothing I could do about my bike tonight. In the morning, I could spend time assembling the pieces back together, if they could go back together, that is.

Chapter 16

June spiraled away as July brought with it a wet heat. Summer had become more of a learning process than any school hours. My time at the wildlife habitat became some of the best days of my life.

Over a heavy crackling radio, Carl said, "Hey, Grady, you should come to your apartment and check this out."

Grady pulled the radio from his belt, pressed the button, and said, "And what is it you're doing in my apartment? You better not be trying to nap in my bed again."

"Negative. It's what's on the TV."

"Okay. We're on our way," Grady said and then looked at me. "Not sure if you ever noticed, but Carl smells like fish all the time. I'm not sure why, because we don't have any fish here. But he took a nap in my bed once and infected that rank fish smell all over it. I washed the sheets, and it didn't do a bit of damn good. That smell worked deep into the mattress. Every time I lay down, my weight pushes that disgusting smell from the pores in the memory foam and out into my private world. Makes me want to puke. I may need to burn the mattress. I think I'll dock it from his wages as payback for forcing me to endure night after night of that ungodly odor."

I couldn't help laughing. "Yeah, I noticed. I never wanted to say anything about it. Being rude is not part of my character. Sleeping on a fish mattress is not my idea of a good night's rest. And I do agree with you. If your bed smells like Carl, then a new mattress should definitely be on your list of immediate purchases."

Grady has a cozy one-room apartment at the far back of the main building. When I say "cozy" it's meant with all politeness. Grady could sit on the toilet while making scrambled eggs on the stove, select his next book to read from the small shelf beside the bed, grab a cold drink from the fridge, and place a DVD in the player below the TV all without getting up. Okay, maybe it wasn't that small, but it was far too tight for a large man like Grady.

Carl was standing back from the TV, with his hands on his hips and his head slightly shaking. We pushed in so we could see what he was talking about. The news was on. It was the weather report segment, where a rather attractive meteorologist was showing the viewing public the storm brewing across the Atlantic. She described how the warm ocean water and moist air were feeding a tropical cyclone, turning this ocean storm front into a hurricane. The models showed a growing intensity as it barreled past the Bahamas, setting its sights on southern Florida.

Grady, Carl, and I watched the projected path of the hurricane roll across the screen. They predicted it would make an expected hard northern change in trajectory before reaching the Bahamas. With that all said, Florida's eastern coast should expect a category four. The meteorologist estimated wind speeds to reach one hundred and forty miles per hour along the coast, accompanied by significant rainfall. The only good news I heard was that Hurricane Francine was a fast mover.

"That sounds awful. I've never been stuck in a hurricane before. Is a category four really bad?"

"Well, it's a little worse than category three, but not as bad as category five," Grady said and winked at me.

Carl said, "Relax, Jayce. Francine won't reach far enough inland to do us much harm. The wind is gonna be about the only thing we need to worry about."

"But you never really know for sure until she makes landfall. That's when she'll show her teeth," Grady added.

"Will there be an evacuation?" I asked.

"Not here. But those in the eastern coastal towns should get out if they have a lick of sense. Nearly everything they possess is replaceable, except their lives. Too many people wait until the last minute. Next thing they know, the highways and interstates running out of town are a bumper-to-bumper mess," Grady said.

Although Paper Moon sat deep inland, it wasn't immune to the effects of a hurricane coming either from the Atlantic side or the Gulf Coast. By the time Wednesday rolled around, people along the entire state prepared for the event with an almost ritualistic behavior, as if simply buttoning up the house just before bedtime. The newscast said that around our area should expect an estimated wind speed to reach near one hundred miles an hour and heavy downpour when the storm really got going.

All of our neighbors were outside. So, we went out as well and began picking up everything around the front and back yard that the wind might grab up. Josh pulled his battered truck into the garage. We also dragged in my bike, the grill, battered lawn chairs, and the garbage cans.

When the task was done and we were sure we had everything, Josh said that we could be useful and help the neighbors. We started with Mr. and Mrs. Emmerson next door. They were an elderly couple somewhere in their seventies who had lived in Paper Moon their entire lives. I had only spoken to them a few times. They were always very nice, and I was happy to help them out. The funny thing about the Emmerson's was that they seemed completely normal. Of course, I didn't know what went on behind closed doors, but when outside their home, they were very basic people.

I thought of Kat. She had once claimed that the longer people stayed in Paper Moon, the more bizarre they became. The Emmersons had lived in Paper Moon their entire lives, and there certainly wasn't anything strange about them.

Josh had gone around the back to help Mrs. Emmerson bring in her potted plants and lawn furniture. I stayed out front with Mr. Emmerson. He had an ancient, kind face that reminded me of my own grandfather, who lived outside Denver.

"Are you looking forward to school in August?" he asked.

"No, sir," I admitted.

He laughed and said, "You can call me Virgil. I never could stand school myself. I wasn't very good at most of the subjects. So, I never went to college when high school was over. I went into construction like your brother. I liked it for a good long while, but after a time it gets to wear you down. You see how I'm moving, and this is a good pace for me. Your brother is young and can handle it, but I don't think he should devote his entire life to it. Are you planning college after?"

"I don't know. I haven't really thought of it," I said honestly.

"Maybe you could be a fireman or a superhero for the way you went running into that burning house without a second thought about your own skin," he said and winked.

"I did think about it. If Josh hadn't gone inside, I don't think I would have. He's the brave one. I'm the stupid one who followed."

"Don't you dare say that. You're a hero in my book. Your brother couldn't have pulled them both out. One of them might not have made it out alive if you hadn't gone into action. You have my gratitude and respect for being that guy who does the right thing when he's faced with a tough choice."

I knew at that moment I had been brave, but I hadn't realized the impact of what I had done meant so much to the townspeople who weren't even affected by the fire.

Josh and I soon left and made our way down one side of the block and back up the other until we were home again. We met a variety of our neighbors. Like the Emmersons, some of them were perfectly normal, and others were completely off their rockers. They weren't rude or threatening, just odd in the way the town barber, Sir Reginald Spree, was with his medieval clothing and a sword at his waist.

We walked through the front door into the welcoming embrace of the air-conditioning, leaving the warm, wet air outside.

Josh went to the sink and filled a glass of water. He watched me as I collapsed on the couch.

He said, "You know, I never realized how many weird people live in this town. Some of them seem downright crazy in a nonhostile way. But, man, it's almost like the state's looney bin opened its doors and just let everyone go, and they all wound up here."

"You don't know the half of it," I said with my face pressed against a cushion. "You leave here and go straight to work in another town, then come home. I've biked all over this town for a couple of months. I've seen the oddest of the odd."

He took a seat in the ratty burgundy armchair and said, "I can imagine."

Josh turned on the television. The news report was showing the hurricane had slammed into the east coast just north of Miami an hour ago. Video footage of the area showed intense winds and crashing waves were tearing apart buildings, pushing cars down the streets, and throwing debris skyward.

"I guess it's a good thing I didn't get a job along the coastline. It looks like those people are going to lose almost everything they own. I hope everyone listened to the evacuation notice and got out before it got bad," Josh said.

The entire house trembled. Josh looked at the ceiling as if it were going to come right off. Something knocked hard against the outside of the house. I went to the front window and peered out. A small branch freshly torn loose from its tree collided with the siding. I watched the wind play hard with the treetops. They were bowing under the increasing eastern wind.

"Tree branch," I told Josh. "It's picking up out there. I think there's going to be a lot of damage to houses when the wind gets to its full strength."

"You need to keep away from the windows. If something comes crashing through, you're going to be pulling slivers of glass from your skin until Christmas."

"Maybe we should have boarded up the windows like I saw some people doing," I said.

"If the wind wants to tear this house apart, then that's exactly what it will do. Besides, I don't think it's gonna get—"

A horrible crash that sounded like a meteorite touching down in our front yard cut Josh off. He offered a stream of curses as he grabbed me and yanked me to the floor. After a moment of realizing we were all right, we stood and carefully went to a window. We didn't immediately see what had made all the racket. Then I stepped closer to the glass and looked at a sharper angle down the block.

Two houses down, across the street, the storm had uprooted a large tree. It had come down through power lines, partially crushing a car parked in the street.

"The wind just tore a tree down," I said.

Then the power blinked away and left us in a growing darkness as heavy storm clouds pushed closer. We slid the couch near the far wall and crouched behind it, making a barrier to protect us from possible flying glass and anything else that may become airborne.

We spent that time having brief conversations about unimportant subjects to help keep our minds off what was happening outside. Our voices went silent every time something large pounded down the street, pushed by a brutal wind. The house continued to groan as it resisted coming apart. I prayed that a company who prided themselves on quality, and not one who might skimp on material and labor for a better profit, had built our house.

I drifted off after a while. I think Josh did too. I believe it was, above all, a defense mechanism in our minds to remove us temporarily from the situation in order to help reduce stress.

When the storm had eased, Josh and I stepped out from behind the couch. It was too dark outside to check for any damage. Besides, the rain was still coming in steadily. We went to our rooms as three in the morning came around. I lost consciousness almost immediately. The exhaustion of the evening was too great to fight against, and I was out like a dying lightbulb as soon as my body found the mattress.

My dreams were a tortured show. They came fast and hard and constantly forced me to briefly wake with an unpleasant moan. But they pulled me back in again and again. I dreamed about devastation to houses, vehicles, and even people being beaten down and lost by the relentless wind and rising waves towering like skyscrapers. The brute force of wind and water washed away entire cities and small towns. A flood found my house and ripped me through the bedroom window and washed me out to sea. As much as I tried to swim back to shore, the water just pulled at me more and more. I went underwater when my strength finally failed, and then I sank with one last breath to the bottom. Through the far-off moonlight above me, I saw debris floating on the surface knocking against each other as the sea claimed them. Knocking, knocking against...

It was this knocking that broke the dream state. Sleepily, I opened my eyes. I had thought it was the wind at first. Then my mind told me in that semiconscious state that it must be a tree branch rattling against the window in rhythm with the howling wind of a dying storm. It took several long moments to pull me from the darkened recess of bad dreams to realize that it wasn't the wind at all, but the almost frantic knocking of a fist.

Sleep dazed, I pulled the covers off and went to my bedroom door and opened it. There was nothing but a dark, empty hallway waiting for me.

When I walked to the bed and was about to slide back under the sheets, the tapping came again. The noise hadn't come from the door as I'd first thought, but from the window. Full dread of yet again finding Deputy Kline outside of my house seized me as I pulled open the curtain, drew up the mini blinds, and looked into the blackness. The face at the window scared me enough that I stepped back, my feet tangled, and I fell to the floor.

The shadows had covered most of the features, but those I saw were recognizable. It was Kat at my bedroom window at four o'clock in the morning. She had come to my house in the aftermath of a hurricane for reasons that were beyond my understanding. The fading rain had soaked her hair and clothes. Her eyes were wide and scared. I thought this would be the first and only time I'd see her wearing a look of fear.

I pushed myself from the floor and went to the window with annoyance.

I unlatched it and whispered, "Do you have any idea what time it is? Why would you come here at four in the morning? If Josh sees you here, he'll freak out."

"I'm worried about Mr. Bixby," Kat said.

"What about him?"

"His house isn't very strong. You've seen how the roof is sagging. I'm worried the hurricane could have damaged his house," she said.

"I'm sure he's fine. You're just worrying too much."

"What if the roof caved in?" she asked.

"Josh will kill me if I ride my bike across town just to check on someone."

"There isn't time to ride our bikes. That will take too long."

"So, if I decided to go with you, how would we get there?" I asked.

Kat was biting her thumbnail in thought. Then an obvious idea struck her. What she said next stunned me.

"We'll have to borrow your brother's truck."

"Are you insane?" I asked in a frantic whisper. "Josh will crucify me if I get caught."

"So, we won't get caught."

"No," I said defiantly. "Just call the sheriff and have him send out a deputy to check on Mr. Bixby. It'll be easier for everyone. You need to go before you wake Josh."

"There's one major problem with calling the sheriff. If they go there to check on him and everything is fine, they'll see that he doesn't have working house lights. They'll see the condition of his house. If they know those two things, they'll figure he's unfit to take care of himself and force him to live in a retirement home. What if he answers the door with Mrs. Bixby? If they see a talking mannequin head on his shoulder, they'll lock him up in a loony bin."

"Maybe it would be for the best if they did," I told her.

Her face immediately changed to a look of pure anger.

She said, "Fine. I'll go by myself if you don't care so much."

"How will you get there?"

"I didn't ride my bike over, so I suppose I'm walking," she said. Then she turned and began climbing back down the tree beside the house.

I could tell she was furious with me. I was sure a long walk across town in the drizzling rain would steam her even more. If I didn't help her with this fool's quest, she would no doubt ignore me for the next month. Part of me thought that wasn't such a bad idea.

"Stop. Come inside. You'll kill yourself trying to climb back down the tree."

After ten minutes of trying to talk Kat out of it and failing, I snuck into Josh's room and stole his keys to the rust bucket. After silently rolling up the garage door, I put the truck into neutral, and we rolled it halfway down the street before jumping in and starting the engine. Even though Josh slept like the dead, I wanted to make sure we were far from the house before kicking over the clattering engine and possibly waking him.

In the aftermath of the hurricane, there were utility crews repairing downed power lines. There were no other vehicles besides the work trucks. It felt more like an obstacle course than a casual drive across town. Fallen branches and trashcans covered the streets.

"Have you ever driven before?" Kat asked.

"Just bicycles."

"You're doing pretty well for a first-timer."

This may have been the first compliment Kat ever shot my way without following it with a crude remark.

"Especially with your eyes closed," she concluded.

"My eyes are open. I'd like to see you do better with all this stuff in the street."

"Sorry, I didn't mean that. I'm just worried about Mr. Bixby," she said.

"The worry is almost over. We're nearly there," I said as I could see the turnoff of Mr. Bixby's long gravel driveway.

Even in the light rain and darkness, I knew something wasn't right as soon as the truck reached the clearing in which Mr. Bixby's house stood. Actually, in which Mr. Bixby's house had once stood.

"No," Kat whispered in a terror of understanding.

Kat's fear of the hurricane doing substantial damage to Mr. Bixby's home had become a reality. I could only guess that the roof had given in first. Without the cross supports, the exterior walls would have no choice but to collapse under the extreme winds. It didn't even closely resemble a house anymore. Instead, it looked like a pile of wreckage that could have once been anything created by man, now left here to rot under all weather conditions.

Kat was out of the truck before I came to a full stop. She ran in an awkward shuffle in the mud and slid to a halt at the house's foundation.

"Mr. Bixby? Can you hear me?" she yelled.

I stopped beside her. I quickly grabbed her arm as she began climbing the rubble.

"Stop. It's too dangerous. You could fall in a hole or step on nails," I said.

The truth was that I didn't want her to go. I didn't want her to find what was buried in the collapsed house. I was sure no one could have survived this kind of disaster. I had little belief that Mr. Bixby was still alive.

"If you were trapped in there, he'd come searching for you. Now stop wasting time and help me look," Kat said and pulled away from my grip.

She was right. When I didn't immediately climb onto the wreckage and search for her friend, I felt cowardly. I was ashamed by my lack of action. There was only one way to make it up to her. I carefully began climbing the mountain of splintered wood and debris.

It was difficult to keep our footing on the wet wood, but so far, we managed to prevent a painful fall. Our calls into the rainy night went on for long minutes. We continuously paused, hoping to hear some kind of response, and then went on calling again.

I said, "We should go get the sheriff. They have people who can come in here and start pulling this stuff out of the way. We need help if we have any chance—"

"Quiet. I thought I heard something over there."

Kat stumbled to the other side of the house. She paused every few steps and listened. Then she was quickly on the move.

"Jayce, get over here."

I didn't need to be told twice. I shuffled through the crisscross of fractured wood and Mr. Bixby's belongings. Kat was on her knees, and she began ripping everything loose and throwing it over her shoulder.

"Mr. Bixby, can you hear us?" Kat called.

It was a muffled sound at first and then grew stronger as the hope of breaking free from the rubble was possible. Mr. Bixby said, "I'm here, Katrina."

Splinters and rusted nails bit into our hands as we took fistfuls and threw them out of the way. Something broke free from the collapsed remains of Mr. Bixby's house. At first, I thought it was a torn piece of colorful paper that was grabbed by the wind, but then realized exactly what it was.

A yellow butterfly with a pink string attached took flight. One of Mrs. Bixby's pets had survived the wrath of the hurricane. In the gentle rain, it headed for the cover of trees and soon vanished into the darkness.

When I reached inside the black hole to seize more material to clear away, something chomped down on my forefinger.

"Ugh!" I screamed as I quickly pulled my hand back. Working the skin from the end of my finger was a small creation that resembled a demonic metal dog from hell. Although the thing was small enough to fit in my palm and operated by cleverly wound rubber bands and springs, my mind, under the circumstances, convinced me that the thing was a Rottweiler on a rampage.

In frustration, Kat reached out and tore the thing from my hand. Unfortunately, the miniature metal guard dog took a good chunk of skin with it. Kat heaved the thing against the closest tree, where the toy came apart, but not before offering a final defying clack of its metal teeth.

"Jayce, could you move to your left? You're crushing my chest," Mr. Bixby said in a raspy breath.

"Oh, sorry," I said and quickly moved.

We had freed enough stuff that we could now see Mr. Bixby's face. He looked relieved, exhausted, and terrified all at once. After a few more minutes, Kat and I had made a large hole in which we could get our hands around Mr. Bixby's arms to pull him free.

"Do you have any broken bones?" I asked Mr. Bixby. I knew that moving a person with broken or fractured bones could do more harm than good.

"My left leg hurt quite a bit when the house fell on me, but now it's more of an aching numbness than pain. I'm not sure if it's broken," he said.

"We should get a rescue squad. We shouldn't move him," I said.

"No. Don't you dare leave me out here. I can get out, but I'll need your help," Mr. Bixby pleaded.

Kat watched me make up my mind.

I kneeled again and took Mr. Bixby's right arm, and, with almost shocking ease, we were able to pull him from his confinement.

"Oh, no," Kat whispered.

I also saw it right away. Mr. Bixby had survived the hurricane, even one of the butterflies had survived, but Mrs. Bixby had taken the full weight of the house on her pale, wooden head. The attachment that frequently sat on Mr. Bixby's right shoulder had sustained enough damage that even the most skilled craftsman could never mend it.

The head appeared as if it had imploded. The nose, cheekbones, and upper and lower jaws were now pressed into the hollow void of her skull. One blue eye had gone missing, but the other dangled by a piece of string from the broken socket. The straps that fixed Mrs. Bixby to her husband had either snapped or come undone. The head hung awkwardly against Mr. Bixby's arm. A network of strings that operated the eyes and jaw ran from the bottom of her head to the collar of Mr. Bixby's shirt and disappeared inside.

"Oh, my God," Mr. Bixby said. With his left hand, he reached out and cradled the severed head, as one might hold an injured animal.

"I'm so sorry," Kat said and gently touched his shoulder.

Of course, I thought the whole scene was ridiculous. It was a mannequin head, for crying out loud, not a real person who had lost her life due to the collapsing house. I wouldn't learn of the significance of Mrs. Bixby until much later. I would also later learn that everything, great and small, has important meaning.

"I called your father a bit ago. He said he'd be on his way when he could," Sheriff Prescott told Kat. He turned to me and said, "I've called your brother. Since he doesn't have a vehicle to get to the clinic, he said it would be all right for me to take you home when we're finished up here. I'll have one of my deputies drive his truck home for him."

I winced in pain. The rubbing alcohol the nurse was applying to the countless cuts on my hands and arms stung like hell, but the dread of what Josh was going to say when I got home caused the worst pain.

"Thank you, Sheriff," Kat said.

"You should have called the police. One of you could have been seriously hurt trying to get him out of that collapsed house," Sheriff Prescott told us.

"We won't ever do it again," Kat promised, knowing full well that such a circumstance happening twice was astronomical.

The doctor came into the room and offered a smile.

"How's Mr. Bixby?" Kat asked.

"Well, the bad news is that he has a compound fracture in his leg, a mild concussion, and more cuts and bruises than anyone should endure in a lifetime, but the good news is that he'll be just fine after everything heals."

"That's good to hear," I said.

"Sheriff, could I see you in the hallway for a minute?" the doctor said.

Both men moved into the hallway, and, with hushed voices, they began an unknown discussion.

Curiosity got the better of Kat as she slinked over to the doorway and listened. The nurse's focus was entirely on my wounds. When the men came back into the room, Kat acted as if she were studying a landscape picture on the wall.

"That just about does it," the nurse said as she finished torturing me.

"Thanks," I muttered.

"You've got a lot of explaining to do, young lady," a husky, slurred voice said from the doorway.

We all turned and looked at a mountain of a man. He was large enough to fill the entire doorway. It was obvious that the man had a once been in top physical shape. There were still ripples of muscles throughout his arms and chest. But now his once-well-defined stomach muscles had stretched out to what I could only consider a beer belly.

Several of us looked at Kat. She hung her head low. Her eyes focused on the green tiles. There was a redness on her cheeks that was either anger or shame.

"I'm sorry," she said simply.

"Damn straight you're sorry, but not as much as you're going to be," Mr. Mossgrove said.

"These two saved a man's life today, Mr. Mossgrove. Now, I'm not saying I approve of the method they used, but a man is going to be all right because they took the initiative to make sure he was okay after the hurricane came through," Sheriff Prescott said.

"I don't care much about that, Sheriff. She went out in the middle of the night without a word to anyone. Not even Anderson knew where she had gone, and she tells him everything. Don't you, peach?" There was obvious anger in Mr. Mossgrove's voice.

He grabbed Kat's forearm firmly and pulled her toward the hallway.

"Bye," she said softly, and a second later, they were gone from sight.

"Well, doesn't that beat all? The man isn't even proud that his daughter helped save someone," Sheriff Prescott said and rubbed his chin in puzzlement.

The sheriff knew a great deal about the town and its inhabitants, but I knew from Kat that her father's drinking was a private thing. I suppose everyone deserves at least one secret, even in a town as small as Paper Moon.

"I'm ready to go home now, Sheriff," I said.

"Yep, I suppose we need to get you home. You've got to be pretty tired," he said.

I agreed that I was, and then Sheriff Prescott and I left the clinic.

Chapter 17

As it goes every year, summer blinked away far too quickly. School was already back in session. I wasn't looking forward to dealing with Regan again. Fortunately, I hadn't heard or seen him since his embarrassment at the tournament. He was keeping a low profile, hoping people would forget the worst day of his life.

I felt depleted, as if I'd just run a marathon instead of two miles around the school track. I was getting used to our daily practice now. I didn't get winded nearly as fast. Keeping up with the rest of the group was easy. Of course, no one could keep up with Anderson when he turned on the juice, leaving everyone in the dust when he felt like it.

On the bleachers, I pulled off my worn-out running shoes and put on my school shoes. As I was stuffing the shoes inside my backpack, I saw Anderson walking toward me.

"Well, you've done it again," I said.

"What?"

"Left me in embarrassment. You nearly lapped the rest of us."

"It's just my thing," he said and shrugged.

Anderson was a kid who didn't speak very much. He was timid like a mouse and stayed away from groups of people, except those on the track. I honestly didn't know much about him other than what Kat told me, which was very little. Most of what I knew had come from school rumors. I wanted to get to connect with him more.

"Do you want to walk with me until Rest Easy Street?" I asked. The street was dead flat and straight as an arrow. It was the street where Kat and I had to part ways when going home.

He shrugged. "Sure."

We went around the front where I could get my bike, but I walked beside it instead of riding.

"How'd you get to be so fast? It's like you're shot out of a cannon and picking up speed all the way," I asked.

He shrugged again. "I just imagine a pack of blood-thirsty dogs on my heels."

I laughed at that, because I remembered once thinking that running should be reserved for an out-of-control bus barreling at you or something eager to tear you apart.

I thought of something, and I wasn't sure if it was a subject I should bring up. I never knew if classmates created stories or if it was something Anderson really believed he could do. I decided to go ahead and ask, since we were somewhat friends after a couple of months.

"I've heard rumors about you," I said.

One of his eyebrows arched a little in interest.

"I've heard from several kids that you have the ability to time travel."

The left corner of his mouth went up in a smile. "Is that what they say?"

"That's the rumor. So, is it true? Can you really just vanish from our time and appear some other place in the past?"

This was not the usual conversation two teenaged boys had, but I was excited to find out what Anderson had to say about it.

"I didn't ask for it. There are times I even don't like having it. I don't have a choice because I'm stuck with it. Maybe I'll have it for the rest of my life, or maybe tomorrow it'll be gone. Who knows? All I can say is that I deal with it like I'm supposed to." He focused straight ahead, maybe in his mind reliving experiences I couldn't imagine.

"So, tell me all about it. I'm dying to know. Where do you go? How do you get there? Can you control the place and time you land?"

He smiled. "Slow down. I'll tell you what answers I have. No, I can't control it. One second, I might be watching television or mowing the yard, and then I start to feel it."

"Feel what?"

"A sort of pull. It's almost like someone worked a large hand into the center of my body, gripped hard, and yanked me somewhere else. All I can remember is bright, colorful tunnels that I'm flowing through like a water slide. They split off into thousands of directions, and I have no control over which tunnel I'm sent."

"Wow. Would you mind telling me about some of the stuff you've seen, some of the stuff you've done?"

"I don't mind at all. Most people think I'm out of my head and that's why they leave me alone. It's nice when someone other than Kat wants to know where I've been."

"I don't think you're out of your head. I think you've got a purpose that some supreme being wants you to accomplish."

"All right, where do I start?" he said, mostly to himself. "I'm not sure if Kat told you this one, but I believe I have a lot to do with the Nazis losing the Second World War. A little over a year ago, I was pushed back to the streets of Berlin in 1932. A man with wild hair who was walking back from the market was in front of me. He saw me appear out of thin air. He went into hysterics, talking to me in German, which I don't speak. He was grabbing at me, maybe to make sure I was real."

"What did you do?" I asked.

"I freaked out. I hit him in the face with a right hook. I guess you could say I sucker-punched him, because he certainly wasn't expecting it. Well, he dropped his groceries, fell back, and hit his head on the base of a lamppost. I just wanted him to get off me. I wasn't really intending to hurt him. The next thing I know, I'm being pulled back here. My mission was done. I was only there a little over a minute."

I scratched my head. "I don't get it. How did that change the outcome of the Second World War?"

"I wondered that as well. I had to go to the library and do research. It was a lot of digging, but I found what I was looking for. The man I punched was Albert Einstein."

"You sucker-punched Einstein?" I nearly shouted, but no one was around, anyway.

He nodded. "I suppose if I had known at that time who he was, I wouldn't have done that."

I didn't know how to respond to all this. So I said, "But why would the being controlling you want this done?"

Anderson said, "Well, as you can imagine, I was very curious about that. From what I researched, I found out that only two days after I attacked him, Mr. Einstein moved from Berlin to the U.S. and became a citizen."

"So, punching Albert Einstein scared him enough to move to somewhere safer, which altered the outcome of the Second World War?" I asked. My head was spinning, trying to gather all this information together where it made perfect sense.

"Maybe. He could have worried that since he was a theoretical physicist, the Germans would force him to help their scientists in harnessing atomic power and creating nuclear weapons. It could have completely changed the direction of the war if the Germans had that power first. Or maybe it was the sight of me suddenly appearing from nowhere that freaked him out. Maybe he thought the Germans were able to create invisibility and were planning on weaponizing this new technology. I really don't know for sure. The point is that my arrival at that point in time scared him enough to flee Germany and stay clear from the grasp of the Nazis. I've only been able to guess why I'm forced to do the things I've done. Whoever controls me must be doing it from the future."

"Why do you think that?"

"Because they know about all the good and bad turns mankind has made. They're altering the past so that the future still exists. Only they can know how the future would have played out if Germany and Japan had won the war. Things would be greatly different from what they are now. At least that's my theory."

We stopped at the corner of Rest Easy Street. This was where we had to part ways, but I wasn't ready to head home just yet.

"Do you remember when I came here at the end of the last school year?" I asked.

"I think so."

"On my third day here, I saw you at lunch. You were by yourself, leaning against a tree."

"That's usually where I have lunch when we're outside."

"Well, you got this weird look on your face. I turned away, and when I looked back, you were gone. Your juice box had tipped over, and your half-eaten sandwich was on the paper bag where you had been sitting."

He nodded. "It happens in a split-second."

"My questions are, where did you go that time and when did you come back?"

His eyes stared at the ground, maybe trying to remember four months back. He was silent for a while before he said, "There was an apartment fire, and the flames trapped a young boy inside. They sent me to get him out. I don't know who he was or even what city I was in. I got him out and then they transported me back here."

"Where did you come back to?"

"What do you mean?"

"I guess what I'm not understanding is why these supreme beings don't put you right back where you were a microsecond after they took you. Then it would appear as if you never left."

He suddenly looked angry. "So, you're just another one who doesn't believe me? You try to act like my friend and then you're going to go off and make fun of me with other kids? I don't have the answers you want. I don't know why they picked me. I don't know why they do it in certain ways and who or why I save some people but not others. I really did think you were trying to be close to me like you are with my sister," he said, and then walked down the road alone.

I called out after him. "Wait! I'm not making fun of you. I really do believe you. I just had questions, that's all."

He didn't turn around and quickened his pace. A moment later, the neighborhood swallowed him up. I figured Kat was going to give me a black eye when she heard about this.

I truly wanted to believe in a time-traveling kid. The idea of it was like a wonderful movie that suspended disbelief, giving us the opportunity that all things are possible. I wanted to believe that the universe has important missions for a kid like Anderson. I really did. But like with all eagerness to believe, there's a degree of doubt that creeps in. It threw its anchors into my brain and wouldn't release, no matter how hard I tried to work it free.

There are rules to time travel called paradoxes. For example, if the controllers of Anderson's missions sent him back to alter the winner of the war, then how could they know that changing that past wasn't really dooming the world in some other way? Changing time has a ripple effect. One small change in someone's life in Wichita, Kansas, could turn out to be a catastrophic alteration to the entire country of Brazil. Or was it that the future had been where Germany and Japan had won? So, Anderson goes back to change it. But then, that would have always been our history. The future would have never known any other outcome. Anderson couldn't have gone back to change anything. It was all a paradox.

Now I was giving myself a headache trying to figure all this out.

As I got on my bike and started to push off, a metallic blue sports car cut in front of me, nearly clipping my front tire. I looked at the driver and saw a face of death. His skin was sickly pale against his slicked black hair, and his eyes were the blackness of a hard, oncoming storm. The last time I'd seen him was when he'd been running around completely nude at the tournament with his younger brother. His hands had been covering the part of himself that no child in the arena should have seen. Back then, he'd been wild-eyed, fearful, and embarrassed. Now his eyes narrowed, and a meanness grew across his face. The look turned my blood into an icy river.

When I heard the door latch pop, I pushed off, but his hand instantly seized my handlebar with a vise grip.

"Well, well, if it isn't my brother's new best friend. You're not trying to run off somewhere, are you? I wanted to have a little chat with you about some people you might know. You see, I know you told people what my brother and I did to you. Was it so terrible that I acted like I was going to run you over that you had to squeal to a couple of rednecks? I know you were there at the games. I know you saw what they did to me and my brother in front of the entire town. I can hardly show my face around town anymore."

I saw something from the corner of my eye. What I saw gave me hope that I wasn't going to be beaten into a pulpy mass.

It was the reason I said, "It isn't your face they'll recognize, but your bony butt scrambling around in circles."

He hit me lightning fast. The first one was a shot on the left cheek. The other one crunched my nose. Blood drooled from my nostrils and into my mouth. My head swam with fuzziness. I felt near passing out, but I pushed myself to stay alert, because I badly wanted to see what happened next.

"That mouth just keeps getting you in more and more trouble."

I thought he was going to say something else, but his mouth and eyes froze when he heard the brief wail of the police siren. The sheriff's car had been coming down the road when I decided to antagonize him. Maybe it had been stupid on my part, but I knew the sheriff had seen everything that had happened.

The police cruiser slid over to the shoulder, and the window rolled down. Sheriff Prescott was a large man, and I figured he didn't want to get out of the car if he didn't have to. He looked me over and focused on the blood leaking from my nose.

"Take your hand off of him," he ordered.

"We were about to play a game, Sheriff. Just me and my friend Jayce. Nothing wrong with that, is there?"

"I said remove your hand before I get unhappy."

"No worries. No worries at all. You see, I saw this young man crash his bike just now, and because I'm a good-natured person, I pulled over to help him up and see if he was all right. There's nothing against the law helping someone, is there?"

Rory's hand released my shirt. As a pathetic method of fooling the sheriff, he began dusting me off.

"I've got a very different story. You're an adult and he's a minor. It's far more than a scuffle between schoolboys. It's called assault, and it carries with it prison time. I'm sure by now you're very familiar with the term of prison time. So, get into the back of my cruiser and we'll head on down to the station. I'll have a tow truck come collect your car later in the day."

I knew what was going to happen before it did. I suspect the sheriff knew it, too.

"Make it easy on yourself, Rory. You don't always have to choose the hard way," Sheriff Prescott said.

"I don't know any other way to be," the black-haired devil said.

Just like that, his body slid into the driver's seat, and the engine roared to life with enough power to vibrate the street. There was a roll of white smoke as his tires grabbed the road. Gravel blew at me like shotgun pellets. The blue racer ate up concrete and all but disappeared by the time the dust cleared.

The sheriff was smiling. He said, "Are you okay, Jayce?"

"Yes, sir," I told him.

"You know, I knew he was going to do that. That's why I didn't even bother getting out of my car. I'll be in contact after I go catch this bird," he said. His siren and roof lights went on again. The cruiser then peeled its tires as the sheriff flipped the car around and gave chase.

I could hear the distant growl of engines and the hard squealing of tires as they took corners at dangerous speeds. As I wiped blood from my nose with my shirt, I got on my bike and aimed for home. My destination was quickly changed when I heard a noise that told me the chase was already over. The sound of Rory's dragster going at high speed was quickly silenced just after the groaning twist of metal and the crunch of whatever it had hit.

I turned my front wheel and started down Likeitornot Street. At the far end of the block, I could see Rory's car had crashed right into the corner house. The house swallowed up the front end of his car. The engine was somehow still idling. The reverse lights came on, and he hammered the gas, trying to pull away from that damaged mess.

The broken foundation blocks had a firm grip on the car's undercarriage, refusing to let go. I saw the sheriff pull up to the curb in front of the house. As I said, he was a large man, and it took him a bit to work himself from the car. Realizing the handcuffs were close to being slapped on, Rory opened the driver's door. The person who stepped out no longer looked like the mean kid who had socked me twice in the face. There was blood covering most of his face. I guessed he hadn't bothered buckling up before the chase began. Tough guys never did use that life-saving belt. A car like Rory's was built before the existence of air bags, so he undoubtedly went face-first into the steering wheel when the car suddenly stopped.

He looked around wildly, spotting the sheriff walking toward him. He was suddenly on the move, trying to keep himself from a prison cell. Because of the high fences circling the neighborhood backyards, Rory only had a couple of directions he could go. I saw the choice in his eyes. He was going to run down Tower Terrace where, at the end of that street, was the edge of town and a thick growth of trees beyond.

I don't know why I did it. Maybe I hated the idea of a punk bully getting away. Maybe I felt sorry for Sheriff Prescott, because there was no way his legs could ever carry him fast enough. Or maybe because my head was still swelling with an untapped fury caused by Rory's fist.

I pedaled hard. When Rory's feet hit the road, I stepped off my bike, held the handlebars on a straight path, and gave my bike a hard shove. The bike didn't wobble a bit. The timing couldn't have been more perfect. Rory stepped right into an unexpected collision. His feet tangled up in the spinning pedal, and then the wheels. He grabbed the bike for some sort of balance, but it was already falling over. I saw a look of terror on his bloody face as he realized he was going to meet the concrete in a painful, jarring halt.

He landed on my bike first, and then his body bounced over it to find the street waiting. I automatically winced, because I knew that had to hurt. Sheriff Prescott didn't have to walk far to grab the young man's arms, helping him to his feet, all the while slipping on handcuffs like a magic trick.

Rory fought all the way to the police cruiser. Even after the sheriff stuffed him into the back, he kicked at the steel cage covering the windows. He cursed a storm of foul words at us, but the glass muffled most of them.

I picked up my bike and looked it over. It had taken a good hit, but there were only minor scratches on the frame. I figured these additional war wounds spoke of another interesting battle.

"I appreciate the assistance, Mr. Graham. I suppose that was payback for the two jabs."

I shrugged. "I suppose so."

The sheriff excused himself and went toward the homeowners. The couple stood outside, staring at the hot rod partially parked inside their house.

As I started off, I glanced inside the back seat of the cruiser. Rory briefly stopped his tirade of kicking at the glass partition to stare back at me. I didn't like what I saw in those eyes. I could read them clearly. They said that if we should ever meet again, Heaven had an open spot for me, but I'd be facing a lot of pain and suffering before finding that blissful place.

I couldn't help it. I smiled and waved at him as I passed.

Before I got home, I thought of Regan. I was sure he'd eventually find out that I was the one to blame for his brother's imprisonment. When Regan found out, I would spend my time in Paper Moon dodging and hiding from my next beating.

When I got home, I pulled an ice pack from the freezer and then went to the bathroom mirror to see what damage he had inflicted. My teeth still looked firm in their sockets, but my gums on the left side bled a little. The blood from my nose had stopped, but the bridge and cheekbones swelled a bit.

I watched television and held the ice pack against my face until I heard the truck rattle into the driveway.

The look on Josh's face was not one of great surprise. I'd been in plenty of fights in the many towns we'd lived in. I assured him this time I had not started the fight, and that I hadn't even thrown a single punch. I rolled out the entire story in such detail as if it had been an exciting movie I had just gotten done watching.

"Well, I'm glad to hear that punk will be sitting in a cell for quite some time," Josh said as he tried to put something together for dinner. "This town doesn't need someone like that tearing up the streets and causing problems just because he feels like it."

The sheriff showed up a little after six o'clock. Josh let him in and offered him a glass of iced tea.

"It seems to me," the sheriff said as he settled in the dining room chair, "for a couple of new guys in town, you're keeping yourselves involved. This is the second time I've been to this house in so many months. I'm just glad it's for good reasons that I came here and not the other. Aside from this mess with the arsonist, the biggest part of my job is stopping fights between schoolboys or neighborhood disputes. With only about five thousand people in town, there really isn't much mischief going on. Of course, sometimes it's the drunks being obnoxious, or kids racing cars in the streets, or even small things like finding lost pets. This deal with Rory Evans is the most excitement I've had all week. Don't tell anyone I said this, but it's a shame he crashed his car so quickly, because I was up for a good long chase. Well, anyway, let's get down to it."

Sheriff Prescott took paperwork from the case he'd brought and asked his questions. I gave answers to the best of my knowledge. There wasn't much to tell, anyway.

Rory had stopped me. I antagonized him a bit until he'd socked me twice in the face. I'd also assisted in his capture. End of story.

The sheriff put the paperwork away, gulped down the last of his iced tea, and stood.

He shook our hands and said, "You're a couple of good young men. You've both got a strong moral compass for doing what's right and fair. Your parents would be proud of what you've become."

"Thank you," Josh said.

As he walked toward the door, I started to say something but quickly bit my tongue. I had wanted to ask if he believed in Mr. Reynolds' claims of innocence.

"Well, if I ever need to deputize you, I figure you'd be up for it, huh?" Sheriff Prescott asked.

I smiled and said I would. It wasn't such a bad idea. I was certainly developing keen insights into the people of Paper Moon.

It was another night I woke to the phantom smell of fire. I went to my window and opened it. Even with the sun sunk far below the horizon, waterlogged August heat rolled in. The only thing I smelled was the sweet aroma of the trees and flowers. There was no fire tonight. There was only a town deep in slumber.

Ever since the police arrested Mr. Reynolds again, there hadn't been any more fires. I really did believe in his statement that he loved Paper Moon with all his heart. No one who loves something so much would set it to burn. So, the lingering question still remained. Were my suspicions correct about Deputy Kline, and if so, why those particular buildings?

One thing I thought of was how the real arsonist loved fire. So, would it be possible for him to frame Mr. Reynolds and no longer set things to burn? Something like that was an addiction, and addictions are hard to beat. I didn't know why, but I didn't think we'd seen the last house or business take to flames. If I was right, something else would burn, and burn soon.

Chapter 18

Late Sunday night, someone was shaking me. In the darkness of my bedroom, only slightly lit by the street-lamp glowing through the window, a figure hovered over my bed. In the confusion of the moment, I wanted to either scream, throw a punch, or run from the house. But what I did was stare at that figure with confused terror until it spoke.

"I need you to come with me, Jayce."

Of course, I knew the voice, and it didn't surprise me to find Kat in my bedroom in the middle of the night. What had brought her here was a mystery, but as you know, I'm a kid who thrives on a good mystery. Only tonight I felt tired and wanted to go back to sleep.

I rolled away from her, faced the wall, closed my eyes, and said, "Whatever it is can wait until morning. Be careful when you leave. The tree is wet and slippery."

She poked me hard in the side and said, "It's serious. Anderson has disappeared."

This wasn't news to me or anyone else in town. A kid who could blink out of this existence and appear at another place and time wasn't anything new to the residents of Paper Moon. Anderson had a talent for being there one second and gone the next.

"You don't understand. Get dressed, you're coming with me."

I started to protest, but she grabbed my bare foot and pulled me out of bed. I hit the floor hard on my back, which nearly knocked the wind out of me. Kat had a way of getting on my nerves well enough when she wanted something until I had no choice but to give in.

I was only wearing my underwear. I told her to turn around until I got dressed.

She didn't, of course, but instead said, "I have no interest in seeing your scrawny butt. Get your pants on and let's go."

"I'm not stealing Josh's truck again. He'll hang me up by my thumbs for a week if I even think about it. I don't know about you, but I can't time travel. So how are we supposed to find him?" I asked as I pulled on my shorts, shirt, and socks.

"Sometimes you can be so dense, Mr. Graham."

I was working my shoes on when she went out the window and began maneuvering down the tree. Carefully, I followed. I retrieved my bike from the back porch, and we headed down Twisted Trail.

We rode in silence part of the way, and then Kat said, "It's a bad one this time. My dad was heavy in his sickness tonight."

I looked at her, confused. I had no idea what her father and Anderson's time traveling had to do with each other.

"You know, don't you?" she asked.

I only shrugged. I didn't want Kat to know that I was, in fact, dense as she claimed.

"Anderson antagonizes dad when he gets this way, so that my dad will leave me alone. Anderson is like a guardian angel to me. It hurts me to see and hear it happen. But Anderson said he will never let it happen to me as long as he lives. He's far braver than I could ever be."

I offered a small grunt to acknowledge that I was listening and understanding. I didn't understand, not any of it. I knew that soon Kat would get to the heart of the matter in her own time. I just didn't want to push her there.

We rode on and took a left on Rainbow Road. I had no idea where we were going and didn't bother pushing for information. It was a strange night and a strange conversation, but like I said, I loved a good mystery.

The sound of a car engine on the next block disrupted the stillness of the streets. When we spotted headlights breaking through the night ahead of us on Santa Clause Way, Kat said, "Over here. We've got to hide."

She directed her bike up the closest driveway and disappeared behind the hedges. I followed.

A patrol car turned on Rainbow Road and slowly drove past our hiding spot. I saw that behind the wheel was Deputy Kline. The same man I had an insane fixation on lately.

"Why are we hiding?" I whispered. "The police can help us find Anderson."

Kat turned quickly and said, "Don't you dare tell anyone about this. You swear it on your parents' grave?"

I didn't bother pointing out that my parents didn't have a grave, unless she considered watery bones moving with the tides a grave.

"Yeah, I swear it," I said. Then I had to ask. "Where are we going?"

"Anderson has a place he goes when he gets panicked or scared. We built it years ago. It's his hideaway place."

We watched as the patrol car turned left on Blink Street and was gone.

Getting back on our bikes, I said, "I don't understand anything that's going on."

Kat looked at me as if I were the dumbest person on the planet. "You will when we find Anderson," she said, and we peddled on.

I didn't like the thought of going into a black forest as I stood at the tree line. There were all sorts of noises breaking through the darkness. I had a hundred images running through my head of every scary movie I'd ever seen. There was nothing but suffering and a gruesome death in such an evil place. I thought that if Anderson had wandered into the blackness of the forest, then he was surely dead already, and Kat and I should turn around and go home.

I've stated before that I am no hero or a kid with a huge supply of bravery. Most of the time when it comes to a fight-or-flight situation, I do believe I could actually grow wings in my quest to get away.

"You first," Kat said and slapped me on the shoulder. I was happy to know I wasn't the only reluctant one.

"I have no idea where we're going. I'm following you. Remember? I can't believe you didn't even bring a flashlight if you knew we were going into the dark woods."

"I didn't think about it at the time. All I thought was that I needed to find Anderson. I guess now we know that women are far braver than men," Kat said and began walking into that gloomy forest.

I didn't argue with her, but I did follow. The wall of trees closed around us like a black glove. It was almost suffocating knowing that the thick forest pulled us in so easily, and I believed it would be reluctant to let us go.

I thought of the time I cut through a forest alone to reach Grady's Wildlife Retreat and had gotten lost in broad daylight. This was another unfamiliar forest, and I couldn't even see the leaves at my feet. I was starting to think that following Kat anywhere would lead me to either the hospital or a morgue. In fact, I had already ended up at the hospital on one occasion.

Something made a jarring crash to our right, and both of us jumped.

"What was that?" Kat asked in a frantic whisper.

The creature quickly scurried away through the dead leaves. I saw a moonlight glow of its eyes as the thing looked back at us, then must have decided to leave us alone.

"It's gone," I said. "I think it was something sitting on a branch. The branch must have broken, and it fell to the ground."

An owl hooted, and again we jumped. The imagination of a kid could make you believe that beautiful common things seen in daylight were actually torturous beasts out for blood when night fell.

"Just an owl that time. What were you thinking when you built a clubhouse in the damnation forest?"

"It's quite beautiful during the day," she said.

"How far is this place? And don't tell me it's miles instead of yards."

She never answered, because we reached a wide tree that possibly grew to the sun. There was a series of boards screwed to the trunk that led to a small shack resting on the first level of branches.

Anderson's journey alone into a midnight forest was far braver than my nerves would have handled. Of course, fear of one thing can override the brain when fleeing from something far meaner.

Kat grabbed the first rung, and I saw it wobble loosely under her weight as she began climbing. I could imagine being nearly to the top when a rung gave out and my body plummeted to the forest floor. Then I would be lying there with two broken legs when something slipped from the shadows, briefly studying me before its massive jaws opened and clapped down on my face and pulled me into its den to be devoured.

"Quit stalling and get up here," Kat demanded.

Kat spoke in a soft voice before I was halfway up the ladder. I couldn't understand what was being said, but I could tell that we had found Anderson.

I made Kat move off to the side a bit so that I could get onto the small deck surrounding the equally small treehouse. She was half inside, whispering as if she were trying to calm down a frightened kitten. I saw the beam of a light move inside and realized Anderson had been smart enough to bring a flashlight.

"I'm here now. It's all over. I want you to come out and come home with me. We'll get through this together like we always do."

I heard whimpering coming from inside the treehouse. Nearly five minutes went by, but Kat was unable to lure him from his safe house.

She slithered out the narrow door, looking deflated from her attempt. She studied me for a long moment as if mentally asking me *what should we do now*?

"Can I talk to him? Maybe he'll see that he has another friend here to help him through this."

Kat made a motion for me to go ahead and try. I was by no means a large kid, but the doorway in the treehouse made me feel giant. I had to rotate one shoulder down and in just to get the first part of my body through. There certainly wasn't enough room for all three of us. Even two people inside was going to be a snug fit. We weren't exactly on top of each other, but there wasn't enough space to stretch out. I leaned against the wall and pulled my legs in.

"May I?" I asked as I held out my hand for the flash-light. "I'd like to get a look at the interior of this place you and Kat built."

Anderson had himself scrunched into a tight ball. His hand came out from the tangle of arms and legs to offer the light.

I took it and worked the beam around and around. As I said, there wasn't much to the place, but for any young kid, this treehouse was a castle high enough in the treetops that it played among the clouds. I hadn't realized there was a small loft area until the light chased away the shadows.

"What's up there?" I asked. "Must be like a sleeping area or a lookout or something, huh?"

I focused the light on Anderson then, and what I said I will never remember. Like many shocking moments in my life, my brain leaves out all the unimportant things. However, what I saw forever etched itself into my mind.

Anderson's face was a mass of purple, black, and red. Dark bruising marked most of the left side of his face. His upper and lower lips had split open from whatever had caused all that damage. The blood had come to a stop, but the lacerations desperately needed stitches. My own slightly mangled face, made so by Rory's fist, didn't compare to the punishment Anderson had endured.

"It'll be all right. Give it some time and everything will heal," I said. It was probably the dumbest thing ever to leave my mouth.

I realized just then, well, everything. Anderson was unfortunately one of those children I'd read about online or saw on the television. He was a kid tortured by the hand of a parent who was only supposed to be loving and never vicious. At least not to this degree. I thought about what Kat had said during the bike ride. She had explained eve-rything, but I was too deaf to hear the truth.

Had I really believed all this time that Anderson was really an unusual kid who had an extraordinary ability to vanish from our existence and propel himself back in time to correct a corrupted future? Well, yes, and no. I'd always been a kid wanting to believe in fantastic possibilities, no matter how extreme they seemed to be. But my deep beliefs knew that such a thing couldn't be real.

Now I understood that Anderson had become a kid with perfect timing. He had the ability to know the exact moment when no one was looking at him, so that he could do his vanishing act so perfectly that it really seemed possible that he was there one second and gone the next. It was an ability born from moments of extreme anxiety when he couldn't handle the overwhelming thoughts of living in an abusive household.

Gently, I touched his knee. It was the only thing I could think of to comfort him.

"Your father did this to you?"

He pulled himself in tighter, trying to shrink away even from the touch of a friend.

Then he spoke in a low voice that I could hardly catch. "I'm a disappointing son. I didn't do the dishes or have dinner ready like I was supposed to."

I had the very same chores at home, but never in a million years would Josh strike me for failing to do them. Heck, he wouldn't even raise his voice. He'd just tell me to get it done.

"I think we need to get you to the clinic. Those cuts on your lips are gonna need tending to by a doctor."

Kat poked her head in. She looked frightened.

"We can't go to the hospital, Jayce. Things would get even worse if somebody else knew," she said.

"He's hurt pretty bad. This isn't something he can hide from everyone. He's gonna need stitches for those cuts to heal properly. You know there's no way around it," I said as I watched her.

Her eyes found the treehouse floor as her brain tried to work out a solution that didn't involve a hospital. I saw the defeat in her eyes as she realized I was right.

Kat held out her hand, and Anderson took it calmly.

"He's right. We need to get you looked at." She backed out of the doorway, and Anderson followed.

We left the forest. I slowly pedaled my bike. Kat sat Anderson on her bike, and she walked beside him as she slowly pushed and steered for him.

Kat said, "Look."

It appeared as if the sun had lost its way and was now rising in the west. Orange light glowed over the rooftops of Showboat Lane. As we were trying to get an understanding of this strangeness, a patrol car zoomed down the adjoining street in front of us, heading east. It was heading in the opposite direction of the light attraction.

"What do you think it is?" Anderson asked through swollen and split lips.

I knew exactly what it was, and I said so. "It's another fire. Something else is burning. Even though Mr. Reynolds is back in prison, the real arsonist can't stop himself."

Then we heard the distant sirens of a fire truck trying to get to the scene of the blaze. Help was on the way, and there was no reason for us to go check it out. Given the situation, I didn't think I would ever be brave enough to run into a burning house again. My heroics still haunted my dreams from time to time. Sometimes the dreams ended all right, sometimes they didn't. Sometimes they ended with either Josh or me or both of us burned to cinders.

"Sounds like they've got it covered. Let's get to the clinic," I said.

Even though Paper Moon was a tiny spot on the map, it did have a twenty-four-hour medical clinic. It was the same clinic where we spent a brief period after we had pulled Mr. Bixby from the wreckage of his house. The nearest actual hospital was about twenty-five miles away in Coral Key. We had no way of getting to the hospital, so the clinic would have to do.

The lights of the clinic were all lit up at the end of Tango Waltz Drive. We went through the front door and had to call down the corridor because the front desk was empty. A woman somewhere in her sixties exited a room and slowly made her way to us. She grimaced when she got a good look at what we'd dragged inside.

"My heavens! What in the world were you up to? You look like you picked a fight with an oncoming train," she told Anderson.

Mr. Mossgrove had a body built like a train and possessed the destructive power of one derailed at high speed.

None of us answered. What could we honestly say?

"Well, can you at least tell me your name?" the lady asked.

"Anderson Mossgrove," he told her through a tortured mouth. Even though he had been born here, Anderson was a fly on the wall in his own hometown.

She grabbed a clipboard with a form on it. "Then that's a start," she said and wrote it down. "And who are the two of you?" She was not the same woman who had been on duty the other time Kat and I had visited.

"I'm his sister Katrina. This is our friend Jayce Graham."

"What exactly are the three of you doing out this late? What happened to this boy?"

"We just need to know if you can help him and that's all," Kat said.

The woman studied us for a good long moment and then said, "Well, I can get the doctor to look at him. He might need some X-rays. Where are your parents?"

"Our mom went to the moon with no plans to come back. Our father has been living in his own personal hell for the last three years, if you really want to know," Kat said defiantly.

The woman watched Kat carefully, and I think she instantly understood everything. "My name is Mrs. Rollins. You don't need to be defensive with me, young lady. It's my job to understand everything that's happened, so we know what kind of injuries to look for."

"I heard you talking out here. Oh, you two are back again. What kind of heroics have gone on tonight?" a man said.

I recognized him as Dr. Harrison, the same doctor who had tended to Mr. Bixby after we had pulled a collapsed building off him.

"It's my brother, Dr. Harrison. He, um, he fell down the stairs."

The doctor wore a pained expression when he stepped up to Anderson and got a closer look.

"Fell down the stairs, huh? And was there a brick wall at the bottom that you went face-first into? Then suddenly, a group of thugs with bats and chains showed up and worked you over until their arms were tired?" The doctor's attempt at humor didn't liven the moment.

"Ah, you bet," Kat said before Anderson answered.

"Well, you better come on back so I can look you over. Mary, can you get Mr. Mossgrove on the phone and tell him he better come on down?"

"Ah, please don't do that," Kat said instantly. "Our father isn't feeling so well tonight. Would it be all right if we could just walk home after you tend to Anderson?"

"Well, we do still have your insurance information on file, so no need to do more paperwork. I suppose it's going to depend on what I find wrong with him."

I could tell by the expression on Dr. Harrison's face that he understood the true circumstances that had brought Anderson here. I remembered him seeming confused when Mr. Mossgrove showed up to retrieve Kat from the clinic, not much caring if she was all right or impressed that she had helped save a life.

"Follow me, young man. The two of you can wait out here," Dr. Harrison said, and they disappeared into the back.

I was having a hard time finding words as Kat and I sat on hard plastic chairs in the waiting room.

"You should have been straight with me from the beginning. I never thought your dad was like that," I said finally.

"It wasn't something I was going to confess to the new kid in town. None of my other friends even know. My father might be drunk most of the time, but not drunk enough that he ever hits Anderson in a place where it will show. Not until tonight, anyway. Tonight, he was more out of his head than he's ever been. He's getting worse, Jayce. When my mom left, he started drinking a few beers a night. Before too long, he had to finish off a twelve pack just to get himself screwed up enough. A while back, he switched to hard liquor. It made him mean toward everything and everyone."

"Has he ever, you know, hit you?"

Kat's eyes found the plain white tiled floor. She nodded as a few tears slipped loose. She said, "Yeah, in the beginning. Then Anderson would begin antagonizing him so that dad's focus stayed off me. Anderson knew I was having a hard time taking it. We both were, but Anderson is far stronger in body and mind than I'll ever be. I don't know how to stop it. I don't have any answers."

"I'm sorry. I don't either."

We didn't talk much for the next hour until Anderson came out from the exam room.

"Well, from what I can see, he doesn't have a concussion. Which is a relief. I had to throw three stitches in his top lip and four in the bottom. Keep those cuts dry and clean to avoid infection. The other bruising will heal over the next couple of weeks and should be gone without leaving any permanent marks. I should be calling someone to come and get you, but I believe you'll make it home okay. The three of you take care of yourselves."

We thanked him and went out the front door to our bikes. As we were getting ready to ride away, I looked back. Through the window of the front door, I saw Dr. Harrison walk up to the front deck and pick up the phone. I'd never seen a more serious look on someone's face as he began speaking to the person on the other end.

The following day, while the three of us were at school, four of the town's men, armed with an uncorked anger, entered the Mossgrove residence through the unlocked front door and offered Mr. Mossgrove the beating of his life.

Chapter 19

Four days after finding Anderson in the woods, there was an all-too-familiar smell in the air. The smell was one I recognized from my first week in Paper Moon. It was the smell of chaos. It was the smell of personal items being eaten away to nothingness. It was another Paper Moon structure being decimated to a heap of black ash that would never again resemble what it once was.

I heard the fire truck off in the distance. After I filled my bowl with cereal, Josh and I simply looked at each other over our breakfast. The sirens and the smell of fire seemed to be a constant thing as our time here went on. It was sad to think that most people in town were acting just as we were. There was no more surprise to the acts of arson. I wondered if anyone really cared unless it was their own house or business disappearing in a black cloud.

Josh shook his head in disgust. He said, "So, the arsonist is in prison, yet the fires have continued?"

"The news speculated that Mr. Reynolds is the original arsonist. They believe a copycat set the last fire four days ago. They think it's someone who knows Mr. Reynolds, and that person hatched a plan to begin the fires again to mislead the authorities, making them second-guess their evidence and force them to release Mr. Reynolds. I don't believe that at all. They actually have an innocent man in prison. The real arsonist can't stop himself from setting things to burn. He set up Mr. Reynolds to take the fall, but the arsonist couldn't step away from the temptation to destroy more. So, it sounds and smells like he was hard at work early this morning."

Josh was watching me closely. I realized how much I had gone to Mr. Reynolds' defense.

"What are you neglecting to tell me?"

"What do you mean?"

"I just get the feeling you're leaving something out."

"I'm not. I'm just repeating what the news said, and then put my own twist on things. I'm a weird kid. Deal with it," I said and winked.

I'd never told Josh about my friendly encounter with Mr. Reynolds as I stumbled through endless woods.

"Uh-huh. I know that, but you're still hiding something."

I put my bowl in the dishwasher, grabbed my backpack, and slapped Josh on the shoulder.

"I'm off. Have a great day."

"You, too, kiddo. We can talk anytime you want," he called after me as I slipped out the back door.

I began riding south. I stopped and looked over my shoulder. Thick black smoke filled the early morning sky to the northwest. I decided to take an alternate route to school. It would most likely make me late, but that was nothing unusual.

I soon realized I was heading toward downtown. The shop owners on U Buy N Buy Street were all outside, looking west. I didn't slow down to ask questions, I just turned toward the rolling black smoke. A few blocks later, I stopped beside a police cruiser with its lights swirling on the roof. A large crowd had gathered here, making it difficult to see over them. All I could see was the top floor of the yellow house and blackness billowing out the windows.

I knew this house. I didn't know who owned it, but I had been here before. It had been on the day I'd followed—

Just then, the crowd cheered, and their hands went up as they applauded. The crowd took a unified sigh of relief at whatever it was they witnessed.

I laid my bike down and stepped onto the rear bumper of the cruiser. Deputy Kline was running down the front porch steps. In his arms was a small boy about four or five years of age. They both coughed hard, trying to get fresh air into their lungs. I knew that feeling. I remembered the hot smoke that tried to suffocate me.

Deputy Kline handed the boy off to one of the volunteer firefighters. Then, the deputy fell to his knees, gasping and coughing as if he had something lodged in his throat and was trying to force it out. A medic placed an oxygen mask over the deputy's mouth and nose, and he sucked in with easing relief.

"Deputy Kline saved that little boy," a large woman in a nightgown said to someone.

"That poor boy would have burned to death if the deputy hadn't gotten here in time. The man is a hero," the other woman replied.

I wasn't thinking anything of the sort. It was true he might have saved that boy from being consumed by flames, but I was sure that the deputy's hands had set the fire. A hero he certainly wasn't. This was the same house Deputy Kline had stopped in front of and taken a picture of on the day I briefly spoke to him in front of the ruined business of Clean Sweep. That was also the day I followed him home, spied through his basement window, and pedaled for my life when he spotted me watching.

To most residents, it would seem that Deputy Kline had a knack for being instantly there when the arsonist had just struck. As far as I was aware, he was the first to respond to every fire the arsonist had started.

"Don't you ever do that again, Sammy. Don't you ever sleep anywhere else in the house except your bed. Your father and I couldn't find you anywhere and thought you ran outside when you saw the fire," the mother told her son, and then hugged him.

Deputy Kline pulled the oxygen mask away from his face and said, "He was sleeping in his bedroom closet under a bunch of blankets, Mrs. Mahoney."

"Thank you so very much, Tom. If there's anything you ever need from us, you just ask," she told him and squeezed the deputy's hand.

He said, "It's all part of the job. I wasn't sure when the fire truck would get here. When you said you couldn't find Sammy, I knew we had little time to find him if he was still inside." He sucked in more oxygen.

I snorted with disbelief at his boasting. There was a lot going on, and I knew no one had heard me. My suspicions were moving into place like the tumblers inside a lock, ready to fall into harmony and reveal its secrets. There were simply too many coincidences happening to go unnoticed by a kid like me who enjoyed paying attention.

Deputy Kline looked at me. Our eyes connected briefly before I stepped down off his bumper and disappeared into the crowd. I didn't like the look in his eyes. There was an immediate meanness on his face when only a moment before there had been nothing but joy as the people praised him.

I decided I didn't want to stick around. I had a fear he was going to snag me by the collar in front of all these people and take me away in the patrol car. That would likely be the last time anyone ever saw me.

Right now, the biggest question on my mind was who could I share my suspicions with? Who would believe the new kid in town when he told them that Deputy Kline was the Paper Moon arsonist? I didn't even have solid proof, only a lame theory that would be subject to ridicule by almost everyone.

They would tell me that yes, Deputy Kline was usually the first one at each burning structure because he was the officer on the overnight shift. He was the one who answered the calls when they came in. On the night of the first fire across the street from my house, I threw up on the deputy's shoes. What I hadn't noticed at that time was what my vomit splattered onto. It had been a clear gel that stank of hard chemicals. I was never sure if it was the fire, adrenaline or the hard chemical smell that made me lose my dinner all over those shoes.

Where had the gel come from?

There were only two people I could think of to help me figure things out. Josh was a good brother and a great listener when I had something to say. But I didn't think there was any way I could convince him the town's deputy was really the man behind the burning chaos. Kat was the only other person who might see things from my point of view.

I realized the time and began pedaling toward school.

The hallways were already buzzing about the fire consuming the yellow house. I overheard many people speculate about who the real arsonist was and why he or she did such things. I didn't know the reason, but I became more confident now that I knew who was behind it all. He drove around in a patrol vehicle during the late-night hours.

I didn't think anyone knew the real face of Deputy Kline. He wore the mask of a hero, a guardian, and a friend to the community. My beliefs were that he became the exact opposite of the public's perspective. He had a seething hate for the population of Paper Moon.

I decided I needed to know why. The urge to investigate could land me in some serious hot water if I got caught. Time in a juvenile facility also held a place in the deal, depending on how I went about getting the information I wanted. The town needed answers. The town needed the madness to stop before there was nothing left besides blackened ruins where a thriving town used to be.

I started formulating a plan during classes when my brain was supposed to be focused on my studies. Teachers caught me on several occasions with a wandering mind. As punishment, the teachers embarrassed me in front of the class when I didn't have the answer they were looking for. It was all right. I figured a little embarrassment was worth saving homes from destruction.

I didn't see Kat all day at school. In fact, I didn't see Anderson either. I wondered if they'd caught a nasty bug and had to stay home. I wanted to share my idea about Deputy Kline being the arsonist. I really wanted her point of view on things. She wouldn't have issues telling me that I was either on to something good or just desperately looking to pin the fires on anyone other than Mr. Reynolds.

After the final bell rang, I unlocked my bike and headed west. I couldn't go home just yet. I wanted to stop at Kat's house and see why she wasn't at school. I leaned my bike against the rickety porch railing and went to the door. I rang the doorbell and then knocked. I did this three times but never received an answer.

I went around the side of the house and peered through the kitchen window. The lights were out. Unlike my bedroom window, which was accessible by a large oak, Kat's bedroom had no easy way to get to it other than a trampoline if there was one. I searched the yard for small pebbles and found a few. One by one, I tossed them at her window. They made a soft *tink* off the glass before bouncing back at me.

There was no answer. It was strange that Kat and Anderson hadn't made it to school, and now neither of them was at home. Mr. Mossgrove didn't have a job as far as I knew. I somewhat remembered Kat telling me he'd suffered an injury at his last job and was receiving monthly compensation. Even Mr. Mossgrove didn't come out the door to holler at me to stop ringing the bell.

I supposed I'd speak with Kat tomorrow at school. I headed toward home.

The rust bucket was in the driveway as I made my way down our street. It was an unusual thing for Josh to get home before me. As I went inside to the thankfully cool blast of air-conditioning, I found Josh sitting on the couch. The television was off, but he stared at it as if some program held his full attention.

I didn't like the look on his face. His features were pale and unsmiling. His hands were rubbing together in deep thought. He looked like a man carrying a burden, but who didn't know how to shrug it off.

"You're home early," I said as I dropped my backpack on the kitchen table.

Josh said, "Your friend Anderson called our landlord today to get my cell number. Anderson then called me at work. Something bad has happened."

Chapter 20

I stared at Josh, having no idea why Anderson would go to such lengths to reach out.

"Apparently, your friend Kat was getting the mail yesterday. Um, a car going down the street was going too fast, and a dog or something ran out. Well, the lady saw the dog, but didn't see Kat standing at the mailbox. I'm sorry to tell you that the car hit her."

I quickly sat on the dining room chair as my vision seemed to pull away from me. I thought a blackout was right around the corner. A quick movie reel ran across my mind. Kat standing in front of her mailbox, a car rolling steadily down the road, a dog coming out of nowhere, and a two-thousand-pound vehicle suddenly running down my only friend.

The question came out in a stammer. "Is she dead?"

"No. But she's suffered a lot. She was in for a second surgery when Anderson called. He didn't know the full extent of the damage, but it sounds pretty bad. The car, um, went over her."

I ran for the sink, because there was no stopping it. The vomit came out in a hot rush, an impossible amount, too. Josh was instantly at my side, rubbing my back until I finished. After the last of it came out and I spit the remains from my mouth, Josh filled a glass of water. I swished it around and spat back out the first two mouthfuls. The rest of the glass went down my throat to wash away the scorching bile.

I knew why Kat was getting the mail. For her, it had become a ritual after school. She had become obsessed with receiving the letter from the facility that was testing her water samples she'd sent off months ago. The process had taken far longer than she had hoped. Obviously, the business didn't consider her request a priority.

"I have to go to the hospital. I need to see her."

"Jayce, she's got a long recovery time. Not even her family will be able to see her for a while."

"But I have to do something. I can't just sit around and wait for her to die."

"Don't you dare say that. Don't even think it," Josh snapped. "You can't let your mind go there until you know exactly what's going on. Even then, you shouldn't let your thoughts go to that place. Not even Anderson knows how bad it is."

But Anderson did know. He knew better than anyone I'd ever met how much a body could take. He had endured years of abuse by his drunken father's fists.

The hours ticked away, and I felt completely useless. I felt as though I should be doing something productive, something to help Kat in some sort of way. Six o'clock came around, and Josh called from downstairs that dinner was ready. I called back to say that I wasn't hungry. Food was the farthest thing from my mind. My nerves were jittery as I longed to get off my bed, quit staring at the ceiling, and do something.

I left my room, went downstairs, and found Josh sprawled out on the couch watching the news. Our town picked up Coral Key stations because Paper Moon was too small to have its own local news. I didn't figure they'd report Kat's accident, as it wasn't Coral Key breaking news.

"I'm going out for a bit."

"Jayce, there's no way for you to get to the hospital up north."

"No, I know. I wasn't even going to try. I just need to get out of the house. I want to clear my head. Maybe I'll just walk around the block, if that's all right."

He watched me for a long moment. He said, "As long as you don't plan on attempting to walk all the way to Coral Key."

"I definitely won't do that. I'll be back soon."

Walking down each street, I wondered if any of the people inside their homes knew what had happened to Kat. I wanted to knock on doors and tell them. I wanted to ask for their prayers that she would make it through just fine. Kat was a well-liked girl around town. I had no doubt everyone's concern would be genuine.

It was an unintentional thing, but I found myself wandering along Kat's neighborhood. A dog barked in the distance, but that was all the street had to offer. No lights shone through the windows as I stepped up onto the sagging porch and went to the door. I had hoped that at least Anderson would be home, dropped off by his father, because he could do little good while his sister recovered. I would likely find him tucked in tightly against a wall, sitting alone in the dark, because that was how he dealt with tragedy. It didn't surprise me when no one answered. I sat on the porch step and looked at the mailbox. Much like the house, the mailbox was in need of repair. It hung limply from the post. When someone opened the lid, the mail would naturally slide right out. Was that the reason the woman in the car failed to see Kat? Had Kat not caught the mail as gravity pulled at it and it fell onto the street?

Crouched low to retrieve the mail, Kat had made herself less visible.

As I sat there wondering why any God would allow a child to be run down in the street, I saw movement from the corner of my eye. It was a piece of paper at the far end of the yard. I stood from the steps and walked over to it. As I picked it up, I realized it was mail. It was addressed to Mr. Mossgrove. A bill from the power company. I planned to put it back in the mailbox when I saw another letter against the backyard fence. It was addressed to Katrina Mossgrove. The return address was from an environmental lab in Atlanta. It was the letter Kat had been waiting months to receive. I turned it over, and the flap was partially opened, as if Kat had eagerly dug a finger inside to tear away the envelope because the information was too great to wait another second.

Did I dare finish opening it? I didn't think Kat would care, especially in her current condition, if I knew the environmental results. I peeled the tear all the way open. There was a chart marked with baseline numbers. The results from each vial Kat supplied were in the adjoining four columns. I slide my finger across the numbers and compared them to the normal ranges. After studying the results, I had my answer. So did Kat. Whether she liked it or not, the answer was definitive.

The next day passed. I went through classes in a zombie state of mind. I wasn't learning. I was simply a body in place, as my mind was far from where it was supposed to be. Anderson had called Josh's cell again. I spoke with him briefly before he had to go. Kat's surgery was only the second of many. I heard the hurt in his voice, the terror of losing the one person he could rely on. I think Kat's pain was his own. Kat's shoulder was the one Anderson could always lean on when his father used his slapping hand to punctuate his disappointment.

Two days after the accident, I still wasn't able to see Kat. It wasn't fair. She needed a friend as much as she needed family. So, I got an idea in my head and couldn't shake it free when Josh swung my door open to say good-night.

"Have you been sleeping all right?"

"Not really," I said.

"I could call the school tomorrow and have you stay home sick, if you like. I could let you sleep in as late as you like."

"Yeah, that might be a possibility. I'll let you know in the morning."

I hugged Josh goodnight and smiled as I closed my bedroom door. My master plan had begun without a hitch.

After situating my pillows under my bedsheet, I stepped back and surveyed my decoy. I didn't think Josh would check up on me during the night, but it was just in case he did. I slid the window up and stepped onto the roof and then onto the overhanging branches of the oak. My bike lay against the front porch. Hopping on, I peddled south. There was no way I was going to steal Josh's truck again. I couldn't bike my way to Coral Key either. Earlier in the day, an idea struck me to locate a vehicle that wouldn't be missed for a while.

The bike ride to Mr. Bixby's property felt good under the cool Florida night sky. There was no traffic, and not a soul was outside. Twenty minutes later, I reached the gravel drive. Moonlight through the trees revealed the wreckage of Mr. Bixby's home. The tangled mess of wood, metal, and forgotten personal items remained since the hurricane winds collapsed the house. His car must have been three decades old. The thing was as long as a boat, and I knew it was going to be a challenge to maneuver down the highway.

As I had hoped, the keys were lying in the ashtray. It took some finesse, but the engine finally kicked over. The tank of a car rolled off the property as I directed it across town and toward the highway. I saw no state troopers during the drive, which helped keep my anxiety levels down. Coral Key was easy enough to find, but the hospital wasn't. With no phone, I didn't have a helpful app to direct me. I was sure the hospital would be on one of the major roads. I must have covered half the town before I found my destination.

After parking in the lot, I hurried inside. I didn't know the layout of the hospital, but if I could find the ICU, I'd find Kat. I got many glances from employees as I searched each corridor. Thankfully, no one asked me what I was doing here at this hour. When I found the ICU, there was one nurse at the duty desk. I waited around the corner until she picked up a clipboard and headed down the hallway to do rounds. Slipping behind the desk, I found a list of patients and room numbers. Kat's room was three doors down from the nurses' station.

It was dark inside except for the glow of the monitors. One of them showed the steady rhythm of Kat's heartbeat.

"Visiting hours ended four hours ago, young man," Kat said in a slightly croaked whisper.

I had to smile at that. Even in a busted-up condition, her humor didn't fade.

"I had to see you. I couldn't wait any longer."

"I'm flattered. I'm glad you came. Come over here and sit on this side of the bed. If the nurse comes in, you can crouch down there. They'll kick you out if they catch you. Maybe even chain you up in the basement dungeons for a year or two."

Her speech was labored. I thought that it must hurt to talk and realized I'd made a bad judgement call to come here. Kat wasn't well enough for visitors. She shouldn't be talking or laughing at her own wisecracks.

"Is there a lot of pain?"

"Some. Mostly a dull ache. I've got fantastic drugs pumping through me right now. I don't want to talk about any of that. What I want to know is how Mr. Jayce Graham Cracker made it all the way to Coral Key. Did your brother bring you?"

"Not exactly," I said and told her my master plan.

She clicked her tongue with disappointment.

"Shame, shame. You won't be able to pin this one on me when they haul you off to the slammer."

"Getting caught isn't part of my plan."

"It never is, is it? Yet for you, it seems to happen often."

"Oh, I'm just a stupid kid who doesn't know what he's doing," I said innocently.

"You definitely have the intelligence of a two-year-old."

"Score one for Kat," I said. It was good to have Kat's attitude back to normal. I even eagerly accepted her harsh comment about my immaturity.

"I know why you got hit by that car."

"Because I was stupidly standing in the street."

"Because you were getting the mail. You must have gotten excited when you saw the results letter for the water and dirt samples you sent off. You forgot to step off the street. I found the letter along with other mail the next day when I went to your house. I hope you don't mind, but I opened it."

If Kat's eyes could brighten in her current condition, I was sure they would have.

"What did it say?"

I looked at the monitor. Her heartbeat became a little more frantic in anticipation of the results.

"You were right all along. The samples showed high levels of, oh, I can't remember the long name of the chemical. But such levels can bring on paranoia and erratic behavior."

Kat coughed into her hand. When she pulled it away, there was blood on her palm.

"Oh, my God. You're bleeding," I said a little too loudly, a little too panicky.

She pulled a tissue from the box on the nightstand. Wiping the blood from her palm and mouth, she said, "Don't worry about it. I had some internal injuries. The doctor said this would happen as my body tries to recoup from surgery. I'm very tired though. It's a funny thing. Now that I know the test results, I'm not so sure I want anything to change. I love the town the way it is. I love its weirdness. The interesting things people do bring a wonderful uniqueness to our daily lives. I think maybe I don't want things to become normal like you see on TV. I think it would crush me. Pun intended."

I couldn't help smiling. "I always thought that. Paper Moon is one of the most fantastic places I've ever been. You're right. This place is unique, and unique things should never change."

"I couldn't have said it better myself."

More blood came with a wrenching cough.

"I'm getting the doctor."

"No. Don't. I just need rest. You should get Mr. Bixby's car back and get yourself home."

"You're probably right. Well, I guess I'll see you as soon as I can."

Kat held out her hand. I wasn't sure what she was expecting until she said, "Take it, dummy."

I did. Her skin was smooth, cold, and her grip had very little strength.

"Thank you for coming. And thanks for finding that letter. But you know, I'd love for you to keep the results to yourself. Paper Moon needs to stay as precious as it is."

"I will. Consider the letter burned to nothingness as soon as I can. Get some rest. I'm sure Josh can bring me back up here in a day or two when you're feeling better. I'm glad I came, even if I do get into trouble for it."

"Lawbreaker," Kat whispered as her eyes grew heavy.

Our hands slipped from each other.

I wasn't sure what to say back, so I settled on, "I'll see you real soon."

"Goodbye, Jayce."

There was something so final in her words that it hurt my heart. I slipped quietly from the room and left the hospital. I took flight south in Mr. Bixby's car and soon came in for a Paper Moon landing.

Chapter 21

At the hospital, I wanted to tell Kat that I thought I knew who the real arsonist was. My theory was lame and my proof was nonexistent. I honestly had nothing to go on except a hunch. I had to do something before another structure burned, and maybe this time someone would die. I didn't think I could live with myself if that happened, especially if I had done nothing to prevent it.

Deputy Kline always worked nights. The fires always took place at night during his shift. Of course, most people had the brains to do wrong things under the cover of darkness.

Deputy Kline had a foul-smelling gel and mud on his shoes the night Josh and I ran into a burning house. The sheriff's department said that whatever was used to get the fires going had resistance to water, which was why all the structures were totaled. I didn't know if Deputy Kline had a background in chemistry. In fact, I didn't know anything about him. What was the gel, and why was there mud on his shoes when he had been driving around all night in his patrol car?

It was impossible to catch him in the act, because I didn't know where his next target was. I couldn't tell anyone, because word might get out that Jayce Graham was going around town accusing him of being the true arsonist. That might be the day I disappeared forever.

What it came down to was simple. I needed solid proof before I could point my finger and confidently say that he was the one we were all looking for. How on earth was I going to find proof?

Two days after I visited Kat in the hospital, the answer was so obvious that it could have slapped me in the face. I was going to have to break the law.

I looked at the glowing red numbers on the clock, which read 2:13. Deputy Kline would most likely be at work unless today was his day off. I had to make sure of that before I did the gutsy move I was thinking.

I slid out of bed, dressed, and quietly opened my bedroom door. Josh's door was closed, and I could hear his soft snoring. The floorboards creaked a little as I made my way to the front door. I waited a minute for any sounds coming from down the hall. I decided it was clear and went out the front door.

I decided to head to the small sheriff's station first. I had to make sure Deputy Kline's car was in the lot before I went to the next move. There were no lights on at any of the businesses along U Buy N Buy Street. There was an eerie feeling to being alone on the town roads, especially at night. It was a strange sense of not just being alone, but being the only person left alive on the planet. It was as if something traumatic had happened during my time alone in my bedroom, and during that time the world was vacated and everyone forgot to wake me so that I might join them on the spaceship out of here.

I passed the grocery store, the Off the Top barber shop owned by a knight, and the junk shop that had just about everything mankind had once created. The sheriff's office was located at the end of Uphold Law Road. As I pedaled closer, I saw two vehicles in the parking lot. I knew the yellow Charger was owned by Deputy Kline, as I had seen it parked in his driveway on the day I followed him home and got caught peeking through his window. There was a four-door car parked next to it, and I figured this was owned by a secretary who answered the late-night emergency calls.

I leaned my bike against the side of the building and crept to the front windows. Someone passed by the window as I started to peer inside, which quickly made me crouch again. There were several parking lot lights on, and if I wasn't careful, the deputy would catch me peeping inside. I doubted I would be able to come up with a suitable explanation about why I was at the sheriff's office at nearly three in the morning.

When I thought the coast was clear, I rose a few inches. It was just enough to allow me a view through the mini blinds, which were partially open. A blonde woman in a flower dress walked to a desk at the far corner, grabbed a stack of papers, and then returned to her desk in the center of the room. A minute later, Deputy Kline came out from the back hallway and sidled up to the woman's desk. I couldn't hear what was said, but he must have told a joke, because the woman cackled loud like a witch.

Okay, I told myself, he's definitely here. So now I've got to get going.

I wasn't sure what time the deputy got off work, but I figured I had at least three more hours before the sheriff came in to take over.

It felt as if I had a heavy weight keeping me rooted to the spot. My nerves were jumping as my entire body trembled. I couldn't believe I was doing this. I couldn't believe I was pursuing my own investigation into the arsonist of Paper Moon. I also couldn't believe that my one and only suspect was the town's deputy. I had to see this through, no matter what the results were.

I headed back to my bike, hopped on, and rode toward Deputy Kline's place to find the evidence I needed.

It only took ten minutes to reach the two-story forest-green house on a corner lot. I stopped at the driveway and looked at the dark, empty house. I studied each house closest to the one I was about to enter illegally. I didn't spot a single light coming from any of them. I was worried that there might be a night owl currently awake, but the blackened windows told me otherwise.

I went to the side of the house and laid my bike on the grass. Again, I searched the neighborhood for any watching eyes. When I felt that my trespassing went unobserved, I scurried around back. Earlier, I hadn't thought about Deputy Kline having a dog, but now I did. I gave a light whistle that would have immediately sent any dog into a barking fit, but no four-legged beast responded.

The backyard was as dark as a cave. I hadn't given a thought to grabbing a flashlight before leaving the house. Again, I was heading into darkness, much like the time Kat and I had headed into the black woods to find her brother. The canopy of trees even obscured the moonlight. I tried to look through several windows and even the one on the back door, but the darkness prevented anything from being seen.

I checked the door and the windows within reach, but they were all locked. I remembered hearing about small towns and how the residents always felt safe enough to leave their houses unlocked at all hours of the day and night. Things had recently changed in Paper Moon. The arsonist had scared the townspeople enough that no one felt the security they once had.

Deputy Kline lacked the necessary fear to begin locking his doors. He likely began locking them long before the first blaze happened on my block. There was possibly a secret inside that he didn't want to share with anyone. If there was a secret to be had, I was going to uncover it tonight.

I had no choice. With no other option, I had to break in. I pulled a dirty, weather-beaten cushion from the lawn chair on the back porch and went to one of the basement windows. I firmly placed it against the glass. I searched the darkened backyards of the neighbors, and then I kicked hard. The cushion whiffed, and the window rattled but stayed intact. I delivered three more kicks before I heard the satisfying tinkle of glass finding concrete in the basement. It wasn't a loud sound, but to me, it equaled a marching band at halftime. I waited. No neighboring house lights flickered to life. No one yelled out questions about what was going on over here. I was in the clear.

I threw the cushion aside, kneeled, and looked in the basement cloaked in shadows. I couldn't make out anything except where the walls were and objects that could have been anything. Carefully, I pulled the remaining fragments of glass from the frame. My heart was thundering in a near-panicked rhythm. I rotated and stuck my feet inside. Slithering backwards on my belly, I let gravity slowly pull me inside. I hung there for a good long moment with my body half in and half out of the house. My feet searched for purchase on anything that would take my weight. Finding nothing to stand on, I slid inside. My arms couldn't hold me any longer. Dropping down the inside wall, I smashed my chin on the window frame hard enough to bite the tip of my tongue.

My body hit the basement floor like a sack of grain. I sat there rubbing my chin and working my tooth-stung tongue against the roof of my mouth. There was a slickness on my palm as I pulled my hand away. I had cut my chin open. How bad it was, I couldn't tell. The blood wasn't exactly flowing, but it hurt like hell. Depending on how this night turned out, I didn't know what excuse I could give Josh. *How did you cut yourself sleeping in bed?* he would ask in the morning.

The little things couldn't be worried about right now. With a mission to finish, I had to find the answers to so many questions. Mr. Reynolds needed help to be set free. I was a blind kid searching the cave for a treasure that would not bring wealth, but peace to all the land.

I decided to turn on a light. I wouldn't discover anything without a light to show me exactly what I needed to find.

I went up a dozen steps before reaching the basement door. On the wall was the switch, and I flicked it on. The basement was full of old furniture, boxes of papers, and worn-out stereos and televisions. The deputy was a man in desperate need of a yard sale or a large dumpster.

I made my way through the piles of rubble, looking left and right as I walked down the narrow paths. I was about to head upstairs when I noticed something odd. Most people wouldn't have noticed it, but I was a kid desperately searching for a secret. The basement was missing space. From what I knew of the house's size and how it sat on the lot, there was a wall where there shouldn't be one. I made my way to the other side of the room. Cheap wood paneling covered the area. Stacked boxes of old newspapers, crates of records, and tubs of musty-smelling clothes lined this side of the basement.

On the floor were marks in the dust where he had moved some of the boxes away from the wall and then put them back. There were also shoe prints walking into and away from the wall. I grabbed the edge of the bottom box and pulled. The entire thing almost toppled onto me, but my hand quickly steadied it. There was a crease where one section of paneling met another. Coming from that crease was a faint chemical smell that caused me to step back. The small whiff I had caught had scorched my nostrils.

I tried pushing on the wall, and then I tried sliding it. It wouldn't move. Then I saw a small hole at the bottom edge. I slipped my finger inside, curled it, and pulled. The wall rotated open on hidden hinges. The smell hit me like a hammer. It was a familiar smell that I remembered associating with an inferno and a black pair of uniform shoes. I knew that whatever secret hid inside this room was exactly what I'd been hoping to find. Even before I discovered the light switch to chase away the darkness, I knew the evidence in this room would uncage Mr. Reynolds and land Deputy Kline in his place.

The switch went on, and light flooded the room. It wasn't a large room, maybe only about ten by ten feet. Work benches ran along two of the walls, and stacks of notebooks and tools littered the surfaces. I opened the top journal and thumbed through the pages. The handwritten entries were a direct admission of guilt, simmering with anger that he had yet to complete his agenda. There were long rants about how justice would come full-circle to those who had wronged him one way or another. It was the writing of a man who had lost all common sense and taken a path of lunacy.

The books were an arsonist's dream collection. Filled with pages of information about how to create fire using nearly any combination of household chemicals. There were also books of bomb-making, and I shuddered when I looked through those. I knew then that Deputy Kline was nowhere near done destroying Paper Moon. He had framed Mr. Reynolds and sent the man to prison. But whatever cruelty thrived in Deputy Kline was far from satisfied. He could not put his hatred for this town to rest. I believed he was preparing to turn this wonderful town and all its people into a destruction of fire and chaos unmatched by anything previously done.

Under the benches were cabinets. I opened them one after another. The last set held the source of the hard chemical odor. Inside were gallon jugs. There were no labels on them. The deputy must have removed them to keep nosy people like me from finding out what kind of concoction he had created.

Common sense resisted, but I forced myself to uncap each bottle and take a quick whiff. The third bottle was a familiar scent. I remembered it from a night of fire, followed by hard vomiting. The smell covering Deputy Kline's shoes and the one inside this jug was the same. I was sure of it.

Something moved upstairs. I hit the light switch, killing the glow in the small workroom. The sound of a door squawking on rusty hinges, followed by squeaking floorboards from above, filled my ears.

I ran for the stairs and nearly crashed into a stack of boxes before reaching the steps. Quietly, I took each step and, reaching the door, flicked off the light. A yellow glow from the kitchen snaked under the basement door. I knew it hadn't been on before, but now I knew Deputy Kline had come home. I prayed he had only stopped by to use the bathroom. Shadows broke the glow beneath the door, two of which looked very much like a pair of shoes. Another floorboard creaked.

While I backed down the steps, the doorknob turned. I hit the landing and slinked into the blackness. Mountains of clutter bumped into my backside. I kept shifting direction until I found a wall. The door rotated open, spilling light down the steps. After a quick moment, the world went pitch-black as Deputy Kline killed the kitchen light.

The steps groaned, and then the door clicked shut. I could hear him carefully making his way downstairs.

The voice that broke the stillness nearly caused me to wet myself. It was a knowing and threatening voice.

"I bet you wonder how I knew you were here. I was doing my rounds, and, strangely enough, I saw light coming through my basement windows. I never leave the lights on. I hate wasting electricity. So, I wandered around back and peeked through my broken window. I can't say I'm surprised to see you here or that you uncovered my hidden room. You're a clever one, aren't you, Jayce?"

Shards of ice slid through my veins when I heard my name. Of course, he knew who I was when he saw me. The whole town knew me as either the hero or idiot kid who ran into a blazing house fire. But Deputy Kline knew me as the kid who took a particular interest in him. The kid who had followed him around town and spied on him through the basement window. He had probably thought his warning at my house was enough to get me to back off. But it took more than the destruction of my bike and an intimidating stare-down from the street to get me to stop my pursuit.

"I'm not blind or stupid. I realized long ago you've had your eye on me. I've seen you watching me far longer than anyone with a bit of curiosity should. I'll tell you what, why don't we play ourselves a game? If you can get by me in the dark, either through a window or the door, then I'll let you go. If you make it, I won't try to stop you from going to the sheriff. I'll give you a fighting chance to save your own life." A flashlight pointed at the ceiling clicked on and then off, on and then off. "I won't even use this to cheat. Make your way out of my basement of terrors and you've won your freedom."

Shoes moved from wood boards to concrete.

I didn't want to play any game. It was impossible to believe a man who thrived on destroying things could be held at his word.

"Smart thinking by not talking. Don't move around too much or I'll find you and—" he said, then abruptly stopped as something crashed. Stacked boxes went over like dominos. He cursed furiously as he thrashed around. He must have tripped over the tangled mess.

This was my one shot to get away. I took it. The sound of my shoes on concrete was untraceable under the noise Deputy Kline was making. The path narrowed to where I had to turn sideways to get through. I found the stairs easy enough and then the door at the top. If it was possible, my blood ran even colder than before. He had locked the deadbolt before coming down. I wrenched the knob and pressed, trying to force the lock or doorframe to give under pressure. They wouldn't.

A laugh erupted in an almost horror-movie moment. It was the sound of a maniac who had won a depraved game.

I just stood there. My mind ran over half a dozen chances that had been there moments ago, but now only one remained.

"I didn't say I couldn't cheat by locking the door. Did you really believe I would play fair? The key is right here if you want to come get it."

His voice was at the bottom of the stairs now. The boards spoke as he approached. I was a trapped animal trying to fight or flee for the sake of my own skin.

When I heard a board squeak just in front of me, my body reacted before my brain knew what was going on. My right leg came up and out in the hardest kick of my life, as if aiming for a field goal a hundred yards away. Even in the dark, my aim couldn't have been better. Deputy Kline must have been just a couple of steps below me, because I was sure my foot found his face. He offered a scream of surprise, and I heard him fall backwards, hit the stairs, and tumble to the bottom. The kick had sent a painful ripple throughout my body. I didn't have time to think about it. I seized my remaining opportunity.

I bolted down the stairs, and my foot stepped on Deputy Kline's leg. I instinctively leaped. I cleared his sprawled body but went crashing into something on the other side. I went down hard. Fear moved me. I was up and searching for the window. I knew about where it was, but not even moonlight offered assistance to show me the way out.

My sneaker kicked something that skittered across the floor. Standing on broken glass, I found the wall and looked up. Though I knew the window was somewhere above my head, my searching hands couldn't find it.

Chapter 22

Deputy Kline offered a moan of pain as I heard him push up from the bottom of the steps.

He said from the darkness, "I'm going to punish you real bad for that."

My grip found the frame of the window. I managed to get halfway up the boxes before a hand seized my left foot and pulled me back. My other foot had a hold on the wooden crates, but Deputy Kline was strong. He brought me back to the ground and the stacked crates came with me. A corner of one crate cracked me on top of the head before rolling along my backside and down my legs. A blinding pain flashed white in my eyes in the basement's darkness. I thought I was going to black out, but I fought it all the way. If I went unconscious now, Deputy Kline would guarantee that Josh would never see me again. I heard the wood crate catch him, and it must have either been from surprise or pain, but he offered a loud grunt. His grip released me.

The haze left my sight, and I fought for life. My ladder of crates was gone except for the bottom one. I crawled up it, hooked my hands in the open window frame, and began pulling myself from the house of terror.

He was cursing with wild anger as his hand was on me again. His grip was nearly hard enough to break ankle bones. I cried out in fear and pain, and then I started kicking. My sneaker hit something with a direct blow, because there was a crunch and a cry of pain that was not mine. The hand released again, and I finished scrambling out the window. Broken glass bit into my hands as I clawed my way out, but I paid no attention. I only had to focus on getting away.

When I was making a run from the house, I heard Deputy Kline crashing through the junk of his basement, followed by the thundering of footsteps going up the stairs. I was deep in the blackness of the backyard when he hammered through the rear door. The screen door flew open and slammed against the house. I found my bike where I'd left it, started pedaling, and aimed for the road. If I could quickly flag someone down for help, then maybe Deputy Kline would know his only chance now was to flee the state.

A dark figure moved to my left, and that figure had a very large grasping hand. Before he could pull me down, he slipped on the wet grass and let out a loud gush of air as the ground forced the breath from him.

I pedaled hard, telling myself not to look back. Taking my eyes away from what was in front of me could instantly cause a crash. I bounced my tires from the grass, off the curb, and onto the pavement. Making sure nothing was in front of me, I had the opportunity, and I took it. I looked over my shoulder and saw nothing except a street barely lit by outside house lights.

I flopped down on the seat and drew in slow, easy breaths. I had gotten away from the madman, the real arsonist of Paper Moon. Now I didn't know where to go from here. How could I know if Sheriff Prescott wasn't also involved? How could a sheriff be so blind and not realize that it was his own deputy burning down the buildings in town? I wasn't sure how Josh could help me. The city offices would be closed. I also didn't know where the mayor lived, so going there wasn't an option.

As I angled my bike toward Wicked Way Terrace, I heard a scream of tires on the pavement. I looked back and saw Deputy Kline's patrol car peel out of his driveway and tear off after me. I forced all my weight down on the pedals but instantly knew I had no chance of outrunning anything with an engine. I moved onto the nearest driveway and cut through the yard and then another yard until I reached the next block. I heard tires bark again, taking a corner as Deputy Kline tried to cut me off. I went through yard after yard, block after block, and even doubled back, trying to throw him off my trail. In the distance, I heard the engine racing down a street as he desperately tried to find me.

I didn't think the neighbors would give it much thought, looking out windows with sleepy eyes, only figuring Deputy Kline was heading off somewhere to the rescue. Only tonight he was truly attempting to silence a fourteen-year-old boy forever.

After fifteen minutes of constantly changing directions and then hiding in bushes, I set my sights on Kat's place. As I rolled up to her house, I felt very confused to find her outside in the dark, sitting on her bike as if awaiting my arrival.

"How is it possible they already released you from the hospital? You just had surgery a couple of days ago," I said. I couldn't help smiling despite the terror following me.

"Nearly good as new. It wasn't as bad as everyone made it out to be. Just a little banged up is all. I'm a tough girl and you know it," she said and offered a smile I rarely saw.

"Well, that certainly is good. You should be inside resting, though."

"Naw. I was for a while, but something told me I needed to come outside, and now here you are. Are you in some kind of trouble again?"

"The worst kind. The real arsonist is Deputy Kline. I have the proof, but I don't know who I can trust."

"Well then, we'll figure it out together."

I heard the revving engine several blocks away coming toward us. It was as if Deputy Kline had a tracking device on me and nowhere was safe.

"I've got an idea if you're up for it," I said.

"So, you trust me to go along with this?"

"All the way," I told her. "We have to keep him on our tail, but not close enough to catch us."

"Show me what you've got in mind. I'm up for one final adventure."

We pedaled into the darkness of Broken Bow Lane. As I looked over my shoulder, the patrol car took a corner so quickly it went into a sideways slide and nearly ended up in someone's yard. Deputy Kline hammered the gas as his headlights captured us.

"He sees us. Quick, cut through this yard," I said.

Kat and I jumped the curb, shot through the side yard, and nearly crashed right into a large sleeping dog. Our yelling and skidding on the grass woke the thing. Even sleepy-eyed, the dog was ready to attack any intruders. It released a series of ferocious barks and pulled itself all the way to the end of its chain, trying to snag us.

We made it through to the next block, and from that point, we were sure to hold Deputy Kline's attention.

Kat grinned as we pedaled for Gator Alley Way. She said, "Now I'm starting to get part of your plan. You've got some meanness in you, Graham Cracker."

I guess I did. Of course, my meanness didn't compare to the man nipping at our heels. I had thought of giving the man a taste of what it was like to be a victim, a person who had no control over what happened next. I just hoped I didn't get Kat, or myself, killed in the process of exacting justice.

As we turned down the gravel road, the streetlights disappeared, but our journey toward Grady's was brightly lit by the headlights of the chasing car.

Kat was puffing hard, her body sluggish at fighting the pedals.

"Are you all right?" I asked, worried that she still had a long road to recovery.

"Doing fine. We're here." She got off her bike and let it fall to the ground.

Grady's place had a taste of wonderful magic in the daytime, but at night, it was an eerie, secluded cove of trees and buildings. There were noises of birds, deep-throated groans of alligators, and many other animal sounds I instantly identified.

I dropped my bike on top of Kat's, and we ran to the front entrance. I moved a potted plant beside the front door and took the key that was hidden beneath. I unlocked the door. Moving inside, I purposely left the door open for Deputy Kline to follow.

Behind us, the cruiser came to a grinding halt in the driveway, and the vehicle door flew open. As Kat and I moved through the entrance and passed the gift shop, there were quick feet on the gravel outside. At the front door, Deputy Kline's flashlight clicked on. The beam scanned the interior, trying to find two kids evading the hand of a crooked lawman.

We hunkered down and slinked along the wall of various dimly lit snake cages.

"You can't keep running. You know I'll eventually find you," Deputy Kline said as he moved inside.

Every few steps, he paused and listened. He was waiting for us to give ourselves away with a loud noise. Every time he paused, we paused. It was like the slowest police chase in history.

"You know, it didn't have to come to this if you had just kept out of my business. I'm not sure who the hell you think you are, breaking into a police officer's home, but you've got yourself in a serious spot of trouble now. I'm sure going to hate to do it, but you do understand I'm probably going to have to make you disappear permanently. I can't have people asking me questions about those fires and poking around my house. You should understand that I won't let them take me to prison. A police officer has no place in prison with criminals. That's why you need to step out and we'll end this thing now."

Kat tapped me on the shoulder. I looked at her and she pointed to a door off to our left, which was Grady's apartment. I started to head in that direction, but Kat held me back. I looked at her with questioning eyes. She then pointed to a small ceramic statue of a red and blue macaw sitting on a pedestal. She made a motion for me to pick it up and throw it across the room. Again, I gave her questioning eyes. She only nodded.

So, I did. I grabbed the statue when Deputy Kline searched the area to his right. I tossed it fifteen feet from our position. It made a jarring crash when ceramic met stone flooring. Deputy Kline was at the spot in a heartbeat. His flashlight studied the fragments.

The apartment door suddenly burst open, and a large man with a metal baseball bat filled the doorway. The crash had woken Grady, a man who stood at six and a half feet tall and strong enough to wrestle full-sized gators.

Instantly, he had snagged a weapon and was ready to bust someone's head for disrupting his sleep.

Deputy Kline whirled around to face the owner.

"You might want to get that light out of my eyes if you know what's good for you," Grady told him as he walked to the unknown man.

"Sorry about that," Deputy Kline said as he lowered the flashlight beam. "Didn't mean to alarm you. It's Deputy Kline."

"None of that explains why you broke into my place of business."

"No, I didn't. I was making a routine drive-by and saw the front door open. I wasn't aware you slept here."

"I live here. I've got my own apartment in the back. The door was open, you say?"

"Yes, sir. Thought I'd come check it out in case someone was up to no good."

When Grady took another step, he spotted us crouched behind a large iguana cage. He did a wonderful job of only making a passing glance and showing no hints that he saw something that wasn't supposed to be there.

Grady walked casually toward Deputy Kline. "Did you happen to notice your face is leaking blood? You should also know that I have excellent hearing. Before the crashing sound, your yammering woke me. I heard you mention something about making someone disappear, as well as the fires and possibly incriminating evidence found in your house. Would you have been referring to the arsonist who destroyed about ten buildings around town?"

Grady was now so close he could have swung the bat and knocked Deputy Kline's head right out of the park. I saw Deputy Kline rest his palm on the butt of his firearm, which sat in its holster.

"Who exactly are you chasing and why? I know you didn't just happen by on a routine check and see the door open. You see, my place of business is not within the town limits. I also have never seen a police officer in my neck of the woods. In fact, I called the sheriff three months ago about an unruly customer who kept throwing garbage at my animals. The man put up a fight when I went to throw him out. The sheriff, your boss, said that my business was not in his jurisdiction and that I needed to call the state patrol if I had a problem. So, I ask again, who are you chasing and why?"

"Well, I—" Deputy Kline began, but he must have decided he was all out of excuses. The gun came free from its holster just like that. He was as fast as an Old West gunfighter, but Grady was a dash quicker.

Grady snagged the hand holding the gun, forced its lethal end away from him, and used his other arm to bring the bat around. Deputy Kline saw this coming and started to pull his head back, but he wasn't fast enough. The metal bat caught him with a glancing blow off his skull. I heard it, and it reminded me of every ballpark I'd ever been to. It wasn't an out-of-the-park hit, but a bunt. Deputy Kline still grunted in pain as he fought to get the gun loose from Grady's giant hand.

The two went to the ground, and I knew it was over, because Grady was a man who took no crap from even the largest gators the Everglades could produce. When the gunshot rang out, I heard Grady grunt in pain and perhaps a bit of fear as the situation instantly took a terrible turn. In the wide flashlight beam, I saw a growing crimson spread across Grady's right shoulder.

Deputy Kline wormed out from beneath the big man, cocked his gun arm back, and delivered a skull-cracking blow to the side of Grady's face.

"I'll deal with you later," he said as he tried to catch his breath.

I looked at Kat. We didn't have to say anything. We knew we had to get out of this situation fast. At first, we tried it quietly, but the flashlight found us in seconds. We bolted for the sake of our skin. I pointed to the right, and Kat kept in that direction. I was going to keep on track of my original plan. If it was going to work, I didn't know, but it was the only plan to reach my thoughts at this hectic moment.

As we stepped up to the double doors at the rear, I opened the drawer of a small table and retrieved a ring of keys. The only light offered was the moon, and in that pale beam, I found the correct key.

"Better hurry. He's coming fast," Kat whispered.

I slid the key in and turned. Stumbling footsteps, unfamiliar with the layout of the building, maneuvered behind us. I pushed Kat through and followed. Here came the final stop of my oddly designed plan. We ran down the concrete path, making enough noise to wake all the animals resting in their cages. It could have been mistaken for the sounds of the jungle when the majestic birds from half a world away began cawing at each other.

I saw the wavering flashlight as Deputy Kline studied each cage he passed. As we reached our destination, I looked at Kat. She smiled and nodded, giving me the go-ahead. I unclasped the lock, put it in my pocket, and swung the gate all the way open. Next, Kat and I ran around the cage to the rear. We waited, and we waited. I thought maybe we had gotten too far ahead, and I was worried that Deputy Kline had gotten lost somewhere on the other side of the property, but then I spotted him. His steps switched from cautious to desperate as the flashlight barely cut through the darkness. He paused when the light found the open gate.

When he began turning around to go another way, I said in a low voice, "Shh, he's right there."

He stopped and faced the cage again. I thought I saw a smile forming. Unsnapping the strap and pulling his gun, he walked inside the cage. The light moved across all corners of the cage, trying to find us.

"Get down, get down," I said in an urgent whisper.

Deputy Kline had his sights on my voice. Like a shot from a cannon, he ran at us. Then things went terribly wrong. The solid ground gave out to a patch of slick moss, causing his feet to slide. The rest of him wobbled for balance as he fell toward the small body of water. The flashlight disappeared underwater, so I didn't see it, but I heard it. His body slapped the concrete, resulting in a yelp and then a splash.

I grabbed Kat, and we quickly rounded the cage to the front. I had the padlock out. When the gate slammed shut, the lock clicked in place.

"Where is it?" he said as he thrashed around in the water. "Where is it?"

I knew what he was looking for. He had lost grip of his gun while going down into that slimy water. Now he searched for it with desperation so that he might be able to shoot our brains out before we could make a getaway. Or at least shoot the lock off so that he could get out.

"You've got something more important to worry about," I told him.

"Don't you dare leave. When I find my gun, I'm gonna—" And that was the moment he noticed the low, vibrating sound.

It was a sound that nearly iced my blood the first time I'd heard it. I knew all about the terror that could follow such a sound. Deputy Kline was having his first close encounter with a species so perfectly evolved that they had been virtually unchanged since the days of the dinosaurs.

"What's that?" he asked. I figured it was a question he asked himself more than us.

"I'd like you to meet the Flintstones," I said.

"And Frank," Kat reminded me.

"Oh, yeah, and Frank." I don't know how I could have forgotten the monster that had tried to swallow me whole in the deepness of the Everglades.

In the moonlight, I saw four large shadows with glowing eyes slip like melted butter from dry land and into the water.

Deputy Kline must have quickly realized exactly what kind of cage we'd confined him in. He sprang like a gazelle trying to avoid the teeth of a lion. He backed up, all the time keeping his eyes fixed on the silhouettes illuminated by the underwater flashlight. His back reached the metal cage, and he could go no farther.

The Flintstones and Frank popped up to eye level. Now the funny thing about this situation was that Kat and I knew the family of large reptiles wasn't really interested in feeding on Deputy Kline. Of course, I wasn't too sure about Frank. He still had a touch of the wild in him. But I didn't think they desired to work for food anymore. Inside their tiny reptilian minds, they believed it was time for a chicken meal. However, Deputy Kline knew none of this. His anxiety and terror were right where they were supposed to be, at the forefront of survival mode.

"Get me the hell out of here. Are you trying to kill me?" he pleaded, but his unfortunate pleas fell on deaf ears. I had no pity for him, because he deserved much worse than this for all the mayhem he had caused.

"You all right out here, Jayce?" Grady called from the pathway.

I looked at Kat. She winked and said, "You did a fine job, Jayce. I'm proud of you seeing it through. The people of town are going to be proud of what you've done here."

Then Kat wrapped her arms around me in a rib-cracking hug and let me go.

"Yes, sir. We're just fine as wine," I told Grady.

"We?" he asked. The flashlight's beam found Deputy Kline in the cage. "Oh, you and your friend here?" He couldn't help but laugh at the terror-stricken look on the deputy's face.

This laugh must have triggered something in the Flintstones and Frank. All at once, they pushed from the mossy water and crawled toward Deputy Kline. I had never seen a man move so quickly. He gripped the metal framing and the fence and scrambled up to the highest corner and wedged himself there. His boots, the same boots I had first smelled the odor of homemade napalm on, found a hold on the horizontal crossbar. He poked his fingers through the fence links for an added hold.

"Are you going to be all right?" I asked Grady as I looked at the thin trail of blood coming from his head and the bloom of red spreading across his shoulder.

"It's going to take far more than that to knock me out of the game," he said.

"I think we need to call the sheriff. Maybe even the county sheriff."

"What I need to do is fix my head and shoulder."

"You need a hospital."

"I won't be going to any hospital. I can fix myself up far better than any doctor."

"What about him?"

"How about we let him hang around here for a while before we make any phone calls?"

Grady turned and started walking back to the main building.

I turned to Kat and said, "Come—" but I was speaking to emptiness.

I spun around, trying to figure out where she had gone.

Grady stopped. Looking back, he said, "Is something wrong?"

"Where did she go?"

"Who?"

"Kat. She was here with me."

"She was? Was she hiding somewhere else inside?"

"No. No, she had been hiding right beside me."

He raised an eyebrow in confusion. "I didn't know she was already discharged from the hospital. Well, okay then. I suppose she'll be along soon," he said and turned to go inside.

I gave another glance around. Kat was simply gone. Deputy Kline remained tightly cradled in the upper corner of the cage until someone decided to let him out.

With my best effort, I helped Grady. His wounded shoulder needed immediate mending, so we headed into the back room that had become Grady's apartment. I thought I might vomit, pass out, or both when he worked a long pair of tweezers deep into the oozing hole of his shoulder. He fished around for a bit with the pointed ends and finally found the slug. Gently, he got a grip on it and worked it free with an effort, followed by a slew of hissing bad words. He dropped the slug in a ceramic mug sporting a painted pit viper on its side. It made a *tink* as it disappeared into the sludge-colored coffee and found the bottom.

I turned my sight from the blood trickling out of the hole and tried to focus on patching up his head wound.

Grady eventually got around to calling Sheriff Prescott. The news about his deputy gave him motive to rush right out. The county sheriff, Marcus Bristow, said he had another matter that needed attention first, and then he'd be out as soon as he could get away.

We went out front to wait. As I sat on the front steps, I saw Kat's bike was gone. I recalled how my bike had fallen on top of hers as we ran for the front door. It seemed as if my bike hadn't even moved when she retrieved her bike to leave, and that, in itself, was a strange thing.

Chapter 23

Sheriff Prescott had reached the reserve in record time. He clicked his tongue in amazement as he looked at his deputy pinned in an uncomfortable position inside the gator cage. The Flintstones and Frank were still waiting in close quarters, expecting something to eat. Deputy Kline pleaded to the sheriff to let him out, but Sheriff Prescott told him to hush as Grady and I explained the events of the night.

I told my story of how I had long ago come to suspect Deputy Kline. I looked at the floor as I explained about illegally entering Deputy Kline's home through a rear window and finding the secret room in the basement.

Grady then told his account of overhearing Deputy Kline speaking to me and confessing his plan to burn down Paper Moon one structure at a time.

"Sounds to me as if you got yourself in a tremendous pickle, Tom," Sheriff Prescott said. "Arson, attempted murder on multiple counts, and whatever else I care to ink into my report. I suppose we need to go see the judge in Coral Key and get a search warrant to find all this stuff the young man has mentioned. Come on, you two."

The three of us began walking back to the main building. Deputy Kline started howling about the injustice of being left to such torture. He claimed he would have

Sheriff Prescott fired and he would sue the department over the pain and suffering and indignity of it all.

Sheriff Prescott stopped and said, "Well, as you think about all that, I also want you to think about the vile, inhuman things you've done over the last four months. I want you to think about those families whose homes you destroyed and the lives you nearly took. Think about the businesses you burned, taking away the livelihood of several residents. Then I want you to take a good, long look at the person inside and ask yourself if this is who you really are. I'm going to give you a bit of time to consider all that. By the time I get the search warrant and find the evidence inside your house, I'll grab some coffee and some breakfast, and maybe by then you'll have come to terms with the terrible things you've done. Only at that point will I let you out."

"I can't hold on much longer. My fingers are numb and I'm going to fall."

Grady smiled and said, "If you want to live, you'll hang on. If you can't anymore, then exercise your legs by going in circles around the pond when they come skittering after you."

An hour later, Judge Roy Weaver listened to Sheriff Prescott's accounts. The judge happily issued a search warrant. Deputy Kline's house was now accessible to the authorities of Collier County. I had told Sheriff Prescott where to look in the basement, but the sheriff told me not to worry about it, because all of Deputy Kline's possessions were going to have a serious inspection. I anticipated that once the sheriff and the other patrolmen were done, there would be no secrets remaining in Deputy Kline's life.

I could have gone home, but I wanted to wait and see how this all played out. I wanted to tell Kat everything she hadn't witnessed after she vanished the way she did. I didn't know what had spooked her. We had Deputy Kline locked inside the gator cage, and the police were soon on their way. I thought that maybe the idea of her father discovering she'd snuck out at night had given her a panic attack, much like her brother often suffered.

It had been a long night, and Grady urged me many times to go home and get some rest. I wasn't sure if I was going to attempt a day at school with such a depleted mind. I wanted to see if Kat was going to manage a school day. I needed to know why she had disappeared.

I needed to call Josh. I was about to ask Grady if I could use his phone when Sheriff Prescott's car traveled down the gravel road.

The sheriff slowly got out of the car as if this move pained him. He looked defeated, and maybe a little astonished at what he had discovered about his deputy of three years. The truth is that you can never really know a person through and through. Sometimes the true nature of a person hides deep inside until it's ready to find the surface and cause whatever mayhem it desires.

"Well?" Grady asked.

"It's just as Jayce said. We found pictures of all the houses and businesses hanging on the wall. Pictures before and after they burned. Some of the buildings were ones he luckily hadn't yet set to blaze. We also found a notebook filled with a list of people who had wronged him in some manner or another. There were pages of rants about how he was going to get even with all these people. Now, I think once this all goes to trial, and it will, he would be able to claim he was just interested in photography and just happened to take pictures of the houses that burned. His lawyer would claim a coincidence that those same houses caught on fire. I suppose the lawyer would also say that the booklets were nothing more than a man venting his frustration. The lawyer would say that everyone holds a grudge and gets angered by other people, but that doesn't make his client an arsonist who nearly murdered several people. Sure, that all could be true. Then the lawyer would say you've already got the arsonist in custody," Sheriff Prescott said and sat down on the step beside me.

"But the man attempted to kill me. Surely you can get him on that," Grady said.

"Oh, sure we will. But you haven't let me get to the good part yet. You see, thanks to our young detective friend here, we found the iron-clad evidence we really needed to lock this thing down. No matter what kind of hot-shot lawyer Thomas gets, we've got him in a death pinch. If it hadn't been for Jayce finding that hidden room, we might have overlooked it entirely. It was a clever spot to hide the stash of chemicals he used to set those fires. Basically, the mixture is napalm. Fighting those fires did no good with the hoses. You can't extinguish napalm with water. It burns until it has burned itself out. That's why we couldn't save any structures. Now, I'm positive the lab boys in Coral Key are going to come back and say the chemical mixture found in his house exactly matches the unburned samples taken from each crime scene. What we have is the real arsonist. I feel a great deal stupid over all this. I'm going to take a lot of heat from the residents that the criminal we were looking for the entire time was right there under my supervision. They might claim that I either had something to do with those fires or that I'm simply incompetent. And you know what? They're right about that last part. I feel like the biggest fool ever to walk the planet. I was too blind to see what was right in front of me."

"You couldn't have known," I said. "He hid it well. None of the town's residents suspected him. So why should you?"

"It's my job to know, to figure it out. I'm supposed to suspect everyone. You figured it out, Jayce, and you are brand new to this town. I didn't uncover any of it."

"Only because after the first fire, when I ran out of the house, I puked on his shoes. I smelled that strange odor. It was the homemade mixture he'd made that must have spilled on his shoes when he poured it around the McCreadys' home. Of course, I didn't know it at the time until I smelled it in his basement. There were a couple of other things that started to make me suspicious as well," I told Sheriff Prescott.

"You should be a detective when you get old enough," Grady said. "You've got a knack for figuring things out."

"Well, what do you say we head on back and see if our prisoner is still alive or became tiny bits?" Sheriff Prescott asked and laughed at his own question.

"I figure the man wants to live, so I'll bet you a donut he's still clinging to those bars trying to stay alive," Grady said.

As it turned out, Grady was right. Deputy Kline was still pulled tightly into the top corner of the enclosure. I figured his body was a mass of cramped muscles that pleaded to stretch out. I could see his fingers had started to bleed some, as his fierce grip on the cage hadn't lessened in several hours. I didn't pity him any for his temporary pain.

"Well, I think that's a view you better get used to, Tom. A view through bars is going to be all you get for a long, long while. It seems we uncovered everything we needed to find," Sheriff Prescott told the caged man.

The look Deputy Kline offered us was one of pure exhaustion. The fight had seeped from him. I think he wanted nothing more than to climb down and find a comfortable seat in the back of Sheriff Prescott's squad car.

"Please, just please get me out of here. I'll tell you whatever you want to hear. I can't hang on any longer."

Sheriff Prescott hooked his thumbs into his belt and clicked his tongue a few times. "I sure wish I could do that, but I want to know a few things first. We found your notebooks with resident names and addresses of the houses you burned and the ones you had yet to torch. Just tell us why you targeted those people. Why would you burn away everything they owned, nearly killing several of them in the process?"

"Because they deserved it, that's why. None of those people were ever nice to me. Never once did they show a moment of kindness. Why don't you ask every one of them how they treated me in school? Ask Susan McCready how she laughed in my face when I asked her to prom. That's right. She laughed at me in the hallway in front of dozens of people. When they were young, those people were mean, hateful souls. But I finally got them back. I showed them who's laughing now. I gave them exactly what they deserved. It just took a little time is all," he said, and spat at us through the bars.

"What about Nelson Reynolds? Why frame him for your destruction?"

"You know, when he came to town in my senior year, he took everything from me. His stupid charm, good looks, and athletic abilities stole away my high-school sweetheart. He also stole my popularity, and he replaced me as quarterback. He got me pushed out of the group of popular kids, and I became another unknown and unwanted student during the last year that was supposed to be my biggest triumph before school ended."

Sheriff Prescott slowly shook his head. "It's hard to believe the citizens paid you to protect this town, and all the while you were trying to destroy it. I'm ashamed that I was too blind to see your cruelty. Well, the way I figure it, the judge and jury will give you ample time to consider all your wrongdoings. You might very well spend the rest of your days looking outside at that same dull prison view. I don't feel sorry for you. How could I?"

Sheriff Prescott gave Grady a nod. Grady fished in his pants for the keys I'd given him, and he released the lock. The Flintstones and Frank shifted their attention to us. Without fear or worry, Grady walked past them, and with his good arm, he grabbed Deputy Kline by the belt and yanked him off the cage wall. He collapsed on the concrete and began whimpering.

"Better get on your feet unless you want your face to become the snack they've been waiting for. I won't stop them from tearing you apart, because I think you at least deserve that much," Grady said.

When Deputy Kline saw the gators creeping forward, he was instantly on his feet. Like a coward, he used Grady as a shield. He then saw a small opportunity and made a sprint to the open door but came face-to-barrel with the sheriff's sidearm.

"I'm gonna ask you really nice to turn around and place your hands behind your back. I will not ask twice," Sheriff Prescott said.

I thought that the sheriff was somewhat hoping for a bit of resistance. I could see he had a lot of anger bottled up, and if Deputy Kline resisted arrest, it would uncork that bottle. The deputy would be taking a ride to prison with a lot more pain than he currently experienced.

Deputy Kline did exactly as he was told as he slid into the backseat of the sheriff's car.

"Well, I'll be in touch later today, Jayce. I'll just come to your house and get any information I need for my report. Do you figure you're gonna head to school today?"

I said I was.

"That's fine then. I'll be over about five o'clock if that suits you." He started to walk to the patrol car when he stopped and turned. "I hope you understand that you're in a bit of trouble for your illegal entry into Deputy Kline's house. I'm not gonna be able to hide that from the judge. One way or another, you're gonna have to pay the piper for kicking in his window and going through his personal stuff without permission."

"Yes, sir. I understand," I said.

"It'll be the lightest sentence ever handed out. Probably a dozen hours of community service cleaning up the roadsides."

"Thank you," I told him as he moved down the gravel road.

Just like Rory Evans had, Deputy Kline watched me through the patrol car's window. I thought that if looks really could kill, I'd be a standing corpse. I never did worry about him coming after me, because he had a very long time until he got the scent of freedom again, if ever at all.

Grady looked at me and said, "How about breakfast? I make a mean Cajun omelet."

"No, thank you. I should be getting home. If Josh is awake, he's going to be freaking out that I'm not in my room. I've got a bit of a story to tell him."

"I suspect you do. Well, don't bother coming to work today. You deserve a day of rest. I'll see you on Saturday instead."

I thanked him, got on my bike, and peddled for home.

I didn't want to climb the tree to sneak back into my bedroom. I was too tired and sore. The effort would have been pointless, anyway. Looking through the front window, I saw Josh making breakfast. I knocked on the front door. Josh wore no expression of surprise when he unlocked the door to find me standing there.

"I went to your room to get you up. I figured you were up to no good when I saw the decoy pillows under the sheet and the window partially open. I honestly don't know what to do with you. Are you trying to drive me insane? Do I deserve any of this stressful crap from you?" he asked in a voice completely deflated.

I held up my hand and said, "Wait, just hear me out first."

He waited and listened. He was really good at that. I spent the next twenty minutes explaining my actions. His expression constantly changed, from anger, when I had broken into Deputy Kline's house, and then to fear, as I biked for my life from the deputy. He even offered a small smile when I told him about locking the arsonist in a cage full of hungry gators.

"So, you trapped him in a cage the entire night?" he asked.

"For a few hours at least. He held onto that cage for so long that his fingers even became bloodied."

Josh shook his head and said, "Is there just something in you that craves chaos? Don't you know how to live a normal boyhood life?"

I shrugged. "I don't think it's craving chaos but correcting it. Any trouble I've gotten into since being here was putting things back to where they should be."

After he thought about it, he nodded. "I guess you're right about that. Mom and Dad would be a nervous wreck if they were still alive. You're a complicated kid with too much curiosity. Lucky for you, I'm a reasonable person. I'm also aware that you can take care of yourself. But going after a cop who was also an arsonist and nearly a murderer is something entirely different. You could have got yourself killed. If he had caught up with you, he could have dumped you out in the middle of the Everglades and no one would have ever known what happened to you. I swear you're trying to push me into an early grave."

"Well, I'm here now and I'm all right. Just like you, I'm hoping this is the last of my adventures."

As it turned out, I had one more adventure in me. It was the hardest one of my life. It nearly broke me in mind and soul.

I did go to school that morning. The funny thing about a small town was that word traveled like a lightning bolt through God's telephone. If there are any secrets in town, a single person keeps them because once they mutter it to another, the entire community knew about it before breakfast. Even though the incident with Deputy Kline had only happened a couple of hours before, the school was buzzing with rumors.

My ears had picked up varying accounts of the night's events. I overheard one girl tell a group that Deputy Kline had decided he wasn't going to prison without a fight. Apparently, he had a shootout with the police and ended up with more than twenty holes in him before falling to the ground and giving up the ghost.

I heard one student tell another at an open locker that the deputy had high-tailed it deep into the Everglades, where he was building a cabin and planning to live off the land and dared anyone to come after him. Anyone determined to stop off on his patch of land would get a rear end full of birdshot.

And so on, and so on. I wanted to tell them that Deputy Kline wasn't so brave or smart. He had got himself in a major jam, and then cried like a baby until we let him out. It amazed me that everyone was trying to build up Deputy Kline's reputation as some sort of superstar, or even a hero. He was none of those things. He was a coward, plain and simple. He destroyed whatever he wanted and didn't care who got hurt or killed during his quest.

Rumors bothered me. So, I set the record straight with everyone I could during breaks between class and during lunch. Despite my story, most of them called me a liar. They said I couldn't have been there, because I would have been asleep in bed when all this went down. They said I was just looking for more attention, because the residents had deemed me a hero when I went into that fire and now I had a strong taste for celebrity status. I gave up telling the truth. Sheriff Prescott must have kept his mouth shut about all those involved. That was all right; the true story would eventually come out, and maybe I would get a few apologies for being titled a liar.

I focused on something else. I had been looking for Kat since the first bell but hadn't found her or Anderson. Since she had been feeling better last night, I figured she would be at school. I asked many of my classmates if they had spotted her during the day. Most of them gave me a perplexed answer, stating they didn't know she was out of the hospital and feeling well enough for classes.

I sat through my classes with only half of my attention clinging to what each teacher said. At about 2:30, a half-hour before the final bell rang, the speaker over the chalkboard buzzed to life. Principal Swann cleared his throat and asked for the attention of the students as well as the faculty. He had a special announcement for all. I didn't quite understand what he was saying, his voice a dull hum in my ears as the minutes ticked away on the clock above the door.

When the principal finished, the speaker fell silent. I looked around. My algebra teacher, Mrs. Scott, wiped away tears from her cheeks. She sat at her desk and stared at the wood surface with such intensity. Tracy Willis buried her head in her arms. I saw her body hitch, as if trying to get a breath. George Nevins, who sat behind me, gently patted my back in a display of friendship I didn't know we shared. I simply couldn't understand what was with everyone. Hadn't they heard the same dull buzz coming from the speakers? Had they read something in that electrical humming that I had missed?

When the final bell rang, I left school and headed for my bike. Several students and teachers stopped me to say how sorry they were. I only shrugged at each of them, not understanding a thing they were trying to get across to me.

I'd decided not to head directly home. I wanted to stop by Kat's house and find out why she and Anderson hadn't bothered coming to school. I also wanted to ask her why she left me behind last night when I needed her to confirm the car chase fiasco to Sheriff Prescott.

I dropped my bike on the grass and ran up the sagging front porch. I pushed the bell twice and then hammered a fist on the window. I waited several minutes, but no one answered. I went around back and peered through the kitchen window. The lights were out. I knocked on the back door as well but was still left standing alone.

I thought of asking a neighbor if they had seen the Mossgrove family but decided I didn't want to disturb anyone.

So, I got back on my bike and headed for home.

Chapter 24

"It's never a good sign when you get home before me," I said as I dropped my backpack on the table.

Josh was intently watching the wall. I actually startled him when my bag hit the table's surface. His mind reeled him back to here and now.

He stood and slowly came over to me. Wordlessly, his arms wrapped around me and held me there for a good, long minute.

"I'm so very sorry. Your friend Anderson called me again at work. He said they made an announcement at school."

"Huh? There was an announcement, but the speaker buzzed and clicked so bad I couldn't understand a bit of it."

His head cocked a little as he tried to understand.

"Oh. But your other classmates must have said something. Or maybe your teachers offered condolences. They all knew how close you were. So, the whole thing that happened last night with Deputy Kline, why did you include Kat in your story?"

"What are you talking about?"

"Jayce, Kat passed away early this morning. She wasn't with you when the deputy chased you down. She never even left the hospital. I need you to understand that."

I shook my head. "No, that's a lie, Josh. She was sitting on her bike outside of her house. It's like she was waiting for me."

"I need you to think about what you just said. Why would she be outside? Why would she even be out of the hospital after major surgery? She wouldn't. You know she wasn't there."

Josh cupped the back of my neck and pressed his forehead to mine.

Sure. I'm up for one last adventure.

Kat had said those words to me when I told her about Deputy Kline chasing me down. She had come with me to Grady's. I was sure of it.

"That doesn't make any sense."

"I think it does. Jayce, you were scared. A man was trying to catch and kill you so he could keep his secret. You needed a friend at that moment. So, your mind wanted to believe so much that she was there to help. There isn't any other explanation."

One last adventure.

"If it's true, then what time did she die?"

"Anderson said his father woke him about four in the morning. They've been sleeping in chairs in her room. He said she had just passed as the nurses and doctor came rushing into the room because the monitors notified them something was wrong."

But I was sure of it. Kat had that adventure with me. The last one. Around four in the morning. That was before I'd found her on her bike, a grin covering her face and one last adventure in her heart. It was right before we slinked from yard to yard evading Deputy Kline but also keeping him close. It was just before Grady stepped from his apartment and saw us crouched behind a display. It was right when she hugged me and said what a brave thing I had done and how proud the people of town would be.

Then she was gone.

I don't remember much of what happened after I left the dining room table. I woke up during the night. My head was heavy with sleep as I lay in bed and stared at the ceiling. I wanted my mind to shut down. I wanted to stop the intrusion of thoughts that I hoped couldn't be true but knew in my heart they were.

School confirmed it all. Kat had stepped from this place, this precious jewel of a town, and began new travels. She stepped into a realm I could not follow at this point in time. She became a sole traveler searching for more adventures, all the while leaving us behind.

I didn't take a lunch break with the rest of my grieving classmates. Instead, I stepped off the property to the south and walked into the woods to be alone, a place where my sadness could be a private thing.

I don't remember much else about the following three days. Life had become a blur, and the voices of my teachers were muted. They had nothing important to teach anyway, because life would throw you into a tailspin whenever it wanted. Nothing about this world was ever under our control. So, what was the point of fighting it?

The sadness morphed into an anger that welled inside me on Saturday as Josh and I got dressed in the nicest clothes in our closets.

A cold rain had started by the time Josh and I went out the front door. The blackened sky showed no signs of letting up. We slid into the rust bucket and headed for the funeral home.

"I don't understand why they call it a wake," I said. I'm not sure if I was really looking for an answer, but the uncomfortable silence in the truck was driving me mad.

"It's about keeping watch over the deceased to ward off evil spirits," Josh said without taking his eyes from the road. "That's what Grandpa told me after Mom and Dad passed. Of course, we didn't have a wake for them, since we never found them. Maybe he thought it was easier for me to believe I was watching over them during their funeral service."

I didn't think it was easier to think that way. Kat was dead. She wasn't coming back from whatever place came after this.

"It doesn't change anything. Just like Mom and Dad, she left when things started getting good. Kat gave up the fight because it was the easier thing to do," I shouted and punched the metal dashboard.

A sizzling bolt of lightning ran up from my fist to my shoulder. I opened and closed my hand and then massaged the throbbing knuckles.

Josh turned his sight from the road and offered a look that I figured was one of pity. He angled the truck toward the shoulder of the road, flicked on the flashers and then the dome light. His expression was gentle. I was sure he was searching for comforting words to ease my anger.

"Do we have a flat or something?" I asked.

"No. The truck is fine. I want to tell you something that you deserve to know. You're old enough now to understand. I couldn't tell you before because you were too young. I don't think back then you could have wrapped your mind around it."

I had no idea where Josh was going with his suddenly intense conversation. It made me feel a little aggravated. I wanted to get to the funeral home and get this horrible day over with.

"Just spit it out," I said with more venom than I intended.

"All right. I told Mom and Dad they should go on that sailing trip."

"What?"

"Jayce, Mom had terminal cancer."

All I could do was just stare at him.

"That's a lie."

"No, it isn't. Mom was always talking about the places she wanted to visit. She said that when we grew up and moved away, they planned to do extensive traveling if they could save up the money. They married young and never even had enough money to take a honeymoon. Then when we found out Mom was sick and there was no chance of her getting better, I told them that they should take the honeymoon they never got while Mom was well enough to travel. It took a week to convince them to do this last important thing together. Mom said the thing she always wanted to do the most was sail away across the Atlantic, land somewhere in Europe, stay awhile, and come back home to us."

"So, you're the reason they were sailing across the ocean? You're the reason—"

I couldn't finish what I was about to say, but I didn't have to, because Josh finished it for me.

"Yeah, I'm the reason they're dead, Jayce. Mom and Dad left because I convinced them to go off and live that dream. If I had just kept my mouth shut, Mom could have spent the rest of her time with us, and Dad would still be here. You can hate me if you want. I wouldn't blame you. I think I hate myself enough for both of us. There isn't a day that goes by that I wish I could go back and stop myself from saying anything. But I can't. Mom and Dad are gone, but I'm still here. I'm all you've got, and you're all I've got. Maybe it doesn't seem like much right now, but it's more than some people ever get."

"I can't imagine what it's like to live knowing that because you wanted her to be happy and talked her into doing that one thing, it caused them to die," I said.

I knew exactly how that sounded. It sounded as if I were laying all the blame on Josh. Maybe I was, because I needed someone to blame for the fact that my parents were long gone. Years had passed and now I hardly remembered anything about them. Not only was time forever lost between us, but now I lived with the person who had brought on the tragedy.

I wanted to hate him. I wanted to step out of the car and walk to the funeral home in the rain because it seemed more pleasant than sitting here with him, listening to him feeling sorry for himself and expecting me to feel the same way.

"Why would you wait so long to tell me the truth?"

"I never lied to you, Jayce. I just never told you the whole story. I figured you'd hate my guts and run away in the middle of the night or something more drastic. You're all I have," he said again.

I looked out the window. All I could see were house lights through the falling rain.

"Answer me one thing, and I want you to be honest."

"I've always been honest with you," he said.

"Okay, I have no reason to doubt that. What I want to know is why you gave up your football scholarship. Did you do it out of guilt?"

"No. I gave it up because you're my brother. I'd do whatever it takes to keep you safe. I never would have allowed anyone to send you to foster care. When Mom and

Dad died, it became my responsibility to care for you. I did it because I wanted to. You've always been more important to me than some damn scholarship. I've got to tell you that looking out for you has become a lot harder than I thought. Being an older brother isn't the easiest thing in the world to do."

I continued to look out the window a long time before saying anything.

"I couldn't have imagined living in foster care and not having you around. My only complaint would be that I certainly don't like moving as much as we do. I don't blame you for Mom and Dad dying. There's no way you could have known something bad was going to happen. Terrible things happen all the time. Look at what happened to Kat. She was one of the most responsible people I've ever known. One day, she's getting the mail and steps out into the street at the wrong time. There was no way anyone could have known what was about to happen."

"That's exactly right, Jayce. Kat didn't abandon you. I'm sure she didn't go willingly. I'm sure she gave it a hell of a fight. There are a lot of things in this world we have no control over. The only thing we can do is live life the way that it makes us happiest. That's exactly what Mom and Dad were doing when their time came."

It had seemed as if the entire town had come to say goodbye to Kat. The parking lot and adjacent streets were bumper to bumper with cars. Even with an umbrella, the rain had soaked our lower halves to the bone by the time we ran the two blocks and made it inside. The people crowded inside the front doors were as wet as we were.

As we cut our way through the gathering, there were a few faces I recognized. They were classmates, but I didn't know their names. I offered them a slight nod, which seemed customary during this heartbreaking day. There was no laughing, no genuine smiles, and no happiness whatsoever in a place like this. There was only bleakness, and a silent longing to be anywhere else in the world.

I didn't think Josh recognized a single person. Aside from going to the market once a week, Josh spent all day at work and then relaxing in front of the television for the remainder of each evening. He probably felt more out of place than I did.

A few people acknowledged me as I made my way through the crowd. If someone did say something, I wouldn't have heard it. My focus was on doing what I came here to do. I had to make sure this was real. I had to make sure that the nightmare was a reality. I had to see Kat.

I broke through the gathering. Half a dozen people were standing in front of the casket. As they moved to the right, I saw a lightly colored wooden casket with a white silk lining, and then locks of blonde hair.

My knees got weak, and I probably would have collapsed if Josh hadn't slid his arm into mine and held me up.

He directed me toward a chair and said, "You don't have to go up there, Jayce."

As I could see the soft pale features of one of the best friends I'd ever had, I said in a choked voice, "I do. I really do, Josh. Kat is my friend. I have to say goodbye, no matter how much it hurts."

My wobbly legs somehow pushed me forward. Josh's arm slipped from mine, and alone I went to face death.

"Take your time. I'll wait here for you."

I felt people staring at me as I approached the casket. Even though most of them had never met me, I somehow knew that most of them must have at one time or another noticed Kat and me running around town together. They knew we were close, and in courtesy of our friendship, they turned their attention elsewhere during this private moment that only Kat and I could share.

It may seem strange to say, but Kat didn't seem like Kat. Her long, blonde hair came down both sides of her face in waves. The mortician had lined her eyes with mascara, her cheeks covered in a pink blush, and she wore lipstick the color of a freshly picked apple. The only thing that seemed right about Kat was the dress. Although I'd never seen her in a white dress before.

I don't think Kat ever marked over her natural skin tone. I'd also never seen Kat's hair in any style other than a ponytail. She once told me that the only time she removed the ponytail band was when she went swimming. She said that she loved the feeling of her long, blonde hair moving freely through the water. She said she liked to imagine herself as a mermaid, and she insisted that no self-respecting mermaid would have her hair tied up in a ponytail.

What I meant by saying that Kat didn't seem like Kat was that I'd never seen her look so beautiful. Even though the mortician had done his best to make her look peaceful, I think he failed miserably at capturing her true image. Of course, there was no way for him to know that when she smiled, her left cheek dimpled. When she was nervous, she looked at her feet and often brushed back loose hair behind her ear. When she was angry, her mouth tightened into a pucker, and three vertical lines formed between her eyebrows. When she laughed, her entire body hitched spasmodically, and every so often she would snort with each gasping breath.

I wondered if anyone else here knew these things about Kat, or if it was a privilege that only I was meant to enjoy.

Behind me, people had taken their seats. The reverend looked at me and cleared his throat. I didn't feel much like sitting down then. I didn't want to do anything except stay at my friend's side.

I thought about my time with Kat in the hospital. I thought of my hand in hers, lying in bed with breathing tubes running from her nose. I thought of Kat struggling to keep her eyes open as exhaustion took hold. I thought of one of the last things I'd ever said to her. It had been a lie. It had felt like a necessary lie, but a lie all the same. I wanted her last thought to be that she had finally uncovered the reasoning behind Paper Moon's strangeness. I wanted her to know that this final case, what I figured to be the ending chapter of her conspiracy theory, was closed with an absolute conviction.

That was when I felt the first tear of many spilling down my cheeks.

The reverend decided to not wait for me to find my seat. He began speaking to the large crowd, but I heard none of his words.

My chest hitched with a sob. The tears came faster. I felt no embarrassment, no shame in standing beside my friend, showing all these strangers how much Kat's friendship meant to me. I kneeled and pressed my forehead to the cool wood surface of the casket.

The reverend ceased his sermon. It was evident he was going to give me this moment to grieve.

I heard someone come up behind me. Josh kneeled beside me. He bowed his head, and his large hand gently settled across my shoulder. Another person positioned at my left. I saw Anderson from the corner of my blurry eyes. His hand smoothly slipped into mine.

This became a moment I no longer had to face alone.

The service was bittersweet. I felt no elation afterwards. If anything, I felt worse.

The reverend had spoken of new beginnings for Kat. He said that she was now in God's hands, and God's hands were a place of great comfort and love. As the service ended, people stood, took a final moment to say goodbye to Kat and to offer their condolences to the family. I stayed as the room slowly emptied.

I wondered if Heaven was all it's cracked up to be. A person passing from this world, Paper Moon in particular, was something I couldn't comprehend at this moment. This place held too many great wonders found nowhere else in the universe. I was sure of it.

But now, with Kat gone, this place seemed to have lost its greatest treasure, resulting in a fractured town. It became impossible to determine if it would ever be mended.

Anderson was sitting by himself against the wall. I stood and joined him. As I sat, I tried to think of something comforting to say. I wanted to tell him that everything was going to be all right. But was it? I didn't know if anything would ever be right again, especially for Anderson.

"The world's a funny place," I decided to say.

"Oh? How so?" he asked without looking at me.

I knew how it had sounded. Right now, I was sure Anderson found no humor in the world.

"Well, I was just thinking if my parents hadn't gone sailing, they would have lived. If they had lived, I never would have known this town existed. I'm glad I know about this place and all the wonderful people here. Your sister was the greatest one of all to know. Maybe in reference to the existence of the universe, our time together was extremely brief, but for me, it seemed much longer. It was incredible to know her, and I'm a better person for it."

"What's your point?" Anderson said bitterly.

"I was just thinking about how my parents died and I'm not sure if I ever really knew them. I know they loved me. I'm sure of that. But beyond that, I couldn't say. I never knew about their hopes, dreams, or even fears. Maybe I was too young to know all these things about them. What I'm saying is that I think I knew the part of Kat that she kept hidden from most everyone else. I'm sure you saw it, too. I'm extremely honored she showed it to me," I said.

Anderson's father approached us. When he held out his hand for his son to take, Anderson shrank away from it. He looked as if he'd received a swat to the side of the head instead of being offered the loving hand of his father.

"Come on, son. It's time to get going."

Anderson was looking at the carpet between his feet as if he hadn't heard.

When Mr. Mossgrove kneeled, I saw there were thick tears in his eyes that were ready to tumble down his cheeks. He gently laid his large hand on Anderson's knee. It made me think of a man approaching a frightened animal and assuring it that he meant no harm. In the case of Mr. Mossgrove, I wasn't so sure. I had known only a small amount about the way he treated his son. I thought that finding trust in a man who treated you for so long like a punching bag was a hard thing to bounce back from. It was impossible to know if Anderson would ever trust his father again.

Mr. Mossgrove's tears finally broke through the dam. Small rivers ran down his cheeks to his lower jaw and then onto the burgundy carpet of the funeral home.

I knew this was a moment intended for family privacy.

"I'm going to get going, Anderson." I stood, but before I got a few steps, I turned back. "I truly am sorry about Kat. I will miss her."

Before I turned to join Josh, who waited for me at the entrance, I saw Mr. Mossgrove slowly place his head on his son's lap. He was blubbering like a small child. Through the sobs, I could hear him asking for forgiveness. I wasn't sure if he was asking Anderson or maybe God Himself for condonation. To me, he sounded sincere. I hoped forgiveness was exactly what he would get. Losing a child to death and another one to his own meanness was probably more than any man should ever have to endure.

Anderson slowly pulled his right hand into a fist. The fingers turned white from the blood being forced from them. I was sure he was about to beat that fist against his father's face. In the end, the muscles released, his hand flattened, and he gently placed it against his father's cheek.

Forgiveness was a choice only Anderson could grant him.

"I'm ready to go," I told Josh.

I looked back only once more. I could barely see Kat's face sticking out of the casket. What I saw was angelic. What I said to Anderson was sincere. I was going to miss everything about her.

I turned away, and then Josh and I stepped into the rain and headed for home.

Chapter 25

Another week drifted past, and my school grades began slipping as my focus in class was all over the place, except on the work assignments in front of me. I didn't care about grades or how many times the teachers snapped at me. My friend was gone, so my cares and concerns about anything else going on around me were nonexistent.

Five minutes after the final bell rang, I walked from the back of the school toward the front. When I rounded the corner, a country ham-sized hand grabbed the front of my shirt and jerked me forward. Another ham-sized fist came from down low and arched up. The fist crashed into my nose and upper lip. I'm not going to lie. I saw a wash of flickering stars followed by an ominous cloud rolling through my vision. It took a split-second to shake it away and find some kind of focus on the situation. I figure if I blacked out now, I'd wake up in an emergency room black and blue from toenails to forehead and have countless broken bones.

I'm not stupid. Before I even saw his face, I knew who it was. There was only one gorilla dumb enough to pick a fight on school property. The size of the fist was also a good indication of who had ambushed me.

Regan Evans spun and flung me like a sack of clothes. I crashed into the dirt and nailed my elbow on a small rock.

A painful tingle shot up my arm, and I'm pretty sure I yelled out a foul word, but I don't remember what it was.

"You knew this was coming. What your hick friends did to me and my brother at the games is going to bring you a lot of pain. You also got my brother arrested. You've been nothing but trouble since you got here."

I didn't argue with his inaccuracy. They deserved the embarrassment at the games, and Rory's arrest was his own fault. And me being a constant problem for Regan was only true if he was referring to the fact that I didn't tolerate getting pushed around like my classmates.

"Fight, fight," someone chanted. Then more students picked up the call.

Before the tingling even stopped running up my arm, a band of children had circled us, expecting a good after-school brawl.

It wasn't easy, but I managed to get my feet under me and stood. My nose and upper lip throbbed. I tasted blood in my mouth and spat on the ground. It hadn't been that long ago that I'd finally finished healing from the damage done by Rory's double jabs. Now Regan was taking over where his brother left off.

"Didn't see that one coming, did you, Graham Cracker?" Regan said and looked back at his posse for approval.

"It must be the only way you can win a fight, by hitting someone when they're not expecting it. I never figured you for a fair fight kind of asshole."

Sounds of disbelief at what I had called him moved like a slow wave across the crowd. I didn't care if it was harsh enough to anger Regan even more. In fact, I hoped it had. I decided to no longer tolerate being bullied in any part of life. I no longer cared if my head was going to be beaten so badly that it would swell to the size of a basketball. Just then, I remembered what one of my teachers in Colorado had said about life. He said that life will offer each of us a defining moment. We have the choice to define the moment, or the moment will define us. I now understood exactly what that teacher was telling us. My grandfather called it *showing your mettle*. It was a choice we made that would show ourselves and those around us our true character.

I stood against the injustice of being beaten down for no apparent reason. I stood for every school kid who had suffered Regan's nonstop meanness.

I slid the backpack off my shoulders and tossed it to a group of kids who were not part of Regan's evil gang. I began walking toward him with confidence in my step. I was sure how this fight would finish. As I've said, my fighting skills were non-existent. Of course, I knew how to throw a punch or a kick to unpleasant parts, but even with my blood boiling, I didn't think it would be enough.

Before I reached Regan, I saw Anderson peering over the shoulders of classmates. The look on his face was not telling me to run, but urging me to show this punk kid what it's like to be humiliated. I only hoped I didn't disappoint him. Embarrassing myself in front of the entire school was not part of the plan, but a likely outcome.

This time, I saw the punch coming. Regan was a fat bear, and he moved as slow as one. I had time to move away from the spot the punch was going to land. I lowered my head and ducked the blow. My right fist had a fury behind it, and it sank into Regan's soft gut. The strike pushed his breath from him, making a sound like a foghorn.

The cheering of the crowd momentarily stopped as all the children realized the school bully was now getting a dose of what he relentlessly dished out.

I didn't take much time rejoicing in the fact that I had hurt him. I immediately went for another swing before he got his hands on me. I pivoted around and swung my right fist at the same spot he had nailed me. There wasn't a lot on it, but I managed to find the mark. My knuckles crunched into his nose and upper lip. The shot drove him back. He couldn't keep his feet, and his bulk of a body crashed down to the dirt. Regan put his hand to his mouth, pulled it away, and his eyes went wide when he saw the blood. Then his look turned to one of confusion. I could see his tongue working around and around inside his mouth. He found what he'd been searching for and spit it into his palm. A single bloody tooth landed in his hand. His already swelling lip pulled up in a sneer. There was now a large gap where a yellowish tooth had been. His tongue explored that hole as if disbelieving it was actually there.

There were no more calls from my classmates urging the fight on. They wore stunned expressions, as I had actually knocked a tooth out of Regan's head.

I said the only thing that came to mind. It turned out to be the wrong thing. "Are you done already or are you planning on heading home to cry? This is over between us. You stay the hell away from me."

"Over?" Regan asked, and the air whistled through the new space in his mouth. "It's just starting, Graham Cracker. I'm gonna hurt you real bad now. I might have to put you beneath the ground next to your dead girlfriend."

I looked at Anderson. His usually calm face was beginning to twist into something I'd never seen before. Maybe it was a mix of anger, fear, and sadness at the loss of his sister. Regan's words stung the crowd. Among her classmates, Kat had been well-liked. Her death was a terrible blow to the entire community. Regan's only friends were the four behind him who had become his crew out of terror and not respect. I didn't think even Regan's parents would miss him if he were suddenly gone one day.

"Teach him a lesson, boys," Regan said as he pushed himself off the ground and knocked dirt from his shorts.

They obeyed. They simply had to. The four boys came at me. I didn't run. My running days were behind me. I knew five against one was going to be an epic beat-down, but I was willing to go that route if it meant standing up for what was right in the world.

Two of them grabbed my arms and painfully wrenched them behind my back. I tried to get free, but my strength had already weakened, and the boys were larger than me. The other two stepped in front of me, their fists ready to strike.

"You'll need to leave some for me. Make sure you don't knock him out before I get mine," Regan said.

I looked at my classmates for help. I even looked beyond them, hoping to spot a teacher moving in to break up the crowd, but saw none.

"Remember this," I told the crowd. "Someday it might be you standing here. As long as you allow them to keep pushing, you'll always be afraid."

"Enough with the begging. Hit him."

The boy named Taylor grinned and said, "Don't tell my mom I did this."

The first blow was a wrecking ball that caught me just below the ribs. I felt my stomach sink in and the air forced harshly from my lungs. Immediately following the pain was the panic of not being able to suck in another breath. Just before another punch came, my lungs inflated. Taylor's fist hammered my left cheek. My head went back hard enough that something in my neck crackled like bubble wrap. My knees gave out, but the two boys held me up for more punishment.

"Okay, okay, my turn," Regan said through a bloody mouth.

Both boys backed off.

"It's okay if you tell my mom I did this," Regan said with a red smile.

My left eye took a hit and then my jaw. Then, when I was sure I was going to take the easy way out and slide into unconsciousness, something unexpected happened.

A kid no one ever thought of having a solid backbone went off like a cherry bomb. Anderson came alive. The students watched with mouths gaping in pure amazement as he threaded through the crowd. With a whirling fist that was a blur to watch, he caught Regan in his already damaged mouth. As Regan tried to get his bearings and figure out exactly what had happened, Anderson clambered on his back like a vicious tiger taking down prey. He began delivering one malicious blow after another to Regan's skull.

Regan reached for Anderson but couldn't get a hold of anything. Then he tried to spin the boy off him, but Anderson had clamped on tight like a bear trap.

"Don't just stand there, morons. Get him off me!" Regan howled.

It took a long minute before any of the four boys moved. Maybe they thought of letting the fight go on. Maybe they also wanted to see Regan get a piece of exactly what he deserved for so long. Then the two boys let me go and the other two came unstuck from position.

I collapsed to the ground. My guts and chest resisted taking a breath and bearing the pain. My head throbbed with the perfect timing of my heartbeat. My left eye had nearly swelled shut already, and my left cheek and lips felt like inflated balloons.

Even through all that, I couldn't take my one good eye off my friend. I had never in my life seen anyone fight with such determination. He was an uncorked bottle, and from that spilled every emotion except happiness, because happiness was too alien to him. Even if he did know of it, it had no place here.

Two of the boys grabbed his legs, while the other two tried prying his grip loose from Regan's shirt. One of the boys screamed as he pulled his hand away, now missing flesh. Anderson had clamped his teeth down on anything that dared to come within reach.

I tried to stand. I tried to get up to help my friend. The will was there, but my body resisted everything except rest.

What happened next would forever stick in my mind. It dawned on one kid to help Anderson. Then another kid and another joined in until Regan's group became overwhelmed by schoolmates, all of whom had enough torment from the bullies. Most of the kids simply tried to pull the boys back until the fight left them. However, other kids, whom I assumed had often been knocked around by those punks, took the opportunity to exact justice. They hit, kicked, and even pulled hair to work out their frustration from frequent harassment.

I saw the five boys disappear inside the mob.

"Enough," I called out weakly. My voice was a very small one in the crowd of action. "Enough!" I finally managed to scream at the top of my lungs.

The crowd did stop, as if I had pushed a pause button. Then they slowly turned and watched me, silently asking why I, of all people, would want the beating to stop.

"Just please stop this. No one needs to be hurt anymore. I think they get the point that you're all angry and fed up with being pushed around," I said.

The group parted, moving away from the carnage.

I saw the five boys, all of them on the ground. They were curled into tight knots with their arms shielding their heads.

With Anderson's help, I finally managed to keep myself upright. I went over to the largest bulk of the bunch and looked down at him. I thought the kids had knocked him out cold, because he didn't move. When he heard my feet scrape the dirt next to him, he tightened up, expecting another attack.

"It's over. All of this is over. The way you were before isn't going to be tolerated anymore from anyone," I said, and then held out my hand. "Let me help you up."

He looked at my hand as if it were something unrecognizable. His hand swallowed mine. I did the best I could to pull him to his feet.

"What in the name of sweet Jesus is going on out here?"

I immediately knew whose loudmouth bellow that was. It was Mr. Dexter, the gym teacher. He parted the kids, and following close behind was Principal Swann and the school nurse, Mrs. Jones.

They stopped at the inner circle and surveyed the mangled faces of Regan and his crew, and then studied mine. I had no idea how bad I looked, but the expression on Mrs. Jones' face told me it wasn't good.

"There's zero tolerance for fighting on school grounds," Mr. Swann told the group, then clicked his tongue with disappointment.

"Who started it?" Mr. Dexter asked. His hands were on his hips, and he watched each face, looking for someone to break under pressure.

No one answered. No one wanted to be the one to rat out Regan so that revenge would come about later in some awful way.

"We were just playing football. I think we got too much into it. But we're all fine. My team won, by the way," I told the three adults.

"Football? Football? And where exactly is the ball? Whoever has it, hold it up," Mr. Dexter yelled.

I looked around. "Regan threw it wild. I believe it went out of bounds, way over there. Maybe it's in the bushes or got eaten by a sinkhole." I shrugged. "Stranger things have happened."

Mr. Dexter shook his head, obviously seeing through my brilliant lie. He walked over to me, painfully pinched my right ear—thankfully not the one hammered by a fist—and began leading me to the school doors. We only went a few steps before stopping. He firmly grabbed hold of Regan's left ear and proceeded to drag both of us towards discipline.

We walked into the air-conditioned building. It was the only relief I had, because my entire body seemed to be on fire. I'd had my fair share of scrapes with kids over the years, but nothing of this magnitude. The students just about had an all-out rumble. Kids who had probably never in their life thrown a punch were about ready to help Regan and his crew meet their maker. The class had lost their minds for several minutes. What happened was something I didn't want. Sure, I wanted, and even needed, help from someone since it was five against one. I never thought so many kids would jump into action and follow Anderson's lead.

Being led by our ears, we were ushered down the hallway. I thought that nowadays people could sue the school district for such treatment from a teacher, but I said nothing. I was already in boiling water and didn't want to make matters worse. It could have been worse if Mr. Dexter made Regan and me hold hands in front of our classmates, as he had made Kat and me do on my third day.

We reached the door with the principal's name stenciled on it. Mr. Dexter thankfully released me to open the door. I rubbed my ear and felt a swelling heat coming from it.

"Thank you, Miles. I'll take it from here," Mr. Swann said. "Mr. Evans, as you can see, your usual seat is available. Mr. Graham, you'll stay out here in the hall. I prefer to keep both of you separated. I have a few things to finish up before we chat."

After the secretary pushed a chair out for me, I flopped onto it. I knew I wasn't in trouble. I hadn't started the fight. I was sure at least half a dozen kids could confirm Regan threw the first punch. Even Josh would likely give me praise for standing up for myself. Josh never suffered being bullied, as he had been the high-school quarterback and well-liked by everyone. He was fully aware of how my life was a polar opposite of his high-school glory days.

Several kids eyed me as they headed for the front doors. I didn't say anything but mostly stared at the ground. I wondered what sort of rumors had already circled through the school grapevine. My head was hurting too much to focus on this thought for long.

I was exhausted, and I felt my eyes slipping shut when I heard the clack of heels next to me. Someone held out an ice pack. I looked up at a woman I'd never seen before.

She smiled and said sweetly, "The swelling is well on its way. This will help your head from becoming a balloon."

There was something very familiar about her voice.

"Thank you," I said and placed the ice pack over the left side of my throbbing face.

I couldn't pull my one good eye away from her. She was very pretty. Her smile was warm and genuine. Her eyes were a pale green, like swimming-pool water with the first touch of algae. Her hair was as black as a raven, with thin streaks of white. She dressed casually in blue jeans and a tan tee shirt.

Her smile widened. I knew she must have been reading my mind that I was trying to figure out who she was.

She lifted her hand, and her fingers snapped like a firecracker. "Turn to page thirty-seven, Mr. Graham. Hurry, hurry, the world is waiting on you!"

I blinked because I couldn't believe this was Mrs. Driscoll, my algebra teacher.

"I really had no idea what you looked like. I thought that you were grossly deformed, and you wore the black veil to hide it. I didn't expect you to be so—"

She laughed. It was an angelic laugh that made my heart flutter a bit.

"So... what, Mr. Graham?"

I looked at the floor. In a whisper, I said, "Beautiful."

"Thank you. That's very kind of you to say," she said. Her features then grew sad. "I'm very sorry about Kat. She was a wonderful, outgoing girl. I don't think there was a dry eye in town when the news came out."

"I feel like life tore a big part of me away. I guess I'd say I feel incomplete for the first time since moving here. I don't know what to say, think, or even how to act."

Mrs. Driscoll studied her feet as she searched for words. She said, "I very much know the pain of losing someone. My husband died four years ago. He was only forty-three years old. That day he had off work. He tried to convince me to call in sick so we could drive to Renay Beach and spend the day in the sun. I didn't call in. I always wanted to spend time with my school kids. I told him we had the weekend to enjoy some fun in the sun. Early that afternoon, he decided to head up to Coral Key to pick up lumber to build a shed out back. A truck ran a stop sign, killing my husband instantly."

"I'm so sorry." It was all I could think to say.

"So was I, and every day after. If I had called in sick, he would still be alive today. We could have spent a glorious day at the beach together. Instead, he got no more life to live, and I got to experience the worse moment of my life. It hardly seems fair any twisted way you look at it."

"So that's when you started wearing the black dress and veil?"

"It is. At first, it was because I didn't want the children to see me crying after I returned to class. It later remained because it was during class hours when he left me that final time. I didn't know how to move forward."

"I don't either. When my parents died, I was very young. I didn't understand what death was. Now I know exactly was death is, and I hate it. It's a cruel monster taking away the important things in everybody's life."

Mrs. Driscoll leaned against the wall. She took a deep breath and released it. I could sense her frustration to life's mysteries.

"I've spent the last four years of my life angry and sad. During the last year, I felt like I was beginning to get over it and prepared to move on with my life. Then this tragedy with Kat nearly put me back to square one. I've got an idea, but I can only do it with your help."

"Sure. What can I do?"

"Can you get away tonight? Will your brother let you leave the house around nine o'clock?"

I blinked at her, not sure what she was thinking.

"I don't know. He's always tired and goes to bed early or falls asleep on the couch. I could get away without him even knowing," I said.

"Don't hide it from him. If you can't get away, we can do it over the weekend. I just figured it would be much better at night."

"I'm sure it will be all right with him if it's only for a little while," I said.

She offered a sweet smile. Again, my heart fluttered a bit. If I hadn't been so distraught by Kat's passing, I might have been experiencing a serious crush on Mrs. Driscoll.

"Great! Meet me in front of the school around nine and we'll go from there."

She patted my knee and then disappeared down the hall.

The office door opened, and I looked at Regan. I imagined my face matched his own. His lips were water balloons, his nose still bled a bit, and the signs of a blackening eye were forming.

I don't know why I bothered asking, "Are you all right?"

He looked at me intently, as his seething hatred hadn't yet cooled. He said, "Why do you care, Graham Cracker?"

What makes a kid like Regan mean and hateful toward everyone and everything is anyone's guess. Maybe his parents were the neglecting type. Maybe his home life mirrored Anderson's trauma of having a father treat him as a punching bag. I figure kids handled circumstances such as those in different ways. Anderson dealt with it by having panic attacks and suddenly running away when no one was looking. He did it so smoothly that rumors began about him blinking out of our time and appearing in another. I didn't know what caused Regan's meanness. I decided there was probably no way he'd ever confide in me, especially since I was the one who ultimately made a stand against him.

Mr. Swann pulled me into his office. I tried to remain calm as I stuck to my story about a football game getting wildly out of control. Apparently, Regan muttered the same crooked lie. Mr. Swann simply shook his head. He told me to go home and pack some ice on the swelling. I hoped the matter would be closed. Mr. Swann could easily question any number of kids who were there and get the genuine story. I believe he avoided the truth because then he would be obligated to expel Regan from school. Mean or not, even Regan deserved the chance of a decent education and a future that wasn't behind prison bars.

Josh was home before me. The look on his face was wide-eyed. He had seen bruising on my face before, but never to this degree. I pulled a bag of frozen peas from the freezer and pressed it to my left eye. I sat down and spilled the entire story before he even asked. He just listened and nodded. Josh knew when to speak his mind and when to listen. If he had told me that it was okay to be angry about what happened to Kat, and the fight with Regan was unacceptable, it would only enrage me more. I spoke, and he listened. We were good that way.

Before I went upstairs to shower away the schoolyard dust, I hugged Josh. Two things that happened next didn't surprise me. I began crying in the crook of his shoulder. It was a powerful flood of tears for my friend and the parents I'd never really gotten to know. The second thing was the exhausting relief. I felt loads better as the action sapped away the anger and sadness. I did still miss them, and I hoped that feeling never faded. I knew the memories would never leave. I'd gathered them up and locked them away in a titanium box in my mind. As I would eventually slide into the hectic ways of adulthood, I would occasionally glance back at the memories of my youth, unlock that box, peer inside, and smile.

As I suspected, Josh did turn in early. I figured he would reject my wandering out at night, especially after taking the beating I had. So, I didn't even bother asking.

I thought of Mrs. Driscoll. Now I was one of the few to know the reasoning behind her black dress and veil. I'm sure the other teachers knew, but I'm confident that I was the only student who understood. As I rode toward school, I couldn't get my mind to settle on why she wanted to meet me alone in front of the school. I figured in a few minutes I would find out.

There were a few outside lights glowing on the school grounds. The inside was completely black. One car occupied the lot. The headlights were on, so I figured it had to be Mrs. Driscoll waiting for me. I braked my bike next to the driver's door. Mrs. Driscoll offered her warm, pleasant smile.

"I'm so very glad you could make it out, Jayce," she said.

"Not a problem. My brother was okay with it as long as I'm home by ten." The lie came out so easily.

"Hop on in. It's only a mile down the road."

"What is?"

"It's all right. Really. I want to surprise you by showing you, not telling you."

I didn't really know Mrs. Driscoll. Until earlier, I had never seen her face before. Something was telling me to trust her and go for the short ride.

I slid my front wheel into the bike rack. I didn't bother locking it, because I didn't figure anyone would wander through here the rest of the night.

I opened the passenger door and looked at the interior as the dome light went on. There was no roll of duct tape, no rope or black bag to throw over my head.

She must have sensed my hesitation and read my mind. She said, "I put my kidnapping gear in the trunk. I didn't want you to run off when you saw it." Her voice and laughter were that of an old movie villain, and she rubbed her hands together to punctuate her sinister intentions.

I had to smile. As I got in, I said, "I'm sorry, but this whole thing is a bit weird to me."

"Understandable," she said. "Do you think I often take a student for a drive on weeknights?"

"Well, no, I wouldn't think so."

"Of course not, but the weekends are a different matter," she said and winked.

We drove down The Long-Short Lane, which was a narrow road cut through the dense woods. The nervousness increased again. I had no idea where we were, where we were going, or why. I hated it when people kept secrets, especially when I was obviously jittery because of it.

I heard a soft roar as we pulled into a small gravel parking lot. The headlights lit up a mid-sized river with a boat ramp.

Mrs. Driscoll parked and shut off the engine. The sound of running water was hypnotizing.

"It's been a long time since I came out here. My husband frequently fished off these banks. We have a little boat that he'd sometimes drop in the river and would fish upstream where there's a small spillway. He could spend all day out here when he wasn't working, not catch a single thing, and still come home with a big smile. This was his place of relaxation when life got too hectic. When he did catch a big carp or trout, he'd bring it home and grill it up for dinner."

"It's very peaceful," I admitted.

She nodded. "I've been grieving over his death for many years. It's time I let him go and move on. That's what he'd want most. He wouldn't want me to put off my happiness for so long."

Stepping out, Mrs. Driscoll went around back and popped open the trunk. I followed to see what she was getting. It only took a moment for me to understand.

"After I spoke with you at school, I went home and made these," she said.

The trunk light showed something wonderful.

"They're beautiful," I told her.

She nodded and said, "Well, let's get to it so you don't get home too late. I wouldn't want you to get in trouble. You take that one."

Together, we lifted them out of the trunk. We went to the edge of the dock in the soft glow of the headlights. I studied what was in my hands. Mrs. Driscoll had spent countless hours today making two wreaths. There was a wonderful mix of purple, yellow, and red flowers woven together. Each wreath had a circle of foam wedged in the center and a white paper bag fastened on top. Inside each bag was a candle. Glue had secured a picture of Mrs. Driscoll's husband to one bag and a school picture of Kat to the other.

I had seen this type of in-memoriam done in the movies, but never in real life.

Mrs. Driscoll removed a box of long matches from her shirt pocket. She struck one and carefully reached inside the bag to light the candle. She handed me the matches, and I did the same. A cool breeze rolled off the river's surface, which made the flames flicker.

"Are you ready?" she asked.

"Goodbyes are hard."

"Yes, they are. But you're strong and I'm strong. Together we're a rock."

I nodded, and she nodded back. Simultaneously, we lowered the wreaths onto the water and gave a gentle push. The calm river waves grabbed them. I stared at Kat's picture until the blackness downriver obscured it. Mrs. Driscoll wrapped her arm over my shoulder and pulled me in close. At any other time, it might have been inappropriate for a teacher and student to embrace like this, but tonight, we were two grieving people in need of comfort.

Mrs. Driscoll began crying softly. We watched the glow of the candles fade into the distance until the night fully cloaked them. She wiped away her tears, and we went back to the car.

When we got inside, Mrs. Driscoll said, "I don't know about you, but the relief is definitely there."

"It is. That was a wonderful send-off. Thank you."

She offered her warmest smile yet. "You're very welcome. You're a fascinating young man, Jayce. Kat was lucky to have you as a friend. Now it's time to get you home. There's school tomorrow. I sure hope your homework is done."

Chapter 26

I decided to stay home from school the next day. My head swelled and throbbed all night long. The headache brought on by the beating never really left. It stuck around and reminded me that youth could sometimes be a hard road to travel.

When I had to use the bathroom, I didn't like looking in the mirror. I had seen my reflection earlier this morning. If I didn't know any better, I would have sworn it was really a team of martial arts students that had so badly marked my face instead of school bullies.

The ice packs and aspirin helped. Sleeping away a better part of the day also helped improve my mood and ease the aches some. By early afternoon, I turned on the television out of boredom. I stopped flicking through the channels when I saw a face I personally knew.

Wearing a gray suit with a blue tie, Mr. Reynolds was giving an interview on channel seven, which was broadcast out of Coral Key. He looked a hundred times better than our introduction in the middle of the woods. He appeared unburdened, smiling in that way of his, and happy to be turned loose from a prison cell.

"I'm still not sure why I broke out of prison to begin with. I saw an opportunity and took it. No one, probably not even my lawyer, believed I was innocent. I tried to explain that I would never do harm to any of the people or structures of Paper Moon. I love the place with all my heart. It's a place of magic filled with beautiful people. I just thought that if I could get away for a little while, I could figure out who would frame me and why."

"And what did you find out when you were on the run?" the reporter asked.

He smiled again and looked beyond the reporter as if watching a memory playing on a screen. His eyes lit up.

"In the end, I wasn't the one who figured it out. It was my friend who I'd found lost in the woods where I was hiding. I told him to leave it alone. I told him it was too dangerous to get involved and that if the real arsonist found out, then my friend could get himself hurt. Well, he didn't listen to my advice and got himself wrapped up in trouble. But his persistence put the other man in jail and got me out." He looked right at the camera then and said, "Words cannot do justice to what you have done for me. Thank you so very much, my good friend."

The camera went back to the reporter. She signed off, and then I was looking at the anchorman behind a desk.

"You're very welcome, Mr. Reynolds," I told the television and then clicked it off.

I had nothing to do. I no longer had a job. Because of the incident with Deputy Kline at Grady's place, the sheriff was made aware of my employment. It was in the best interest for everyone that I stepped away from the job to keep Grady out of legal matters for employing a minor.

I was feeling a bit better, so I decided to go for a bike ride. Without fully realizing where I was going until I got there, I found myself riding through the gates of Seven Heavens Cemetery.

The groundskeeper had maintained the property so well that not a single weed grew wild among the tombstones or the trunks of trees. There were fresh, bright flowers left at many of the graves, put there by loved ones who refused to forget those who moved on without them.

As I pedaled down the gravel drive, I spotted a battered car I knew all too well. In fact, I had borrowed that vehicle to drive to Coral Key to visit Kat in the hospital.

As I approached, I saw a man in a blue suit standing beside the freshly covered grave. He used a rainbow-colored umbrella to block the brutal sun. His thin white hair was neatly combed back on his scalp. He was leaning on a crutch because his leg was in a cast. The shocking thing about the man was that he only had one head.

Truth be told, it was good to see Mr. Bixby. I hadn't been able to see him in the hospital after Kat and I had dug him out of the wreckage that had once been called his home.

He smiled as I stepped up to him. He shifted the umbrella so that we both got some relief from the sun.

"I was hoping to see you again," he said.

"Yes, sir. I'm glad to see you're out of the hospital. Are you feeling much better?" I asked.

"Well, old bones don't mend quite as fast as they used to, but I'm up and about now. I tried to see Kat when I heard about the accident. The doctors prohibited me from seeing her because I'm not family and her condition was guarded. I never got a chance to tell her how much her friendship meant to me. I couldn't even tell her goodbye. So, I came here to see her. I think this is a good spot for her, right here on the hillside. She'll be able to see a good part of the town where she was born and raised."

"It is a good spot," I agreed as I took in the view. A headstone had yet to be prepared, so, for the time being, a simple marker was placed at Kat's grave. "I need to confess something. I borrowed your car when you were in the hospital. I drove to Coral Key to see Kat. I had to see her. I hope you're not mad."

He smiled and said, "I'm not mad at all. I'm glad you did. At that time Kat needed a friend. I have no doubt you're the one she would have wanted to see. So how exactly are you doing, Jayce?" The question was soft and sincere. It hung in the air for a long moment. He studied the dark bruises on my face.

"Not so good, sir. I've been having a hard time the last week. My days aren't nearly as fun. I can't even seem to focus on anything for very long. I don't even know what to do with myself," I said and looked at Kat's grave.

"It's a hard thing to carry on once you've lost someone. I've seen the passing of many family and wonderful friends over the years. At a certain point, life stops giving you things and begins taking them away. It never gets any easier. The only comforting thing I can say is that you'll eventually be able to move on. What you need to remember is that you can always keep her alive in your heart and mind. I bet you'll think about her often. She was an extra-special young woman."

"I feel bad about something I said to her."

"Oh? What was that?"

"I told her a lie when she was in the hospital. Do you remember when I was at your house the first time?"

"Of course I do."

"It started with that picture on your wall of the military train wreck that your father photographed. Well, we decided to research it."

"What for?"

"I'm not sure if you know it or not, but Kat was sure that there had to be a reason why the people of Paper Moon act so strangely."

"Who's been acting strangely?" Mr. Bixby asked with a serious expression. His face then cracked, and he began laughing.

I wanted to say that I could think of one person in particular who was in close proximity to me, but I honestly wasn't sure if Mr. Bixby was aware that he was around the bend and through the woods nuts.

"All right. So, what about the train wreck?"

"Well, I had an idea when I saw that photograph of the military cleaning up some sort of mess that leaked from the train cars. You said that the military guys were all wearing protective suits. So, I got to thinking that just maybe what spilled out of those train cars was something serious the military had just cooked up. If the derailment happened during World War II, then maybe that stuff was supposed to be put into bombs and dropped on Germany. I figured there was no way the military could have cleaned up everything that got out. I thought that maybe some of that stuff soaked into the soil and a heavy rain washed most of it deep into the town water supply."

"That sounds like quite a theory," Mr. Bixby said and studied me closely.

"Well, anyway, I thought that whatever chemical it was could have caused mental damage to the people of Paper Moon just by drinking the water. Kat and I went to the library and did some research. We started with the local paper from when the train wrecked and any weird news after. We were trying to find out when people started getting strange ideas or just acting a little odd. We found some articles like that, but the one that convinced us we were on to something was the article about one of the locals getting the idea to construct the medieval arena. No one seemed to question the proposal. The town committee passed it, and the townspeople were okay with their tax dollars going toward building it. Doesn't that sound strange that an entire town would be behind something like that?"

Mr. Bixby thought for a long moment. Then he said, "I've got to say that the arena was one of the best ideas this town ever came up with. You've got to understand that back then were different times. People were tired of hearing about war an ocean away. The planning, construction, and eventually the opening of the arena helped take everyone's mind off what was happening on the other side of the world. I was just four years old when it opened, and I can still vividly remember everything about it. It was like stepping into another world, another time. And every year when the fliers went up, everyone in town came alive with anticipation."

"But how could an arena with sword fighting and jousting help take everyone's mind off of war?"

"Well, I guess at the time it seemed like the best idea out there. Perhaps it was a little foolish to spend such a great deal of money to construct one of the biggest buildings in town that would be rarely used during the year. But I'm pretty sure no one has ever regretted doing so. We've kind of got off track with our conversation. Why was Kat so convinced that something conceived by the military was behind the way people in town act?"

I told Mr. Bixby about my first meeting with Kat and her strange ranting about the oddness of Paper Moon's citizens. I told him how sure she was that either something in the ground, water, or air was causing some sort of mental instability for the residents.

"She was determined to figure it all out. Honestly, I just figured she fit right in with all the other odd people in town."

A peel of lightning scarred the sky, and thunder rolled across the gray clouds as a storm brewed in the east.

I said, "I meant that she fit right in with a brother who supposedly time-traveled. A barber who walks around all the time wearing a tunic and cape, and another man who..." This is where I stopped myself. Without a second head perched on his right shoulder, I had completely forgotten whom I was speaking with.

Mr. Bixby watched me, and when he was sure I wasn't going to continue, he said, "A man with a second head that he claimed to be his wife?"

I looked at Kat's grave. The first droplets of rain pattered the fresh dirt.

I nodded.

"Even in a world with so many people, it can be a very lonely place. When my wife died ten years ago, I withdrew from the world I loved so much. As you know, I became a hermit. I picked up some strange hobbies to occupy my time. Then I created the new Mrs. Bixby. Of course, I knew she was never real, but my lunacy was without shame, because no one else was around to see it. Then Kat came around many years ago while I was working on one of my projects in the garage. I still remember the look on her face when she looked at Mrs. Bixby." He began laughing wildly, and that laugh was infectious, because it got me going.

"I can only imagine it was close to the same expression I gave you," I said.

"I will miss her more than you know," Mr. Bixby said as his laughter faded. There was an awkward silence between us. He said, "What was the lie you told her?"

"Well, Kat had sent water samples to a lab in Miami. She was opening the results letter in the street when the car hit her. I was near her house the day after the accident.

I found the letter hung up in the bushes by the side of her house. I opened it and read the test results. There wasn't anything unusual in the vials of water or dirt she sent. When I went to the hospital and she told me about receiving the letter, I told her I found it. I told her she was right, that there was something bad in the water that was making everyone mentally unstable. I just had a feeling it was the last time I was going to talk to her. I didn't want her to know she was wrong. I thought that if she were going to die, she would die knowing that she solved the mystery she was so determined to uncover. I wanted her to know that Paper Moon would be as normal as every other town once they fixed the tainted water."

I felt the sadness welling in me again. Mr. Bixby wrapped his arm around my shoulder and pulled me closer.

"Do you believe in your heart that it was the right thing to tell her?"

I thought for a long moment and said, "Yes. But in the end, it didn't matter. She insisted that I destroy the results. She'd decided that she didn't want anything here to change. She loved it just the way it is."

"Then it was the right thing to say. You should be happy because you made Kat happy one last time. Come, we should get going. I think the rain is going to get bad."

We walked down the hill to the road. I retrieved my bike from beneath the elm and settled on the seat.

"I don't want you trying to get home in this weather. Why don't we put your bike in the trunk? I'll drive you home."

I shook my head. "Thanks anyway, but a bike ride in the rain is just what I need."

Mr. Bixby nodded. "Boys will be boys, I suppose."

Before I set off, I said, "Where will you go now that the hurricane demolished your house?"

"Oh, I have a daughter up in Tallahassee. She's been begging me for years to come see her. I think family is just what the doctor ordered. You take care of yourself, Jayce," Mr. Bixby said and held out his hand.

"You as well, sir." I held out mine, and we shook.

I started my bike down the path back to the main road. I would never see Mr. Bixby again. I would never visit Kat's grave again. But there was no doubt in my mind that I would think of them often.

Thankfully, the rain hadn't intensified, as Mr. Bixby had guessed. Instead, the steel-colored clouds shifted south, the light drizzle dissipated, and the sun broke out again. The coolness of the day turned mildly warm as I pedaled for town. Before long, I found myself approaching Downside Up Street. Kat first brought me here when she had an idea to get me up close and personal with alligators. We had taken the downward slope of the hill to begin our journey. I remembered how Kat had shot down the hill straight as an arrow, her arms spread like the wings of a majestic eagle, her face turned up to the stunning sky.

Putting fears of crashing aside, I had momentarily attempted the same feat, but the blaring horn of Rory Evans' car had nearly caused a painful body slide.

Although taking the hill to the top and following the road would lead me in the opposite direction, I found myself steering toward that destination. I had to walk my bike to the top because the steepness was too much to manage while riding. Once I crested the peak, I rested a moment. The view was something I hadn't got the chance to take in last time, because Kat had been in too much of a hurry to make the ride.

I could see the distant thunderstorm raging to the south. The tops of the evergreens seemed to stretch all the way to the horizon. Within the fields of green, I spotted the brown and black rooftops of Paper Moon houses.

I settled on the seat, planted my right foot on the pedal, and pushed off. My legs hammered fast. The wheels hummed, and for a moment I felt like I was a jet shooting down a runway.

Even with the pavement wet, I was going to chance the stunt. I steadied the handlebars. Before I completely let go, I made sure there was no wavering with the front tire. My hands pulled back, and my arms spread wide like wings. My head tilted back, mouth open, and my eyes studied the ever-expanding blue. I saw birds flying above me. For precious seconds, I knew that I was one of them.

My bike reached the bottom of the hill and streamed down the long stretch of flat road. I slowly pulled my arms in and gripped the handlebars again. The experience had been as close to flying solo as I would ever come. Now I understood why Kat's face had beamed the first time we had taken this hill. Of course, the Evans brothers had cut short her final experience on this hill. I hated them for that. But the brothers had gotten a dose of the meanness they frequently dished out. For me, that made for a pretty good ending.

Chapter 27

It's funny how life can take so many accidental directions. I don't think any of us are meant to understand the mystic path of destiny. At least I'm sure I'll never understand it. Maybe that's the greatest part of life, the inability to understand what comes next. Since my parents died, I hated relying on Josh. I had often thought of him as irresponsible. The fact that he couldn't keep a job and often forced us to move was something I wasn't meant to understand, because the cosmos simply didn't want me to.

More than fifty percent of the time, there was a neat little surprise around the next corner. Paper Moon had been one of those surprises I hadn't welcomed at first. I had learned to love it, but all things, like love, must come to an end.

Josh's upcoming words were familiar. I had heard them enough times over the last few years to know that the direction of my life was insistent on changing again.

I had come home from school, noticing that the rust bucket was sitting in the driveway. Josh had only missed one day of work since we'd arrived in Paper Moon. That had been the day of Kat's wake. The day I needed him, and like an older brother should, he was there for me.

"We need to talk," Josh said as I came in and dropped my backpack next to the dining room table.

"No," I said flatly and headed for my room.

I closed the door, flopped on the bed, and clamped my eyes shut. I figured if I prayed hard enough, the upcoming conversation would never happen.

There was a soft knock on the door. Josh pushed it open and stepped inside.

"I take it you already know what I'm about to say." Josh moved into the room and sat at the foot of the bed.

"How could you have lost your job again?"

"Hold on. It's different this time. They didn't fire me. I quit."

"It's bad enough that you get fired over and over again, but now you're into quitting good jobs?"

"Listen, Grandpa called here late last night after you had gone to bed. Actually, he called in a favor for me. There's a job for me back in Colorado. He's got a friend who said there's an open supervisor position at the Mountain Grains Company. Basically, Grandpa said that I wouldn't even have to interview. The position is mine if I want it."

"Why don't you get your job back with the construction company? I like it here."

"The job in Colorado is double what I make doing construction. Plus, I'm betting it's a lot easier on my body. Besides, when I get in there, it means stability. We won't have to move again. Grandpa even said that we could stay with him until we get on our feet and find a place of our own. I know you liked living in Colorado. I'm not sure why you're fighting me on this one," Josh said and waited for an answer.

"I did like living in Colorado, but I like this place more. Find somewhere else around here to work."

"I'm sorry, Jayce. I've made up my mind. We're moving again. Hate me if you want, but I'm doing this for you just as much as for myself. It's the smarter thing to do. I think Grandpa needs us around as well. Don't you think it would be better to have more family around?"

I shrugged. "I guess."

Josh's tone grew even more serious. "I know you haven't made many friends here. The only person I've ever heard you talk about was Kat. Now with Kat gone, there's no reason you should be so reluctant to leave Paper Moon."

Even though what Josh had said stung like a wasp, I knew he was right. Kat was gone. Mr. Bixby was heading for greener pastures in Tallahassee. Though there were plenty of interesting people in town, I thought the best of them were gone and never to return.

"What does the company do?" I asked.

"It's primarily a mill. It's not an ideal job, I suppose, but it's a great start to something better. What do you say? Do you want to give it a go?"

I thought it over before giving an answer. My options were nonexistent.

"What do I have to lose?" I asked.

If there is a category in the Guinness Book of World Records for packing the entire bedroom of a teenager based on time and efficiency, I should hold that title. It wasn't that I was enthusiastic about moving and putting Paper Moon in our rearview mirror, but I simply hated packing and, like ripping off a bandage, I did it quickly just to get it over with.

I helped Josh with the rest of the house. The truth was that we owned very little. A couch, coffee table, a rickety entertainment center with a small television on top, and a bookshelf with beat-up paperbacks, and a dining room table set were the only furniture outside of our bedrooms that needed to be moved into the rental trailer.

"I think we've become pros at this," Josh said as we slid the last piece of furniture inside the trailer and finished strapping down the items in the truck's bed.

"Maybe if supervising a mill doesn't work out for you, then you can look into the furniture moving business," I said without looking at him.

He didn't bother with a remark, as he knew my anger was still simmering, but it would soon vanish once Colorado appeared through the windshield.

And so, nearly five months after arriving in Paper Moon, I would be leaving it behind. The memories of this place were like priceless jewels that would stay alive and shine ever brighter the more I thought of the people in this town. This brief stop in a place most people have never heard of was certainly a one-of-a-kind crossroads in my life.

We pulled the rust bucket out of the driveway, towing a trailer with our worldly possessions, and then drove down Paper Moon's streets one final time. We stopped at Mr. Barshell's house and dropped off the keys to the rental house.

"I sure hate to lose a tenant like you. I never had a single complaint, and the rent was always on time," I heard Mr. Barshell tell Josh.

"We hate to be leaving, especially Jayce," he said and nodded toward the truck in which I was sitting. "We've cleaned up the house. It's being left in the same condition from the moment we moved in."

"I have no doubt, Josh. Here is your security deposit back," Mr. Barshell said and handed Josh an envelope.

They shook hands, and Josh came back to the truck. As he settled in the seat and started the engine, Josh opened the envelope and looked at the stack of money.

"I was thinking—" he started.

"That's a first for you." I shot another one of my zingers.

He let this remark go as well.

"We've got some extra traveling cash. What do you say we swing by Six Flags in Texas?"

It was uncharacteristic of Josh to spend money needlessly. This was one of those rare moments when a good offer came along, and if I chose not to seize it, then it might never happen again. The idea did sound fun, although I wasn't going to give him the satisfaction of knowing that I was getting excited about it.

I shrugged and said, "I guess."

We drove down Broken Bow Lane. This was Kat's street. I saw an odd thing from nearly two blocks away. There were two figures running around in the front yard. As we got closer, I saw Anderson and his father playing catch. Anderson took off running and his father put a perfectly spun football directly in his hands. I saw something else I'd only seen twice before. The first time was when I gave him money to purchase a gator on a pig on a peg during the tournament. Also, a short while later, when payback was served, and the Evans brothers found themselves in the arena wearing nothing but their birthday suits. Anderson was now smiling. He also laughed and threw the ball back. Despite being a small kid, he had one heck of an arm. With his amazing speed during track practice and a rocket arm as well, I wondered why he had never tried out for the football or baseball teams.

"Can we stop here for a minute? I want to say goodbye to Anderson," I asked.

Josh consulted his watch and said, "Yeah, but you'll have to make it quick."

They stopped playing as we pulled up to the curb. Anderson's face brightened when he saw me, and then he frowned, as he must have realized the only reason for us to be towing a moving trailer was because I was taking a one-way ride down the highway.

I got out of the truck and walked over to him.

"Moving on already?" he asked.

"Yeah, just when I was beginning to like a new town. I noticed that you've got a nice throwing arm."

"My dad has been showing me the principles of making a perfect throw. Do you think you can stay awhile and play?"

I looked back at the truck. Josh was staring off into the distance. Perhaps he was reliving a particular memory Paper Moon once offered him.

"I'm afraid not. We've got a long journey. You look happy. It's good to see you smile," I said.

In a whisper, Anderson said, "My dad quit drinking. He hasn't hit me either since my sister went into the hospital. He's kept the promise he made to Kat to be a better father. He's different, but different in a good way."

"I'm happy for you. I think everything will be okay from now on. I've got to get going." I hugged Anderson. "I'll write to you as soon as we get settled in Colorado."

"You better."

"I promise." The next thing I said was in a whisper. "No more time-traveling, okay?"

Anderson smiled. "No more. My feet belong right here."

"Good," I said.

I got back in the truck. We waved goodbye to Anderson and Mr. Mossgrove. They waved back and then resumed practice.

Josh and I moved down the road. Soon Paper Moon's town limits approached.

It wasn't a surprise to see her waiting there. She always had a knack for doing unexpected things. That's just who she is.

This was only the second time I'd ever seen her blonde hair unbound. Maybe because now she was free from all of life's restraints.

Josh didn't slow. He couldn't see her like I saw her.

Kat offered the most genuine smile to date. Her blue dress fluttered in the Florida breeze. With both hands raised, she waved her goodbyes to me as I lifted my hand and returned the gesture. As we reached her, I looked out the side window. Our blue eyes caught each other. We needed no words. Hearts can speak to each other if you have the will to listen.

I leaned forward so I could keep sight of her in the side mirror. Kat spun, still waving and smiling, as she faded away into the sunlight.

All that remained was a sign that I read in the mirror's reversing image.

Welcome to Paper Moon
Experience The Wonder!

Just like that, the town became obscured. But like all things, it wasn't really gone. Nothing magical ever dies.

Josh was watching me. He said, "Why are you smiling and waving? You look like a crazy person."

I smiled even more at that. Maybe I did fit in after all in a place like Paper Moon.

"Just saying goodbye to an old friend."

Truthfully, I was happy that Kat was wrong. It hadn't been something in the water, the earth, or the air. There was no government conspiracy to cover up a bad chemical spill due to a train wreck. There wasn't any unnatural reason whatsoever. It just is what it is.

I thought that a place like Paper Moon was like a rare gemstone lying on the ocean floor. Ordinary rocks and pebbles surrounded that one perfect jewel. But for those who searched for it, or by chance happened upon it, that gemstone shined so bright. For those willing enough to dive deep for it, the reward was a lifetime of perfect memories.

If anything, Paper Moon was some sort of magnet for the strange and wonderful things in life. The town pulled in people who wanted a small piece of the magic and in turn shared it with others.

I think Kat's death had fractured the perfect town. The tragic death of a well-liked member of the community, especially one so young, was like the death of a loved one. Everyone felt it. Everyone reacted to it. Everyone suffered a deep sadness because of it. But like everything else, life went on.

One thing that made me happy was Mr. Mossgrove's promise to Kat. Anderson had said that at her hospital bedside, their father had sworn he would give up drinking if she pulled through. Even though Kat had slipped away from life, Mr. Mossgrove had stuck to his promise. It was then when I realized how people could change if their will was great enough.

"So, tell me exactly how Anderson can time travel," Josh said.

I studied him for a moment. "Either you've heard stories from around town or you've got good hearing."

"I didn't know many people around town. I just know when to pay attention. Especially when boys start whispering."

I smiled and said, "It's a long story."

Josh pointed to the endless, empty road ahead of us. "I've got the time."

I thought it over. Just like all the incredible stories out there, I decided exactly where to begin.

"Well, on my third day of school, a girl I'd never seen before grabbed a handful of my shirt and pulled me into a classroom."